TruthSpell

THE TRUTHSEER ARCHIVES
BOOK 2

MIKE SHELTON

TruthSpell
Copyright © 2018 by Michael Shelton
2nd edition © 2020

ISBN: 0-9987935-6-6
ISBN-13: 978-0-9987935-6-6
Library of Congress Control Number: 2018902791
Salem, Oregon

Cover Illustration by Christian Bentulan
https://coversbychristian.com/

Map by Robert Altbauer
www.fantasy-map.net

For More information about Mike Shelton and his books
www.MichaelSheltonBooks.com

mikesheltonbooks@gmail.com
www.MichaelSheltonBooks.com
https://www.facebook.com/groups/MikeSheltonAuthor/
https://www.facebook.com/mikesheltonbooks/
http://www.Twitter.com/msheltonbooks
http://www.Instagram.com/mikesheltonbooks
https://www.pinterest.com/mikesheltonbooks/

ACKNOWLEDGEMENTS

I really appreciate all the support I get in my writing from so many people. All my friends and family have always been so encouraging. My wife, Melissa is of course my biggest support. Her love and encouragement are what drives me forward.

I am always amazed at the skills of my cover designers. Christian Bentulan hit it out of the park once again with this cover! Robert Altbauer continues to create amazing maps for my books. You can see a color version of it on my website.

The editors at Precision Editing (Heather, Crystal, Julie, Lisa) continue to help me be a better author. Their guidance and input has been invaluable.

My daughter Danielle (Danny) helped in providing some research for the stones used in this series.

TruthSpell is a work of fiction. Names, characters, places and incidents are the products of my imagination and are used fictitiously. Any resemblance to actual events, locales, or persons, living or dead, is entirely coincidental. I alone take full responsibility for any errors or omissions in this book.

-Mike-

BOOKS BY MIKE SHELTON

WESTERN CONTINENT BOOKS:

The Cremelino Prophecy:
The Path Of Destiny
The Path Of Decisions
The Path Of Peace
The Blade and the Bow (A prequel novella to The Cremelino Prophecy)

The Alaris Chronicles:
The Dragon Orb
The Dragon Rider
The Dragon King
Prophecy Of The Dragon (A prequel novella to The Alaris Chronicles)

The Dragon Artifacts:
The Golden Dragon
The Golden Scepter
The Golden Empire

The Wizard Academies
Mark of the Medallion
Search for the Medallion
Power of the Medallion

GEMSTONES OF WAYLAND BOOKS:

The TruthSeer Archives:
TruthStone
TruthSpell
TruthSeer
The Stones of Power (A prequel novella to The TruthSeer Archives)

MAP

See Color map at www.MichaelSheltonBooks.com

STONES OF POWER ON WAYLAND

TruthStone—Moldavite—Green—All Kingdoms

IntelligenceStone—Labradorite—Blue—Kingdom of Galena

StrengthStone—Red Jasper—Red—Kingdom of Gabor

SpeedStone—Garnet—Orange—Kingdom of Antioch

HearingStone—Celestite—White—Kingdom of Althea

HealingStone—Azeztulite—Pink—Kingdom of Shema

CHAPTER ONE

Shaeleen stood on the deck above the bow of a sizable sailing ship with her friend Orin, the city of Mistport looming up in front of them. As her long, brown hair blew around her head, she had to put up a hand to keep it from flying over her face. She peered through the mist in front of her, trying to see the outlines of the city. Then she breathed in deeply and allowed the fresh scenery to help her relax.

The three-day trip from Stronghaven had been difficult for Shaeleen. Her brother, Cole, had traveled with her as her wizard guardian and protector—a fact that still made her shake her head. But an even greater shock was that she, the fifteen-year-old daughter of a carpenter, would need a wizard to accompany her.

Ever since she had been given the TruthStone by its Verlynian keeper, now almost a month ago, Shaeleen's life had been turned upside down. She automatically put her hand to her stomach as she remembered the pain that any lie now caused her—whether told from her own lips or from others'.

"Why so gloomy?" Orin said, his unruly, blond hair blowing around his head also.

Shaeleen glanced down at him—something she wasn't able to do often as most people were taller than her. But Orin was two years younger than Shaeleen and hadn't quite hit his growth spurt yet.

"Just thinking about my brother and our errand to Verlyn," Shaeleen said.

"Is Cole still angry at you?" Orin's face grew grim. He didn't seem to like Cole very much.

"It's not that he's angry." Shaeleen grabbed the railing a bit harder and squeezed. "It's his stupid sense of honor and justice and doing what's right—no, what *he* thinks is right—all the time. It gets tiring."

"Do you want me to do something to him? Tie him up? Throw him off the ship?" Orin smiled, rubbing his hands together in glee. "My power of speed is still faster than his."

"No, Orin!" Shaeleen gave him a stern frown. "You can't just go around using your powers for mischief."

"Then you do something. He is sworn to you," Orin said. "You can make him do whatever you want. I've seen you do it to others before."

Shaeleen turned around, making sure no one was listening. "I only did that TruthSpell when I had to. I would never force my brother to tell the truth." Shaeleen paused then let out a small laugh. "Anyway, Cole always tells the truth, so that wouldn't gain me anything."

"I don't know why you brought him along, Shae," Orin continued. "He's doing this for Prince Calix, not for you or Prince Basil."

"And who am I doing this for, Orin?" Her voice had risen, but it was lost in the mist and wind. "Queen Victoria asked me to bring her daughter, Diamonique, back from Verlyn to marry Basil. But now..." She pushed her hands into her stomach and winced. Just thinking about Prince Basil and his twin brother, Prince Calix, brought her pain if she wasn't careful.

Prince Basil had been raised as the heir to the throne of Galena. When his father had passed away, five years earlier, a regent was named. Now Prince Basil was approaching his seventeenth birthday and was preparing to accept the throne as king, which would include announcing his betrothal to Princess Diamonique of Gabor.

But Shaeleen had learned just one week ago that his brother, Prince Calix, was actually the older twin—a fact that Prince Basil was still not aware of, but one that, according to Cole, Prince Calix did know. Shaeleen assumed his mother and the TruthSeer of Galena had finally told Prince Calix. Now Prince Calix was preparing to take the throne away from his brother, Prince Basil, and had sent Cole to fetch the princess for himself to marry.

The outlines of the harbor were growing more distinct in front of them, and the sky began to clear. The warmth of the sun felt good on Shaeleen's back, and she let out a long breath. She reached under her cloak and ran her hand over a pouch that held the TruthStone. Even through this covering, she could feel the power of the TruthStone, along with faint pulses from the small IntelligenceStone and StrengthStone that were now embedded in it.

Behind them a sailor yelled out, and then Shaeleen and Orin were thrown to the hard wooden deck. Without much warning to its passengers, the ship had turned starboard. It was a slight arc, but it was enough to throw them. As Shaeleen tried to get up, she instead found herself sliding across the slippery decking toward the side of the ship.

"Orin!" she yelled out, not knowing what else to do. The railing was coming toward her fast. She was going to hit into it hard. Shaeleen turned and tried to find something to hold on to, but nothing was close by. Her feet were now sliding in front of her. And, at this rate, she would slide right underneath the railing and fall off the deck into the cold seawater!

Just as her feet went under the railing, she flung her hands out to grab a hold of a nearby baluster. At the same time, a flash of light sped by her and then materialized as Orin crashed into the railing right next to her. With one hand on the railing, he stretched his other hand to Shaeleen. She grabbed it and held on, the rest of her body dangling over the deck's edge.

Luckily, at that exact moment the ship began to right itself and straighten out. Shaeleen let Orin pull her back onto the deck. They both sat there, breathing hard.

"Thanks, Orin," Shaeleen said after a few deep breaths. "Your power of the SpeedStone seems to keep saving my life. I'm surprised by how much it flows through your blood."

Orin shrugged and turned his face away from Shaeleen, pulling himself back up onto his feet. Then he reached down and helped Shaeleen stand back up.

They watched through the lifting mist as their large sailing ship passed close by a small fishing boat—the obvious cause of the sailors' quick maneuvering. Then they moved back to the front of the ship, and Shaeleen continued watching the outline of Mistport form in front of them.

"A quick stop in Mistport, then through the Straits of Mist, and on to Sylvermoor," came a voice from behind them.

Shaeleen jumped and then turned around. "Cole!"

"Did I frighten you, Sister?"

"N-no," Shaeleen stammered, and pain grew in her gut.

Cole tilted his head at her as if assessing her answer himself. He stood six feet tall—almost ten inches taller than Shaeleen herself. His eyes were the same shape and pale blue color as hers, but he had darker hair and a broader build.

"You look pale, Cole. Are you feeling any better?" Shaeleen asked him. He had taken sick during their three-day journey from Stronghaven.

Cole shook his head. "A little, though I feel like going back to bed already. But we need to be ready to find Princess Diamonique. We need a plan."

"So anxious to get the princess back to Calix?" Shaeleen said. "You'll have a few more days to rest and plan, until we are in Sylvermoor."

"*Prince* Calix, Shae. He is a prince of Galena," Cole said seriously. "And he asked me to do this for him. I am as bound to follow through with it as are you in your agreements with Queen Victoria and Prince Basil."

"If you remember, Cole, you and I are not bound to anyone." Shaeleen felt so angry at her brother's need for honor sometimes. "The powers we hold put us outside the laws of any one kingdom. If anything, you are bound to me."

Cole's eyes flashed at her. Ever since she'd turned him into a wizard, he'd seemed to become more hardened. "If you remember, Shae, I bound myself to the truth—something that, as a TruthSeer, you should be familiar with."

Shaeleen ground her teeth together. *A TruthSeer! Ha! That's what holding the TruthStone meant she was, but she'd had no training—besides from a few antiquated books and a life lesson or two.* Both Prince Basil of Galena and Queen Victoria of Gabor had said Shaeleen was the prophesied one. They'd been so sure that they'd willingly given her the last remaining bits of their stones of power. This choice was made with the hope that somehow Shaeleen would be the one able to restore all the stones to their former glories.

Orin stepped closer to Cole and glared up at him. "Just leave her alone, Cole. Can't you see you are causing her pain?"

Cole glared back at Orin but then returned his attention to Shaeleen. He put a hand on the railing and seemed to let a bout of his own stomach pain pass before he could continue speaking. Shaeleen could commiserate with that feeling all too well now. When he turned back to her, his eyes had grown softer and he lowered his voice. "I truly do not want to cause you pain, Shae. I'm sorry."

And Shaeleen knew that for the truth. Her brother was a good person and, at seventeen, was still coming to grips with his own powers and place in this new world of theirs. A part of her knew Cole was right about her. She should be the one defending the truth, not hiding it or hiding from it.

But Prince Basil is loved by the people and is kind and would make such a better king than his power-hungry, angry, mean brother, Prince Calix.

She winced again.

"Shae," Cole said to her. "Stop thinking about it. You'll drive yourself crazy. Right now, we are all on the same errand: to bring back Princess Diamonique from Verlyn to Wayland. We will figure the other things out when the time comes."

Shaeleen smiled at him and let out another sigh—something she found herself doing more often of late. But Orin still glared at Cole.

"Orin, let it go. Cole is right. For now, let's focus on finding Diamonique."

The ship slowed down, and all three of them stood watching the crew maneuver the bulky passenger ship into the harbor at Mistport, the capital city of the kingdom of Antioch. Gulls flew over them, squawking, and the smell of fish rose in the air. It wasn't so different from Stronghaven.

"Orin, how long has it been since you were last home?" Shaeleen asked.

"Last time I stepped foot in Mistport was about six months ago, but I haven't been to my true home, east of the city, for over a year." He frowned for a moment.

"And your father?" Shaeleen asked, for she knew Orin had been traveling with him.

"I saw him in Stronghaven," Orin said. "He will be coming through here soon and then down to South Bay."

"And your mother? You've never spoken of her."

Orin grew quiet. "She was not so fond of my abilities. She grew up in the foothills. That's why my father lived outside of the city—closer to her family rather than his own. My family is…uh…*a little complicated.*"

Shaeleen felt there was more to this statement than he was letting on, but there were no lies in what he'd said.

"My father was only able to use a small amount of the SpeedStone," Orin offered. "Once I started showing signs—and a more powerful affinity for the power of speed—things got uncomfortable around my mother and her family. They're not ones for magic."

This was more than Shaeleen had learned about her new friend in the last two weeks, since they'd first met on a ship going to North Bay. His speed abilities had saved her a few times, and they had become friends. Then he had offered to accompany her on this new errand from Prince Basil and Queen Victoria.

The port side of the ship bumped slightly into the dock, and the crew prepared to let people off and pick up new passengers before embarking over to the island of Verlyn. Orin's stomach rumbled, and Shaeleen got an idea.

"Why don't you show me a good place to eat, Orin?"

Cole put his hand up. "We don't have much time, Shae. The ship will leave in a few hours. The captain asked us to stay on board."

"That's enough time, isn't it, Orin?" Shaeleen said, ignoring Cole's reasons for staying put.

Orin's eyes lit up. "Well, I am hungry."

"You're always hungry!" Shaeleen laughed.

"Well, I am a growing boy," Orin said. "But I don't know if it's the sounds of my hunger driving you to shore or if that nose of yours is already smelling something sweet."

Shaeleen laughed, and even Cole smiled. Everyone knew Shaeleen's propensity for sweets.

"Cole?" Shaeleen asked and turned to her brother to see if he wanted to go along.

He shook his head. "No, I cannot eat anything right now, and anyway I need to lie back down. I need to get over this sickness before we get to Sylvermoor so we can accomplish our task. Just be back before the ship leaves."

Shaeleen smiled and motioned Orin forward, saying, "Orin can surely get us back as quick as we need to." With that, the two headed toward where the other passengers were disembarking.

But it was a long and crowded line. As she smiled over at Orin and winked at him, he caught the meaning. He grabbed her hand, and then everything swirled around them. As everyone froze, she and Orin deftly moved between the passengers. In the blink of an eye, they would be on the docks.

Coming back out of the speed, she hoped others didn't notice. However, this was Antioch, the home of the orange Garnet SpeedStone.

"I thought you said not to use my powers frivolously." Orin smiled over at her.

"Well..." Shaeleen thought for a moment. "Nothing should get in the way of a girl and her sweet rolls!"

Orin laughed and proceeded to direct her out of the docks and into the marketplace.

CHAPTER TWO

Maneuvering through the marketplace to find somewhere to eat was harder than Shaeleen would have thought. The streets here, in Mistport, were narrower than the ones in Stronghaven. She was wearing serviceable traveling attire—a long shirt under a leather vest with black leather pants and high boots—which made moving around much easier than the dresses she usually wore. And a burgundy cloak covered the pouch that hung at her waist—a pouch that held the TruthStone, which could be the means to save Wayland from further chaos.

"This way!" Orin called to her and directed her down a small alley, which wound its way back and forth around so many buildings that Shaeleen soon found herself at a loss for which direction they now traveled in.

"Do you actually know where you're going, Orin?" Shaeleen frowned at him. "We do have to get back soon, and you promised to find me something sweet."

Orin laughed. "I've been playing on these streets since I was a babe."

"Oh, for just a few years, then?" Shaeleen teased.

Orin glared at her. "That's not funny."

"I thought you said you lived west of here, by the mountains," Shaeleen said.

"W-well, I…" Orin stammered.

"You do know I can tell when you're lying."

"I'm not lying," Orin said. "I visited my father's family here many times over the years. It's like a second home to me."

As Shaeleen felt no pain, she laughed. "You're getting used to traveling with me, Orin. You're getting better at avoiding the truth without actually lying, better even than the two TruthSeers we've met."

"I'll take that as a compliment." Orin did laugh this time and then pointed to the end of the alleyway. "Almost there."

They emerged out onto a less crowded street—and one that was considerably nicer. Cobblestone walkways led past well-kept three-story homes and shops. The people walking the streets were well dressed—the men wore fancy caps, and the women wore colorful dresses. And the shops were all well marked and clean.

Shaeleen glanced around in wonder. Compared to the docks, where she now stood seemed like another world. "Orin, are you sure we should be here?" Since the streets were less crowded, Shaeleen also felt as if everyone was looking at them. "This neighborhood looks to be far above us."

"Speak for yourself." Orin grinned. "The best bakery in the city is just up ahead."

Shaeleen smelled the sweet aroma now. Her face broke out into a smile. She grabbed Orin by the arm and began skipping ahead. The dark looks they received from passersby did nothing to dampen her mood.

Entering the bakery, Shaeleen took in a deep breath through her nose. Delightful smells of cinnamon, chocolate, sugar, and freshly baked pastries sent her head reeling with delight.

"Orin, you little scoundrel," said the man at the front counter. He was older than Shaeleen's father, with a small paunch. His white apron held stains from baking, and his hands were dusted with flour. "Where have you been hiding?"

Orin grinned. "Out on the sea, Tam."

"Following your father's ways, I see," Tam said. Then he turned to Shaeleen, and his eyes crinkled in a smile. "And how do you find yourself in such pretty company, Orin?"

Shaeleen smiled at the compliment and nodded her head to Tam. "My name is Shaeleen, sir. Orin and I met on a ship, and he has been a good friend ever since."

Tam nodded and then turned back to Orin with a more serious demeanor. "Have you seen your grandfather lately? Or your mother?"

Orin frowned and glanced at Shaeleen before speaking—he appeared nervous. "No, I haven't. We are only here for a short stop. Then we must get back to the ship."

Tam's eyes lingered on Orin for a moment longer, and Shaeleen saw Orin give a short shake of his head. Tam seemed to get the hint and turned back to Shaeleen, smiling widely once again. "I can tell that you are here for some sweets."

Shaeleen forgot all about Orin's behavior for a moment as she moved closer to the counter and eyed all the sweets there, which had been baked fresh that day. Her eyes lingered on each one in turn. It was so hard to decide.

Tam laughed and eyed Orin. "A sweet tooth this one has."

Orin rolled his eyes. "You have no idea!"

"Well then, the special of the house is the only thing good enough for her." Tam winked at Shaeleen before turning around to prepare something.

Orin rubbed his hands together in delight. "Me too, Tam."

Tam just chuckled and continued working. Shaeleen tried to peek out around him, but he seemed to be purposefully blocking her view.

Finally, he turned and motioned the two of them to a small table in the corner. They sat down obediently, Shaeleen's mouth watering with anticipation.

Tam proceeded to carry out a tray with two plates on it and set it down in front of them. Shaeleen sat speechless for a moment. On top of the small plate sat a fat, circular roll with layers of what appeared to be cinnamon and something creamy inside. Drizzled over the top was melted chocolate. She had never seen—or smelled—anything so delicious in all her life. She glanced up at Tam and then back at the creation again.

"Go ahead," Tam urged. "But I warn you, you may never want to leave the city again." He laughed heartily.

Shaeleen scooped it up in her hand and leaned forward to take a bite. Tam hadn't lied; it was the most delicious thing she had eaten in her entire life. Shaeleen took a second bite and then a third before turning her face back up to Tam's.

Tam smiled down at her. "I take it the pastry meets with your pleasure."

"Mmmm, so good," Shaeleen mumbled between mouthfuls.

Orin laughed and stuffed his roll into his mouth almost as quickly as Shaeleen was. Shaeleen ate the balance of hers without any more talking and then sat back in the chair and relished the experience. Her stomach was now full and happy.

When Orin and Shaeleen stood up to go, Tam came around the corner and put his arm around Orin. "It is good to see you again, my boy. But you should really go and see your mother; she is in town."

Orin's eyes shot open. "Here, in Mistport? Why is she here? Is she all right?"

Tam lowered his eyes. "Aye, she is fine—" Before Tam could continue, Shaeleen leaned over in pain. She clutched her stomach with her hands.

"Shaeleen!" Orin moved over to her and put his hand on her arm. "What's wrong?" Then he realized what was happening and turned toward Tam instead. "You lied to me, Tam!"

Tam put a hand up in the air. "What? Orin, I…"

"She can tell," Orin said, pointing at Shaeleen. "What's really going on with my mother?"

Tam let out a long breath. "I don't know, Orin. She's at some sort of compound on the edge of town. No one knows exactly what's going on there, but…" He paused and snuck a glance at Shaeleen.

She stood up straight once again, cursing the lie for fouling up the tasty sweet roll. She was not happy anymore. Shaeleen moved her hand toward Tam. *I could get the truth out of him with a TruthSpell.*

"No, Shae," Orin called out to her. "Don't!"

Shaeleen stopped and gave both of them a stern look. "What's going on here, Orin? What are you and Tam not telling me?"

Tam spoke to Orin again. "Orin, there are things going on in the city that you're not aware of."

Orin motioned for Tam to continue.

"There are those who want to outlaw magic—take away the power of the stones," Tam continued. "Your mother, well…"

Shaeleen's attention was heightened at the mention of the stones. "What about the king and his TruthSeer? They should be protecting the kingdom."

Tam turned to her. "The king has grown weak."

With that statement, Shaeleen knew the truth of things. Then the power of the TruthStone soared through her, and she knew what she needed to do now. "Orin, we need to see the king."

Orin's eyes popped wide. "Oh no, Shae. I can't do that."

"Why not, Orin? What are you hiding?"

Orin ground his teeth at her and, instead of responding to her question, asked one of his own. "Can we see my mother first?"

"Is she involved with the movement to ban magic?" Shaeleen asked Tam.

As the baker started to shrug his shoulder and to lie, Shaeleen could feel the pounding in her head start. She gave a look to Orin, and he knew what it meant.

"Tam," Orin said, "you can tell us."

Tam nodded his head. "Your mother's family is at the heart of it. They have set up a magic-free compound west of the city. Its numbers grow daily."

Shaeleen nodded her head to Orin. That was the truth.

Orin's face fell. Shaeleen had never seen this usually happy young man look so depressed.

"She never did like it much." Orin held his head down low. "That's what drove my father to the sea."

"We don't have much time, Orin," Shaeleen said, catching his eyes. "We must get back to the ship soon."

Orin nodded his understanding.

"I really don't want to face my brother's *I-told-you-to-stay-here* lecture, Orin," Shaeleen said. "That would be worse than the captain's reprimand."

"I will get us back in time," Orin said firmly.

Shaeleen and Orin walked to the door. She gave Tam a smile and thanked him for the sweet roll—though his recent words had already soured the memory of it. "Maybe I will come back someday under better circumstances."

They opened the door, but just before they stepped out, Tam offered one last bit of news to Orin. "Also, your two uncles are missing."

Orin put his hand on the doorframe and almost fell over. His eyes clouded over, and then he went pale.

"Orin, what's wrong?" Shaeleen grabbed onto him. "What's going on here?"

Orin just shook his head. "Later," was all he said as he grabbed her hand and drew upon his power from the SpeedStone that flowed through his blood. He whisked himself and Shaeleen through the streets of town. Houses and strangers blurred around them, not even aware of who sped by. The people stood frozen in place as the two whizzed by. They sped through numerous alleys, and out the back gates of Mistport. Trees, grasslands, and farm animals flew by in mere moments of time. They travelled now toward a large compound encircled by a wall.

Preparing to go through on open gate, they instead fell out of the speed and hit into an invisible wall at the entrance to the compound. Orin fell to the ground, and Shaeleen tripped over him, dazed for a moment, trying to figure out what had happened.

"What happened?" Orin questioned as they untangled themselves. They stood in front of an open gate surrounded by a twenty-foot stone wall. On top of the wall was a walkway, where half a dozen armed men stood with drawn bows, all pointing arrows at the two of them.

Shaeleen raised her eyebrows at Orin. Something had stopped his power of speed.

A hefty man walked out of a small door in the stone wall and greeted them with a smirk, "Welcome to the compound."

Following behind the hefty man at the small door had been three other men, who could only be described as *guards*. They'd held swords in their hands and had scowls on their faces. Without any other words, Shaeleen and Orin were ushered inside, and then the door was closed behind them.

CHAPTER THREE

As soon as they had entered the compound, Shaeleen had immediately felt something different inside of her. Her connection to Cole was now gone. *How can that be?* Maybe it had to do with his sickness.

Shaeleen tried to concentrate on their current condition as she gazed around. Their surroundings were similar to any small village. A main, dirt-packed thoroughfare ran for a few blocks in front of them. Shops lined this road, with other merchants set up under tents in what looked like a town square. Smaller roads led off to the sides, where newly built stone and wooden homes sat—most with small vegetable gardens out front.

She also saw men and women in serviceable, homespun clothes walking around on their daily business. And three children ran in front of her and Orin, laughing.

The town spread out farther than Shaeleen could see, but it appeared to have within its walls everything that people would need to live a comfortable life. And the only things marring its idyllic setting were the guards posted on each corner and the walls that seemed to surround everything.

Then a woman came up to Shaeleen and Orin. She was middle-aged and appeared to be fit. She had dark blond hair that fell just below her shoulders, her green eyes seemed intelligent and serious, and her face held a pleasant but determined look—that was, until she looked at Orin. Then the woman's eyes and expression darkened.

"Orin," the woman said as she let out a sigh.

"Mother," Orin said back as they all stood in the middle of the road.

Mother? Shaeleen wondered as she threw a questioning glance at Orin.

"My mother, Miriam," Orin said. "Mother, this is Shaeleen, a friend of mine."

Miriam glanced at Shaeleen in only a perfunctory way, as if discounting her presence almost immediately. Turning her attention back to her son, Miriam asked, "What are you doing here?"

"I could ask the same of you. What is all of this?" Orin asked as he moved his hand around in front of him.

Miriam's eyes brightened, and she smiled. Shaeleen could see where Orin got his smile from. Miriam was quite a beautiful person when she smiled.

The hefty man who had greeted them at the gate walked up to them now and gave a slight bow to Miriam. "Founder, these two were stopped by the wall. They need to be cleansed."

Cleansed? Shaeleen began to panic. *What does that mean?* It didn't sound good. She needed to find out the truth of what was going on here, for they had to get back to their ship soon, and they still had to see the king. They would have maybe an hour in total—Orin could get them back to their ship fast, but they'd only have a few minutes to see his mother.

So Shaeleen stepped forward. "Miriam—" she started to say but was then grabbed roughly from behind. It was one of the gate guards.

"Miriam is a founder," the guard said. "She will address you when she is ready."

"Mother!" Orin said loudly and moved over closer to Shaeleen. "Shaeleen is my friend. What's going on here?"

"Yes," Shaeleen said, despite the warning not to speak. "What is this place?"

Shaeleen felt the sting of a slap as the guard brought his hand down across her face. She had seen the guard bringing his hand up toward her. But she had watched Orin out of the corner of her eye instead of defending herself, for she knew Orin would speed to her defense and stop the guard. But, instead, Orin had fallen to the ground next to her. Shaeleen pulled her arm free from the guard and bent down by Orin, pushing the pain of the slap to the back of her mind.

"It didn't work," Orin said to Shaeleen. "I'm sorry, my speed didn't work."

Shaeleen stood up, taking two steps toward Miriam. Miriam was taller than Shaeleen by a few inches, but Shaeleen reached to pull on her powers. *I will find the truth of things now.*

But nothing happened, and she couldn't feel her powers. What was going on? Could this place stop magic? And, if so, how? She needed to test it out.

Reaching down to help Orin stand up, she leaned in to him and whispered, "Tell a lie."

He gave her a questioning look. But she urged him on with a look of her own.

"Nice to see you again, Mother," Orin said.

Nothing. No pain. No desire to vomit or throbbing in Shaeleen's head. Maybe Orin *was* happy to see Miriam. No, not with the way they were being greeted.

She had to think of a way out of this. She tried to pull on the power of the small IntelligenceStone she held in the TruthStone. But nothing came. Not feeling a connection to Cole might not have anything to do with his sickness.

Orin's mother motioned for the men to bring Orin and Shaeleen along. Then she turned to Orin. "I really hope you can see that what we do here, Orin, is for the best."

Still no pain. Shaeleen reached inside herself and tried to find the power of truth that had been her constant companion for the last month. Only emptiness met her. She glanced at Orin, and she could see her own thoughts mirrored in his eyes.

Our magic is gone!

She realized that it was going to be difficult to get back to the ship in time.

Cole! she cried out in her mind. But she didn't think he would hear her now.

* * *

An hour later, after Shaeleen and Orin had been left alone in a small, guarded room, a young woman barely older than Orin came in. Orin seemed to perk up in her presence.

"Claire!" Orin rushed to the young woman's side. "What are you doing here?"

Claire watched the guard and then turned back to Orin. Her expression had stayed neutral, except for her eyes. These flashed with joy at seeing Orin. With her back to the guard, she mouthed, "Hello, Orin." But, externally, she said, "The founders have requested your presence."

Claire led Shaeleen and Orin, with two guards following them, out of the room, down a short hallway, and out of another door. They walked for a few moments outdoors toward a larger building. It was made of sturdy logs and looked like it would be able to hold a few hundred people. As they walked this short distance, townspeople turned toward them, a fervor lighting their eyes.

Orin turned, looking about him in quick glances, like he would bolt at any time. Without the use of their individual powers, though, and with the number of guards that stood around them, they wouldn't have much chance of escape. Shaeleen noticed that Orin's eyes softened and steadied when they settled on Claire. Claire only smiled at him and kept them walking forward.

Soon they entered the larger building. At one end of the room sat a rickety table. Shaeleen frowned at its poor workmanship. Her father took much more pride in building the furniture that he sold. Around the table sat five men and three women, including Orin's mother, Miriam. Just before they arrived at the table, Shaeleen noticed as Claire reached over and squeezed Orin's hand, but Claire dropped it as soon as a man arose from the table and walked up to them.

"Claire," the man said, "thank you for bringing the newcomers." The man was not very tall, but he seemed fit. His smile appeared to be genuine, and it had softened when he was addressing Claire. Then he turned to Orin. "I was hoping that, if you saw a familiar face, it would make this transition easier for you. I know you and Claire were good friends."

Orin only nodded at the man, but he didn't speak. Then he turned his attention to the table and glared at his mother.

"You may go now, Claire," the man said.

"Thank you, Papa," Claire said and turned to go. Before leaving the room, she glanced over her shoulder at Shaeleen and Orin but said nothing.

The man led Shaeleen and Orin closer to the table as he said, "Orin knows me. I am Speaker Alain." He paused and then spread his arms out toward the table. "And these are the founders."

Shaeleen and Orin stood at a short end of the table as each of the men and women seated nodded at them.

"And what are you the founders of?" Shaeleen asked, speaking for the first time since entering the room. She knew she couldn't rely on her powers for now. But she hadn't always had them. And speaking up had never been a problem for her before. "We need to leave here right away."

Miriam stood up to answer, "We are the founders of this compound: a society that is pledged to live away from magic and to eradicate its effects from our land. And we determine if and when you will leave here."

The boldness of this statement surprised Shaeleen. Things seemed to be falling apart here, in the kingdom of Antioch, even more than they were in Galena and Gabor.

"And why do you think eradicating magic is the best course of action here?" Shaeleen asked, speaking bravely to the group. "Why can't you just live free from magic on your own and not bother others?"

Alain, still standing, motioned for Miriam to resume her seat. "Founder, these proceedings have an order, as you are aware. The questions asked by these two young people will not determine how we proceed."

Miriam didn't look happy, but she sat down nevertheless, followed by Alain. No chairs were offered to Shaeleen and Orin.

"We will now proceed with the trial of Orin and his friend, Shaeleen," Alain said. "All founders are in attendance, and all are in accord on this matter."

Each founder in turn said, "Aye," until coming to Miriam. She paused for a bit while staring down at the table. When she brought her head up, she peered intently at her son.

Orin held her eyes and didn't flinch.

"Aye," she finally stated.

"A trial for what?" Shaeleen asked.

Without warning, the back of her legs screamed with pain, and she fell to the floor. Up above her stood one of the guards. He held a small polished stick in his hand. The two-foot piece of wood was stained pure black and had been polished to a shine. Shaeleen thought she saw a wispy tendril of black fog surrounding the stick, but the fog dissipated before she could be sure. She didn't know what the stick was, but it had given a staggering shock of pain to her legs.

Orin reached over and helped Shaeleen up. Then his eyes turned to his mother with what seemed to be murderous intent. But his mother wasn't looking at Orin. With pinched lips, she kept her focus on Speaker Alain.

Alain waited patiently until Shaeleen resumed standing before he spoke again. "You will answer our questions when we speak to you. We are not on trial, so we have no obligation to answer your questions. Is that understood?"

Shaeleen nodded.

But Orin did not. "Wait until the king finds out about this," he said, testing their patience. Then he howled in pain as the stick brought him to the floor. From that position, there on the hardwood, he spoke once more—turning his attention toward his mother. "Or wait until my father finds out." He writhed in pain as the guard struck him again. But Shaeleen saw Orin's mother flinch at his words.

Shaeleen helped Orin to his feet. With a look of unspoken agreement, they resumed their stances at the end of the table and stood still as they met the stare of Alain and of each of the founders.

CHAPTER FOUR

"Are you displeased with the question, miss?" Alain asked.

For the past hour, Shaeleen and Orin had both refused to answer any questions. Speaker Alain's patience had seemed to be endless, but the rest of the founders had seemed to be getting restless. Shaeleen hadn't even heard the last question that had been asked. They all had to do with their magic—when it had manifested, what their limits were, what they'd done with it—the list had gone on and on.

The day had grown warmer, and the founders now began to fan themselves. So Speaker Alain called for a brief recess.

Before proceeding any further, a tray of cups and refreshment were brought out for them, and the founders all stood and stretched their legs, filing off in groups of twos and threes to the far corners of the room. Even the guards had turned away to get cups of water. Shaeleen's own mouth felt dry and tasted stale. The only thing she had eaten that day was the sweet roll that morning. But it was now sometime after noon.

Shaeleen knew they had only a very short time left before their ship would leave Mistport, if it hadn't gone already. She wondered if her brother, in his sickened state would even knew they were still on land. Cole had been spending more time practicing his wizard skills. *Something that would be handy at the moment.* This thought brought a frown to her face, for magic didn't seem to work here in the compound.

Shaeleen let out a deep sigh. Thinking of Cole had been a welcome distraction. She'd tried to reason out how these people had blocked her magic, but she couldn't find a solution yet.

With this unanticipated break, Shaeleen turned to Orin and said, "You doing all right?"

Orin's eyes flashed darkly. "I can't believe my mother is involved in this." He waved his hand back toward the founders. "My uncle and grandfather, as well as others from where we used to live, are founders. Alain and his wife Coral and their daughter, Claire, were all good friends of our family."

"How did they take our powers, Orin?" Shaeleen whispered back. "That's what I want to know."

"I don't know," Orin said, moving closer to her. "They haven't seen your stone."

Having the stone here worried Shaeleen. *What if they find it and take it from me?* What would happen then to the kingdoms of Wayland?

She remembered the day about a month previous when the keeper of Verlyn had given Shaeleen the TruthStone and had told her she was prophesied to gather all the stones. Each of the five kingdoms of Wayland held a stone of power, and each had a TruthSeer to protect that kingdom. Shaeleen had gathered two of the five stones already. But what if these were taken from her now?

"Then why do they think I have magic?" Shaeleen asked. "They can't know for sure."

Orin seemed to catch on. "They know about me, because of my mother, and they stopped me when we sped here. But they don't know about you. You can get away, Shaeleen."

"How?" Shaeleen asked. "They won't let me go after this."

They both stood in silence as the founders regrouped and sat down once again. Speaker Alain appeared ready to talk, when Orin suddenly spoke up.

"Speaker, I have something to say," Orin said.

The guard brought the shock stick back up, but Alain held up his hand for him to stop. "Let's hear what the boy has to say. After over an hour of silence, I am curious as to what has finally filled his mind to such importance that he now feels compelled to speak."

Shaeleen shot Orin a sideways look. *What is he doing?*

Orin took a half step in front of Shaeleen, and it almost appeared he would turn toward her, but he didn't. Instead, he faced the founders in an eerily calm manner.

"I will admit to all you have put to me and will submit to your cleansing on one condition," Orin said in a loud and clear voice.

No, Orin! Shaeleen felt what Orin was intending to do.

"You do not set the conditions," shouted out the oldest founder of the group, the man that Shaeleen determined must be Orin's grandfather.

Alain held up his hand in the air. "Let him speak."

Orin took a deep breath before speaking. "I hold the powers of the SpeedStone and have used them recently, even while coming here to visit my mother." Orin glanced at his mother, but her face held no expression. "But my friend Shaeleen was not born with any powers."

Shaeleen had to bite her lip at the way Orin had said that. He was so used to being around her that, even when she couldn't feel the pain of a lie, he proceeded deftly.

"She is the daughter of a carpenter from Stronghaven and had befriended me on a ship sailing from Stronghaven to North Bay. She was accompanying me back to my hometown and was interested in seeing some of the sights of Mistport—especially the bakery in the nobles' district." He smiled, making his performance seem flawless. "She does have a sweet tooth. When Baker Tam saw me, he was kind enough to tell me my mother was close by, and so, before Shaeleen's ship sailed back out, we determined to visit."

There were a few minor lies in his words—Shaeleen knew, not from her powers but because she knew what they had really been doing—but most of what he'd said was true.

"I will submit to your cleansing and stay here with my mother if you let Shaeleen go back to Stronghaven," Orin said in conclusion.

"No!" Shaeleen said without thinking, and the shock stick hit her in the back of her legs.

"Shaeleen," Orin said, looking down at her. She could see compassion and affection in his eyes. "I will be fine. There is no reason for you to stay here. You have no magic in your blood."

Tears stung her eyes, and words choked in her throat. She dared not say anything else. *How can I get Orin to change his mind?*

"The founders will consider your words, young Orin," Alain said. He then turned to Miriam. "Founder Miriam, do you have any other questions or comments to add to this proceeding?"

It grew quiet in the room as all awaited her answer. Then she stood and, after taking a deep breath, turned once again into the stern founder Shaeleen and Orin had encountered upon their entrance into the compound.

"You will not regret this decision, Orin," Miriam said. "This is for the best. Magic has caused heartache in our kingdom. Attaining the favor of the SpeedStone has driven men to do horrible things. And now, the magic is too widespread and the king is too weak to do anything about it." As Miriam spoke, her fervor seemed to grow greater. Her eyes took on a sheen of excitement.

Shaeleen felt the truth of Miriam's words and wondered if, somehow, she was still feeling some influence of the TruthStone.

"King Wayland never intended so many people to hold magic," Miriam continued. "Over the past two hundred years, it has now corrupted us. This place," she spread her arms out to her sides, "this compound, is the start of a new era. The overseer has given us a place without magic. Soon we will spread throughout all of Antioch and then all of Wayland. We will choose our leaders not by the power of the stones they hold but by the type of people they are. Justice, peace, and fairness will prevail."

Shaeleen stood mesmerized by this speech. Who was this overseer Miriam had mentioned? Shaeleen wished she had her powers to help her know if it was all true or not and if Miriam really believed it.

On the surface, it sounded good. But…things were not always what they seemed. Shaeleen's own land of Galena was proof of that. For her entire life—and especially since the last king had died—she had always heard that Prince Basil was the crown prince. And now, to have found out that Prince Calix is the oldest… No, things were not always what they appeared to be.

Prince Calix was mean, self-centered, and would bring destruction to their kingdom, Shaeleen was sure. But the truth of the matter was that Prince Calix was the oldest—a truth she had found out but had kept hidden from Prince Basil. At least, for these last hours in the compound, she hadn't had to feel the pain of that deceit.

"Orin," Miriam continued, "I have always loved you. But, as you know, your powers made me and others uncomfortable. Now, if you are cleansed, you can help us build a bright, new, and wonderful future."

Shaeleen frowned at Miriam's last statements and looked over at Orin. He too had a frown but would not look back at Shaeleen. He only nodded silently at his mother as she sat down.

"This court is dismissed," Alain said. "We will reconvene when a decision has been made."

The two guards took Orin and Shaeleen by their arms and led them back toward the room they had been held in before.

Once they were back in the room, the guard closed the door, and the lock clicked into place. Then Shaeleen turned to

Orin, who was already sitting in one corner. She took a few steps toward him and knelt down in front of him. A rock from the hard-packed dirt floor poked through her pants, and she grimaced a moment before moving a few inches to the side. Then she opened her mouth to speak, but Orin beat her to it.

"Don't say anything, Shae." Orin brought his head up and peered into her eyes. "I know what you're going to say. I know every argument you can use against me. But I thought about this the entire hour of their questions. It's the only way to get you out of here." Orin's words had picked up speed, as if he thought that, by taking a breath, he would lose his train of thought. "I'm not sure what you are or what your powers are meant to be, but I have seen enough to know that you are at the center of everything going on in the kingdoms of Wayland right now."

Shaeleen felt the beginning of tears in her eyes. "Oh, Orin," was all she could say as she gathered him into her arms.

CHAPTER FIVE

There were no windows in the room where they had been sitting. So the passing of time had only been broken by a small meal that had been brought in to them at some point in the evening. A small candle had been left for them but it was hard to tell what time of day it was. After the evening meal Shaeleen and Orin had both slept, but they hadn't talked much—both seeming deep in their own thoughts.

Shaeleen spent most of the next day pacing the tiny wooden room back and forth, trying to think of a way out.

"You'll be out of here soon, Shae," Orin said at one point. "Just stop the pacing, will you?"

After receiving nothing but six small meals, Shaeleen was going stir-crazy. "It helps me think," Shaeleen said, but she stopped moving. "The key to all of this is how they are blocking our magic. Your magic was inherited somehow through your Antioch bloodline—stronger than most, but you don't actually have a stone."

His fingers moved nervously, as if he were hiding something. "Um…well…" he stumbled on his words. But he eventually answered, "No, Shae. I don't have a stone. It just runs in my blood. And I don't like being without it."

"But it must come through your father's line, as your mother obviously doesn't have any of the stone's power—or want any," Shaeleen continued in her line of thinking. Orin wasn't telling her something. She was sure of it. But it was no use forcing the truth out of him—something she couldn't even do at the moment, anyway.

"But your power comes directly from the stone," Orin offered. "So I see what you mean. Our powers come from different sources…or, at least, they came to us in different ways."

"Someone is doing this to us, Orin." Shaeleen hit the wall with her fist. "Someone with magic. That's the only way. If I could just get out of this place and look around—"

Her words were cut off as she heard a sound at the door. Both Shaeleen and Orin moved closer together. The founders must have come to a resolution on the matter. Then a woman with a hood over her head walked into the room.

"Claire!" Orin cried out, recognizing her as his longtime friend.

Claire nodded to the guard behind her and closed the door. She moved over to Orin and gave him a hug. "I'm so sorry, Orin."

"Have they come to a decision yet?" Shaeleen asked.

"Soon, I fear," Claire said. "They were waiting for the overseer to return. But I begged my father to come and spend some time with you."

"Overseer?" Shaeleen asked.

Claire's face grew dark and more distant. "He's in charge here."

Well, that was a place to start, then, Shaeleen thought. She watched Claire, an idea forming in her mind. She realized the younger woman was about her own height, and their hair colors were similar.

"Claire, would you allow me to get out of here and look around?"

"What are you thinking, Shae?" Orin asked.

Claire squinted her eyes at Shaeleen and tilted her head to the side. "I don't know what you mean. You can't leave." Tears began to form at the corners of her eyes. "No one can leave…ever."

Shaeleen put a hand on Claire's arm to try to comfort her. "You could give me your cloak."

"What?" Claire asked. "What do you mean?"

"You could give me your cloak and call for the guard to let you out," Shaeleen said, grabbing onto the first stirrings of hope she had felt in two days. She knew that her brother would be desperately looking for her and that they needed to get to Verlyn—which meant her getting out of the compound as soon as possible. "I could go out in your stead and look around. I need to find whoever is blocking our powers."

Claire's eyes went wide. "So you have the powers of the stones too?"

Shaeleen groaned. She needed to be more careful. "No. Of course not," she lied and felt relief that the lie had caused her no pain. *Maybe life will be easier without the stone.* But she had to at least get Orin out. And, deep inside, she knew she needed to get her powers back, for she had to save Prince Basil's throne. "I'm just worried about Orin, that's all."

Claire didn't seem like she believed Shaeleen much.

"Let her do it, Claire," Orin pleaded. "She can help us and you."

Claire only nodded and slowly took off her cloak and gave it to Shaeleen, who put it on and pulled its hood up over her head, letting her brown hair flow out in a similar fashion as Claire's.

"Any idea who or what is blocking the use of magic in the compound?" Shaeleen asked.

Claire immediately shook her head, but then she scrunched up her eyes and seemed to be thinking for a moment. "Well…" Claire paused. "There is a building in the western back corner of the compound that was recently built—I see smoke come out of its chimney periodically, like food is being cooked inside. We are not allowed in that direction. I…" she choked on her words for a moment. "I've heard maybe the overseer stays there."

Shaeleen smiled and clapped her hands together. "Perfect! That's where I will start."

"Be careful, Shaeleen," Orin warned. "I won't be there to help you get away quickly."

Claire walked up to the door and yelled for the guard to open it. Shaeleen pulled the hood further over her head and nodded her thanks as she left. Claire hid behind the door, remaining inside of the room.

Shaeleen kept her head down as she walked past another guard, who called out Claire's name. She reached a hand up and waved to him, but Shaeleen kept her head down and used a cough to cover up her reason for not vocally responding. Then she left the building and moved out into the compound.

It was early evening, the sun hanging low in the sky. *Another hour of daylight at most.* Shaeleen wiped beads of sweat from her forehead and began walking. The late spring rains had turned the hills that rose up outside of the compound green. She knew these hills led eventually to the Great Mountain Divide—all of which were westward from here, the direction that Claire had said she had seen the newer building.

Keeping to the shadows, Shaeleen crept slowly westward, stopping behind wooden structures to let people pass in front of her. Soon she came to the end of the homes and entered a small pasture. Cows stood eating their shares of grass and paid no attention to Shaeleen as she moved forward. Trees were few and far between here, but she stopped at each one and peered around. Then she heard voices, off in the distance behind her, but no sounds in the direction she was moving, except the light echo of a stream.

As she walked forward again, her hand moved to the pouch that held the TruthStone. She wrapped her hand around it, willing the stone to respond to her touch.

Nothing happened.

Soon she came to a creek, leafy oaks growing along its borders. The creek also ran to the west, toward the hills. She decided to follow it, but then she heard voices in front of her. Moving slowly behind some of the older oaks, she peeked her head around one of them and then pulled it back.

On the banks of the river, three people stood talking, a small home behind them. One she recognized as Alain. Another was a woman that was one of the founders. The third person she couldn't quite see yet.

"The boy definitely has the power of speed," Alain said softly. "He says the girl doesn't have any powers, but I still don't trust her."

"I don't think she is a danger to us," the woman said. "We should let her go. She isn't even from Antioch. What trouble could she cause us? And, what trouble will Galena cause if they find out that we have one of their citizens?"

Shaeleen breathed a sigh of relief. She might be let go after all.

"Tell me about this young woman," a third voice said. It was deep and powerful and held a slight accent, as if this person was not from the local area. Shaeleen peeked around the tree again.

"She is of no consequence, Overseer Georrod," the woman said with a wave of her hand.

What exactly is an overseer? Shaeleen thought for the third time that day.

She took a few steps to her right, behind another tree, for she needed to see who this man was. The sun was still halfway above the horizon and behind the man, making it hard for Shaeleen to see him. Then Shaeleen's foot stepped on a small twig, and it cracked under her weight. She dropped to the ground behind a tree and hoped she wouldn't be noticed.

Peering through a small bush, she watched as Alain and the woman turned around and scanned the area quickly. All three had stopped talking.

"Most likely a squirrel," Alain finally said.

"The girl?" the overseer said once again.

"She is short—no taller than five foot two—and has long, brown hair," the woman founder said. "She is very thin but has a pleasant face. She could be anyone's daughter from Galena."

"And her eyes?" the overseer asked.

"Her eyes?" the woman asked.

Alain stood up straighter and groaned, as if realizing their mistake. "Her eyes, Overseer, are pale blue…the color of your own eyes."

Shaeleen put her hand over her mouth to stifle a gasp and moved another foot to her right. The sun had moved lower, and the overseer took a step toward the two founders. His hair was pale and long—down to his waist—and his face was thin. When he turned his head to the side, the fading sunlight caught his features: upturned ears and brows.

Verlyn! The man was from Verlyn. *How could that be? What would he be doing here?*

"I am glad I returned when I did," the overseer said. "She matches the description we have heard about. If the rumors are believed, she is very powerful."

"Powerful, my lord?" the woman said. "I highly doubt that."

The overseer moved his hand up in front of himself and pointed it at the woman. As Shaeleen watched, black tendrils of power flew from his fingertips and swirled around the founder.

The woman gasped and moved her hands to her neck. "Do you doubt my words?" Then the woman shook her head violently and fell to her knees.

Shaeleen stayed as still as she could on the ground, her mind reeling with what she had just seen. Then she realized what she had been doing: she was holding the TruthStone pouch in her hand. For a brief moment, while the man had been using his powers, Shaeleen thought she had felt warmth come through the pouch onto her hand. She didn't dare open the pouch now, to look, but this experience gave her hope.

"Enough, Overseer," Alain said to the man. "If you remember, magic is not allowed here."

The overseer turned to Alain and nodded his head. "Very well." He pulled his hand back, and the tendrils disappeared.

The woman stayed on her knees and seemed to be gasping for breath.

"We will take care of the girl," Alain said. "She will be cleansed along with the boy."

Shaeleen gulped.

"Soon, all magic will be eradicated from this land and back on Verlyn, where it belongs," the overseer said. "It is too dangerous in your kingdoms' hands."

"Just keep your part of the bargain."

"Don't threaten me, Alain," the overseer said with a sneer. "You will rule at our pleasure. Don't overstep your bounds."

"And the king's sons?" Alain asked.

"The two oldest are gone; only the youngest remains," the overseer said. "He will soon meet with an accident at sea."

The woman rose from the ground, still struggling with her breathing. "Let's go, Alain," she croaked. "The other founders are waiting for us."

With no other words, Alain and the woman turned and took a small trail that Shaeleen hadn't seen before. It followed along the creek, back toward the village. After they had passed by her, she remained where she was hiding, waiting for the man from Verlyn to turn to go back to his home. But he stayed still for a few more minutes and moved his eyes carefully over the copse of trees in front of him—the same one Shaeleen was hiding in. At one point, he seemed to look directly at her. She closed her eyes, knowing they could reflect the final light of day.

Once again, the pouch warmed.

Soon she heard the man's feet rustle over the ground, and she peeked out slowly. He had gone. Letting out a deep breath, she waited a few more minutes before heading back. She needed to get Orin out and then leave and find her brother.

Coming up to the guard, she motioned for him to open the door again. She cleared her voice and tried to sound as close as she could to Claire's voice. "I'm sorry, I'm not feeling well. I need to see the prisoners one last time. The founders are coming for them soon."

The guard looked at her with suspicion but reached toward the door. Somehow, his arm bumped into Shaeleen's head, and the hood on the cloak that she wore slipped back, off her head.

"You are not Claire!" the guard yelled out and moved toward Shaeleen.

Shaeleen tried to duck and kick out at him at the same time, for she was used to having the StrengthStone at her disposal. When her feet didn't do much against the ankles of the guard, she tried to run around him. But the man was too fast. By then, another guard had heard the commotion and had joined them, grabbing her from behind—completely defeating her.

I should have just ran away on my own, Shaeleen thought to herself. Obviously, she wasn't able to pull on the IntelligenceStone at the moment, and her own plan, of returning for Orin, hadn't worked.

Opening the door of the room, the guard shoved Shaeleen inside, causing her to stumble and fall to the floor. Meanwhile, the other guard roughly pulled Claire out.

"Your father will hear about this," growled one of the guards.

Shaeleen turned around and looked up at the guard from the ground. "She didn't have anything to do with it," Shaeleen said. "It was all my plan."

As the second guard began closing the door, Shaeleen heard him say to the first guard, "They will be cleansed soon. Then we'll see how defiant they are."

As the door closed, Shaeleen heard a booming laugh from one of the guards. She stood up with her fists clenched. "How dare they treat us like this, Orin." She breathed in a few deep breaths. "Cleansed! Over my dead body."

CHAPTER SIX

The next morning, Shaeleen and Orin were taken from their prisonlike room and were escorted by a half-dozen guards out to the town square. Morning fog that hadn't yet burned off swirled around the square and reduced visibility down most of the side streets. The temperature had stayed warm overnight, and the warm, sticky air clung now to Shaeleen's face and dampened her hair.

By the looks of it, the entire compound had gathered for the *cleansing*. A few of the older members sat on chairs, but the remainder used crates or stood on their feet. And some enterprising vendor had brought a cart out and was selling drinks and sweet pastries. Their smell tickled Shaeleen's nose and made her mouth water.

"What is this cleansing?" Orin asked, seemingly more to himself than as if expecting an answer from anyone. To Shaeleen, he said, "They should have let you go free. I'm sorry."

"We'll get out of this, Orin," Shaeleen said to try to comfort him. But, in reality, she didn't have a good plan yet. She kept hoping Cole would find them. But, without their magic connection and with Cole never having been in this city before, she couldn't plan on that. *I will have to get out of this myself!*

Everything quieted down as the eight founders walked forward and spread out in a line in front of the group. Orin seemed to try to catch his mother's eyes, but she gazed out over the townspeople along with the rest of the founders.

Then Alain took a step out in front of them and raised a hand up in the air. "Be it known that the two people in front of you—Orin and Shaeleen—have been found guilty of using and holding magic. Their punishment—and their salvation—will be the cleansing." At this, he raised both his hands in the air.

"Cleanse them," the crowd chanted in unison. "Free them from their abomination."

Shaeleen scanned the crowd again. They were being worked up into a frenzy. They began to stomp their feet and yell out in the air. *How many of them had been cleansed?* Shaeleen wondered. There was no way of knowing. A foreboding prescience fell over her, and she turned to Orin with wide eyes.

Then Alain motioned to the side of the crowd, where, through the lingering fog, four men came forward, carrying two long tables. Setting these down in front of Orin and Shaeleen, the men then proceeded to grab her and Orin and forced them onto their backs on the tables.

"No!" Shaeleen yelled as she kicked and screamed. "This is wrong! Let me go!" She flailed her arms, but another guard stepped forward, grabbing her hands, and held her arms to the sides of her body. Meanwhile, the others had tied her legs and her middle to the table's hard wood.

"Mother?" Orin whispered quietly, as if in desperation.

Shaeleen turned her head to the founders and caught Miriam's eyes. For a brief moment, they seemed to hold doubt. Then that look was replaced by hard determination.

Then two doctors, by the look of their white coats, came forward. They each carried a pig bladder, full of something, and a handful of things that looked like tubes made from intestines. One doctor approached Shaeleen, and the other approached Orin. The doctor tied a tight cloth around Shaeleen's right arm and then, with a sharp knife, cut into her vein.

Alain spoke again, a gleeful fervor apparent in his eyes. "Let the bloodletting begin."

The crowd cheered.

"The bloodletting will drain the tainted blood from their bodies, removing any presence of their powers," continued Alain.

Shaeleen turned her head and found Orin already peering in her direction. He seemed to be gritting his teeth to keep from crying out. But his eyes pleaded with her to help him. Shaeleen herself felt no pain, but a light-headedness enveloped her thinking, and she felt herself zone out for a few moments. Alain's voice pulled her from her trance.

"The cleansing!" he yelled out, and the crowd responded in like manner.

"Aaargh!" Orin yelled out in obvious turmoil and pain. His power was in his blood.

"Cleanse them with the pure blood of youth!" Alain shouted out.

Shaeleen felt the doctor cut her other arm and saw him take what looked like the quill of a pen and stick into her arm with a quick jab. She heard screaming and then realized it was her own voice mixed with Orin's. The doctor connected the intestine tubing, which was attached to the pig bladder, to the other end of the quill stuck in her arm. Then he forced through the tubing fresh blood, transferring it into her body.

Looking over at Orin, she saw something else rising from his arm when the new blood hit his body—a black tendril of twisted fog. Then it seemed to move inside of his arm and disappear.

Shaeleen felt warmth growing next to the outside of her thigh, and then she felt her heart skip a beat as she realized that Georrod, the overseer from Verlyn, was there somewhere and the TruthStone was responding to his powers somehow. There was some kind of connection between them that she didn't have time to think about just then. She was just happy that she had her powers back!

Shaeleen tried to concentrate—the bloodletting was making her light-headed. But her power wasn't in her blood; it was in the stone, which had miraculously stayed hidden in the pouch that Prince Basil had given her.

"Shae!" Orin groaned loudly. "I can't take much more of this."

Shaeleen closed her eyes and moved her right hand ever so slightly, to touch the outside of the pouch. As she did so, it became even warmer. The power of the TruthStone was responding somehow to the evil power of the overseer. Shaeleen's power was not in her blood. It came from the still hidden stone at her side. *It will protect us. It has to!*

Digging deep inside for power, she focused on the warmth of the TruthStone and searched for the small Red Jasper StrengthStone embedded in it.

She pulled the StrengthStone's power into her body. As it responded, Shaeleen pulled her arms up into the air and, with a terrible roar of pain, ripped the tubing out of her left arm and pushed the guard away. She almost blacked out, but the power of the StrengthStone held her together.

The founders yelled in astonishment as the crowd surged forward to see what was happening. Guards reached over to try and hold Shaeleen down, but she kicked her legs free of the ropes and then jumped up onto the table itself. All five feet two inches of her stood strong, blood dripping down both her arms and splattering onto her black leather pants. Shaeleen pushed her sweaty bangs out of her eyes. She breathed in deeply and turned around until she found what she was looking for. Down one of the small dirt lanes stood the man from Verlyn. Through the clearing fog, Shaeleen could see his light blue eyes glowing with surprise. "Shaeleen!" Orin roared. "Take this out of me!"

Jumping to Orin's table, Shaeleen grabbed a knife from the belt of one guard and then used her strength to throw him backward a dozen feet. Pushing the doctors away, Shaeleen leaned down and cut the ropes off of Orin, yanking out the tubing. Then she ripped a piece of cloth off of her cloak and gave it to Orin to wrap around the bleeding cut from the bloodletting.

She heard a loud rumble from down the road. As Shaeleen looked up, the overseer walked out of the fog and into the view of all present in the town square. The people lowered their heads in silence in their overseer's presence.

"Behold the menace of magic!" he wailed over their heads. "These two show the danger when common people possess powers of the stones."

Shaeleen reached inside of her pouch and grabbed the egg-sized TruthStone. She felt power roar through her once again. She drew upon the powers of the TruthStone, the small StrengthStone, and the IntelligenceStone, which filled Shaeleen with more power than she had ever held.

"Georrod!" Shaeleen yelled at the overseer. Pointing her other hand out in front of herself, at the oncoming overseer, she chanted the words of a TruthSpell as they flowed through her mind from the IntelligenceStone. Then she flung her fingers out. Bright flashes of green light flew from her fingers, running through the air. Soon red and blue light also shot out and mixed with the green as the streams bore down on the overseer.

"Tell these people the truth!" she and her power demanded of him.

The overseer roared, as if trying to disobey this order from the TruthStone. But her spell was too strong for him, and he fell forward onto his knees. "The truth is…" he paused, gritting his teeth in apparent pain. "The truth is that power corrupts and should not be in the hands of mere commoners."

Shaeleen realized that his statement caused her no pain. She lost her grip on her powers as she took in what the man had just said. The powers of the stones were never intended to be spread throughout the kingdoms. If that was true, what right did any of them have to such powers? She gritted her teeth and shoved these doubts away. The overseer's dark powers were disrupting the clarity of her thoughts and potency of her powers. The overseer stood back up and thrust his hands forward. Black fire shot out toward Shaeleen, but Orin reached up and pushed her to the side, off the table, just in time. As Shaeleen hit the ground, landing hard on her shoulder, she yelled out in pain. Then Orin came to her side and helped her up.

"And what will *you* do when magic is gone?" Shaeleen shouted out.

The overseer stopped—two dozen feet away from her and Orin—and he smiled. "I will leave and let them live in peace, of course."

Shaeleen felt the pain of his lie rip through her gut. Part of her almost regretted restoring the power she now had—the power to know the truth. It had brought her so much pain. But she pushed through the pain now and stood back up.

"Who are you to defy me?" the overseer shouted. The crowd moved back, farther and farther from the power struggle. "I am a keeper from Verlyn. It is my right to have this power. My ancestors found the stones in the lakes and pools of Verlyn—my people, not yours! Then the powers were given to King Wayland, leaving us weaker. Now it is time to return those powers to the land of their origin."

Shaeleen glanced at Orin to silently tell him to be ready.

But he shrugged his shoulders and whispered, "I don't know if I can, Shae." She saw him tremble momentarily, and a tendril of black fog wisped out of the uncovered slice on his arm.

Shaeleen nodded. He had lost a lot of blood—the source of his power. "Just one more time, Orin. That's all."

Then Shaeleen turned back to the overseer and let the TruthStone's power fill her voice. "I am fulfilling prophecy. I have the TruthStone meant to control all stones and will restore strength to Wayland." She brought out the TruthStone in front of herself and held it high above herself and Orin. The stone sent a blinding green light out over the group, causing all of them, including the overseer, to avert their eyes for a moment.

"Now, Orin!" She grabbed Orin's hand. "Take us out of here!"

Orin grimaced as he pulled on her hand. The crowd in front of them froze in place, but Shaeleen and Orin didn't seem to be moving.

"I can't, Shae," Orin yelled in frustration. "There isn't enough of the power left in my blood. That crazed man stole it all!"

"Use my powers, Orin. Just once." Shaeleen sent all the power she had through her hand and into Orin's body. "I can't hold on much longer." She felt drained from the loss of the blood, the new TruthSpells, and holding off the overseer's powers.

There was a sudden whirl around them, and they moved rapidly through the town square and toward the gate. Then Orin screamed, and they stopped, still hundreds of feet from the gate.

The crowd had recovered from the power of the TruthStone and started after them. Shaeleen looked back, over her shoulder, and caught the eyes of the overseer. He was not moving, but he glared at her nonetheless. Then he turned and headed in the opposite direction. Shaeleen knew he wasn't done with her and Orin yet. But, for now, it seemed that she had bested him.

The crowd was getting closer, when all of a sudden a wagon came from a side street, pulled by a horse, and almost ran them over. Shaeleen lifted her hands, to throw a spell, but stopped when she saw Claire.

"Get on!" Claire said to them. "Let's go."

Shaeleen nodded her understanding, but Orin was falling behind. She ran back and grabbed his hand, dragging him to the wagon. Then she pushed him up into the back. As soon as he was in place, she jumped into the wagon and then climbed up closer to the front.

Claire snapped the reins, and the wagon jumped forward. They were coming up quickly to the closed gate. Claire gave Shaeleen a questioning look.

"I don't know if I can." Shaeleen brought up the TruthStone in her hand and drew upon the power of the embedded StrengthStone once again. She briefly wondered if she might use it up before she would get a chance to restore it. With a thrust of her hand, she sent a push of air bolting from her, which smashed into the wooden gate just as the wagon rumbled through it.

Shaeleen fell backward, into the wagon, and breathed hard. The blue sky shone brightly, all traces of the fog now gone. She felt heady with the salty scent of the sea air.

"Where to?" Claire asked.

"To the king," Shaeleen mumbled. She felt so tired. She didn't know how she would get in to see the king, but she had to warn him quickly of what was going on.

Then she closed her eyes and thought about Orin. *Will he be all right without his powers?*

CHAPTER SEVEN

Not much later, Shaeleen heard a voice cry out to her, and she opened her eyes—realizing she must have fallen asleep.

"Shaeleen!" Cole said again, suddenly materializing next to them on the road. He seemed to have been using the power of speed and was taking a moment to recover.

"Claire, stop," Shaeleen yelled out. Then she turned to Cole. "I'm glad to see you!"

Cole appeared shaken. "I tried to find you, Shae! I really did. I was resting on the ship when all of a sudden I felt our link go blank. I didn't know what to do."

Shaeleen smiled and tried to calm him down by saying, "It's fine, Cole." Her stomach lurched with the lie. After recovering from the pain, she shook her head and said, "I guess it's not fine. Get in. We have to get to the king."

Cole climbed onto the front of the wagon and sat next to Claire. But Shaeleen remained in the back with Orin.

"Is he all right?" Cole asked, looking at Orin.

"I don't know." Shaeleen shook her head. "Oh, Cole, it was horrible. A keeper from Verlyn drained our blood and tried to take our powers."

"Drained your blood?" Cole's face went pale, and he seemed angry. "I should have been there for you, Shae, but I couldn't find you. I've never been to this city before. I sped around and around, looking for you, but I couldn't find you until a few minutes ago, when our connection came blazing back."

"The keeper from Verlyn blocked our powers somehow. So you couldn't feel me until we got back out of the compound."

"But I am supposed to be your guardian." Cole's eyes grew hard. "I should have been with you. I will do better in the future, Shae. I promise you."

Shaeleen sat up and put a hand out to touch her brother's shoulder. "Cole, we're not perfect. We are all still learning—it's good that you are here now."

They sat for a few moments in silence. Then Cole stated, "We missed the ship to Verlyn."

"We will get another one and finish our mission, Cole," Shaeleen said. "But, right now, we have to see the king." She slumped back onto the floor of the wagon. She felt exhausted. "I'm glad you're here, Cole," she mumbled as she closed her eyes for a bit.

* * *

Sometime later, Shaeleen was jolted back to reality. She blinked her eyes a few times and sat up in the back of the wagon, its wheels bouncing on a cobblestone road.

Claire turned her head toward Shaeleen with obvious concern.

"Shae, are you all right?" Cole asked.

"We're in the city now and will be at the castle soon," Claire added.

Shaeleen looked around, trying to get her bearings. She saw a few horse-drawn carriages pass by them on the broad street lined with grand homes. Although most were of white painted wood or light rock, they were trimmed in various colors.

As the sun beat down warmly, she pushed her sweaty bangs off of her forehead.

"How is Orin?" Claire asked.

Shaeleen scooted over by him. He had smudges and droplets of blood on his arms and clothes. But she could see his chest rise and fall with regularity, a fact that made her let out a long sigh.

"He seems to be sleeping, but I will wake him up." Moving over next to him, she pushed his shoulder lightly. "Orin. Orin. Wake up."

He stirred and mumbled, but his eyes stayed closed. Shaeleen was about to rock him harder, when the carriage began to slow down.

"We're almost there," Claire mentioned.

"How are we going to get in to see the king, Shae?" Cole asked.

Shaeleen shrugged her shoulders. She looked around the side of the wagon and saw a few carriages in front of them, stopping at a broad, ornate gate. Castle guards and stable boys were busy welcoming the guests and escorting them into the castle grounds while taking their horses off to be fed.

She glanced down at her clothes and groaned. She looked and smelled like a street urchin, hardly fit to step into the grand castle of Mistport.

The castle loomed over its tall rock walls. At the convergence of the Myr River and the Straits of Mist, the castle's light stone walls reflected the morning sun. Uniformed guards also stood at regular intervals along its twenty-foot walls. A few guards frowned down at Shaeleen in her approaching wagon—one that obviously wasn't of noble origin.

Shaeleen smoothed her hair down as best she could, but the dirt and dried blood in it would have to remain. As Claire brought the wagon to a stop, Shaeleen hopped over the side, Cole quickly at her side. The jolt she felt—when her body had hit the ground—hurt more than she had anticipated, and she put a hand on the edge of the wagon to steady herself.

Cole put his arm around her to help hold her up, though Shaeleen was almost as worried about him as he apparently was about her. He obviously hadn't slept much since he had begun looking for her, and his face was pale. He seemed to be trying to hide it to be strong for her.

Taking a deep breath, Shaeleen waited for one of the guards to approach them. The man appeared to be in his mid-twenties and eyed the wagon suspiciously. He had approached Claire first, as she was the driver, but Shaeleen stepped forward and spoke to him in a tired, but clear voice.

"We are here to see the king."

The guard looked from her to Cole and then back to Shaeleen and seemed as if he wanted to laugh but had the sense not to. He instead called over an older gentleman.

"Gad, these youngsters have asked to see the king."

"Please, sir," Shaeleen begged. "It is very important."

"And what is your name, miss?" Gad asked. "Is the king expecting you? Does he even know who you are?"

Shaeleen felt herself growing weaker. Between the magic and the bloodletting, this morning's ordeal had drained her to the point of barely being able to stand or think clearly.

"My sister's name is Shaeleen," Cole said for her. "And my name is Cole." Shaeleen saw that Cole's hand rested on the top of his sword's hilt. "If my sister says it's important, then it must be."

Both of the guards looked at each other. Then the older one said with sympathy in his eyes, "If you need a warm meal and somewhere to sleep, I can arrange that. However, the king has other important business to take care of today."

"Not as important as mine," Shaeleen said, hands on her hips. "I must talk to him."

"I assure you," the younger guard said, "the king's business is more important than yours."

In response, Shaeleen leaned over in pain. *The blasted TruthStone.* These men didn't even know they weren't telling the truth, for they were unaware that nothing the king would do that day would be more important than what she had to tell him.

Hearing a rustle behind her caused Shaeleen to turn around. Orin had sat up in the back of the wagon. His face was pale, his eyes looking hollow, and his hair was plastered to his head. He raised himself up onto his knees and then spoke.

"The king will see me." Orin's voice sounded raspy.

The two guards seemed to become annoyed, and the younger one moved closer to Orin. "Now, look here," he said as he eyed them all. "There is a line of carriages waiting behind you now. Kindly pull forward, and we will give you a few coppers to get cleaned up and find a meal. The king just can't see you today."

"Tell him Orin is here to see him," Orin said.

The younger guard didn't understand.

But Gad stiffened for a brief moment. "What did you say your name was?"

Orin reached inside his shirt and pulled out a ring that he had hanging on the bottom of a silver chain. Shaeleen had never noticed it before and didn't understand what was going on. Her mind felt so foggy and tired.

"My name is Orin." He showed the ring to Gad.

The older man stepped closer, and then his eyes bulged.

Before Orin could say anything more, he fell back down into the wagon.

The two guards moved forward swiftly.

"Make way!" Gad yelled out while shooing other visitors to the side. Then he sent another youngster to run ahead and inform people in the castle. Meanwhile, the younger guard had jumped up into the back of the wagon and had bent over Orin, trying to see what was wrong.

Shaeleen didn't know why this was happening and turned around in circles, trying to figure it all out. She and Cole walked next to the wagon and through the iron gates. Then she looked up at Claire with a questioning glance.

Claire's face colored, but she said nothing.

What does everyone know that I don't?

Soon Claire had the wagon pulled up directly in front of the castle, and then a bustle of activity ensued. Servants helped Claire down from the wagon, and she, Shaeleen, and Cole were guided up a dozen steps and into the foyer of the great castle.

Even though Shaeleen had been in the castles of Stronghaven and of Riverton, the wealth and power she felt each time she stood in one of these grand edifices still took her breath away. Gold-rimmed tapestries hung on the walls. A polished banister stood along the ten-foot-wide stairs to her side. She marveled at the wood's grain, which had been brought out by obviously talented artisans.

At hearing a noise behind her, she turned and watched as two men carefully carried Orin into the castle. His eyes had remained closed, and his breathing seemed to have slowed. He looked so small and vulnerable that Shaeleen choked on emotion.

"Will he be…?" she began, but she couldn't get the full question out.

"Hail the king," yelled out a strong voice that echoed through the foyer.

Shaeleen jumped and turned. Down the stairway came a man in his sixties, if she were to guess. His hair was gray, his eyes dark but alert. He had an athletic build that helped him almost float down the long stairway. A burnt orange glow flew around him momentarily, and then, in an instant, he stood in front of them.

"Hail King Eadric!" all the people shouted.

The SpeedStone! Shaeleen thought, having just seen the man move instantly down the stairs. Now he stood with one hand on the end of the banister and closed his eyes briefly. When he opened them, Shaeleen could see a tiredness in them, and she felt he was much weaker than he was pretending to be.

"Orin!" The king's voice was filled with longing.

Shaeleen wondered if Orin could even hear the king. But then there was a rustle among the guards, and Orin sat up in the arms of one guard, who was holding him. A broad smile covered Orin's face.

"Grandfather," came Orin's whispered reply.

Grandfather? All of a sudden things began to click in Shaeleen's tired mind. She stood speechless. How had she never known? That's what Orin had been hiding all along, she realized. That's why he had avoided too much talk about his family. By not speaking of them, he had dodged having to tell her lies—lies that Shaeleen would have sensed.

The room began to spin around her, and Shaeleen reached out her hand to steady herself against Cole. Then darkness began to close in on her. As her body went limp, Cole lowered her to the ground, and she found herself thinking only that the stone was cool against her arms.

"Grandfather, help her," was the last thing she heard.

CHAPTER EIGHT

Shaeleen could hear voices, but she couldn't understand the words. She seemed to be developing a bad habit of passing out lately. *Too much use of the power*, she surmised.

She opened up her eyes and blinked a few times in the bright room. High above her was an ornately carved ceiling. A chandelier with dozens of candles hung over her head, a head that was resting on a soft pillow.

"Shaeleen," a small voice called to her right.

Turning her head, she saw a smile of relief cross Claire's face. Shaeleen also noticed that Claire had changed clothes and her hair had been freshly washed and combed.

Cole quickly appeared at Claire's side, relief filling his face. He also looked better and wore a simple change of clothes.

Shaeleen smiled at seeing these familiar faces, the prior ordeal flooding back into her mind.

Orin! She sat up quickly and then regretted this decision. As everything swirled around her, she laid her head back down.

Claire came to her side and reached a hand to Shaeleen's forehead. "Her fever broke, Alison," she said to someone behind her.

"Welcome back, miss," said Alison, a middle-aged woman that had now moved into Shaeleen's line of vision. "It was touch and go there for a while."

"Orin?" Shaeleen had mouthed the word. Her lips and throat felt so dry.

Alison brought a cup up to Shaeleen's lips. Shaeleen drank the water down as she looked at her nurse's features—short brown hair, rounded face, green eyes, and a pleasant smile. The water felt good and seemed to give Shaeleen her voice back.

"Where is Orin?" she managed to say. "How is he?"

Alison frowned and glanced at Claire and Cole before turning back to Shaeleen.

Worried, Shaeleen sat up in bed once again, pushing back the darkness that tried to settle in her head again. "What's wrong?"

Don't imagine the worst, she told herself, but tears came to her eyes nevertheless.

Then Shaeleen turned her head, looking around. A few feet away from her, on another bed, lay Orin. She was so happy to see him. She wiped tears from her eyes. He seemed so peaceful under the blankets.

Shaeleen smiled and then let out a small laugh.

Claire and Alison gave her a questioning look.

"It's the neatest I've ever seen his hair be," Shaeleen explained.

Alison smiled and nodded her head. "He always does have a way of keeping it messed up."

"He's going to hate it," Shaeleen said and laughed again. This helped to clear the rest of the tears away. She then reached her hand out to Claire. "Thank you so much. I don't know what we would have done without you. Are you all right?"

"Yes, I am," Claire said. "Your brother carried you up the stairs and hasn't left your side for more than a few moments."

Shaeleen felt a tightening occur in her gut. There was something that wasn't being said. Glancing around, Shaeleen noticed an empty bed on the other side of her own and realized that her brother must have slept there to guard her.

"What are you not saying?" Shaeleen asked.

Claire frowned. "I don't know what you mean."

This time, Shaeleen fell back onto her bed and groaned in pain.

"What's wrong with her?" Claire asked Alison.

The nurse shook her head. "I don't know."

"You're lying," Cole said. "And she can tell." He turned to Shaeleen and tenderly ran his hand over her hair as he said, "She needs to know."

"Know what?" Shaeleen asked. "Cole, you are scaring me." Shaeleen decided to push for an answer. "What's happened? How long have I been out?"

Claire stepped back, away from Shaeleen, and fear crossed her face.

But Alison stepped forward and put her hand on Shaeleen's head. "You just need to rest."

"No. No." Shaeleen shook her head. Then she remembered her pouch and sat back up frantically. She felt around in the bed for it. "Where is it? Where's my pouch? What have you done with it?"

Then Shaeleen moved her feet toward the floor, twisting her body around on the bed.

"What pouch?" Alison asked. "Shaeleen, you need to lie back down. You've been through a lot. The loss of blood…"

All of a sudden, Shaeleen felt something hard against her hip. Reaching her hand under the blankets, she felt the familiar soft pouch, and she brought it out in front of herself.

"Where did you get that?" Alison asked, reaching her hand forward.

Shaeleen pulled it back toward herself, cradling it in her hands against her body.

"Miss, please," Alison said. "You seem confused. Is that what you were searching for? Does it have special meaning for you?"

Shaeleen took a deep breath as she realized that no one must have found the pouch. It had somehow remained with her the entire time. She felt her body relax again, and she smiled, finally feeling the comfort of the stone.

Why is everyone still looking at me that way? she wondered, glancing around.

Alison moved to put Shaeleen's feet back into the bed as Shaeleen lay back down on the pillow. Shaeleen held the pouch tightly in one hand. Then she yawned and closed her eyes. A gleam of sunlight from a nearby window settled on her face, and she basked in its warmth. Then she remembered her previous question.

"Cole, how long?" Shaeleen asked once again.

"Over a week, Shae."

She opened her eyes and stared at him. His lips were tight and concern still filled his face.

"It's been eight days since we arrived," Cole continued.

Eight days! Surprise blasted through Shaeleen's mind. But she couldn't muster enough strength to continue another coherent thought. With her last ounce of strength, she moved the tips of her fingers inside the pouch and felt the familiar warmth and throbbing of the TruthStone.

As Shaeleen fell asleep, she could feel the warmth of the TruthStone join with the sunlight streaming through the window. Soon she found herself in the light, gazing down on her sleeping body. Cole, Alison, and Claire stood next to her bed, speaking softly, but Shaeleen ignored their words.

Peering at the next bed, she watched Orin's chest fall and rise. Worry for her friend made a sob catch in her throat, but she turned her focus away—back toward the sunlight shining into her room. She was drawn back into this light and joined with it again, her spirit flying within the light and out of the window.

She saw the grounds of the castle spread out down below her. Bright red impatiens and purple petunias bloomed around the white walkways, sculptured bushes, and broad trees. Benches were spaced out around fountains and small streams.

Off to the east, the sunlight glittered beautifully off the ocean, which was clear of mists, for once. If she looked far enough, she thought she could catch the faint outlines of the island of Verlyn, but she wasn't quite sure. She knew she needed to get there soon.

Eight days! What could have happened in that much time? Would Princess Diamonique still be there? The princes' birthday was fast approaching, only two weeks away now.

With only a brief thought, she guided her spirit westward, over the city, and recognized the district where Orin had introduced her to Tam, the baker. Her mouth watered at the memory of the delightful, chocolate-covered sweet roll. The city seemed very clean and peaceful from this high up. It was clearly well taken care of.

Periodically, she could see a blur below her—someone using speed to get somewhere quickly. *To do something good or something bad?* She shook her mind away from that. She had more important matters to check on.

Moving farther west, she followed the route she and Orin had taken earlier. Finally, in the distance, she spied it. The walls of the compound rose up below her as she came closer. Now a small army battalion stood in front of the compound—by the looks of it, one sent by the king. She watched for a moment as the men tried to move in quick bursts toward the wall, but they were continually repelled.

The overseer from Verlyn must have reestablished the block on magic once again. The soldiers of Antioch were used to using their speed, and their leaders were sure to be some of their fastest men. Without their powers, though, they didn't seem to know what to do.

Without crossing over the walls, Shaeleen moved around the side of the compound. On the south end, hidden within a large forest, she saw another gate. This one was open and was being guarded heavily. But, into it flowed a fairly large contingent of people, people who were probably being convinced of the evil of magic—not even realizing that this compound, their sanctuary *from magic*, was being created by magic itself.

Clouds began to roll in from over the sea, dimming the light around Shaeleen. She was struggling to stay where she was. But she had one more thing to do here. Moving along any flecks of light she could find, she traveled around the wall to the west side of the compound. Studying this area, she finally found what she was searching for: the small home where the overseer lived.

Shaeleen drew closer to the wall and then tried to move over to it. But, as she did so, she grew weak and had to pull back. *I'm not strong enough yet.*

Then she saw the evil man come out of the home. He glared up in her direction and then smiled.

You are powerful indeed, young TruthSeer, said a deep voice inside her mind—the overseer.

You are deceiving these people, Shaeleen said back to him.

These people are fools, he said. *You are a fool. You trifle with powers you know nothing about. Powers that should stay with those of pure blood in Verlyn.*

Your people gave King Wayland the stones to protect his people and to help them prosper, Shaeleen said.

But now… the overseer said.

Shaeleen watched as the man from Verlyn raised one hand in the air and began gathering black tendrils of power around him.

Now, you know the truth, the overseer said into Shaeleen's mind. *The powers of the stones are too weak. The kingdoms are falling.*

Don't deny it. Now is the time for Verlyn to arise and become the kingdom we were meant to be.

Shaeleen saw the man's other hand go into a pouch at his side, and then she gasped. *He too must have a stone of power*, she thought. *But what stone? It couldn't be a TruthStone.*

Suddenly, he threw a bolt of black lightning at her. In her insubstantial state, she was able to move away in time, but just barely. Doing so caused her to leave the light. The overseer's black tendrils continued past her and into the clouds, growing bigger and blacker.

"It is time for the ShadowStone to take control," the overseer yelled out loud.

Shaeleen's view dimmed, and her power began to weaken. She groaned and pulled upon the TruthStone's strength. Quickly, she turned and tried to get back through the air, struggling to find small pockets of light. The Overseer, who she now knew must be known as a *shadow keeper*, gathered blackness all around him and with menace continued to pour it out at her. She struggled to push through the shadow.

Her thinking dimmed and she felt the evil shadow slither around her. Her only thought was to find light again. In the back of her mind she faintly heard Cole's voice, and she used it to give her a point of focus. Slowly she pushed back the shadow and found the patches of light she needed. Finally, she fell back into the window of the castle.

With a yell of anguish, she rolled over in bed and curled up in pain. Cole was immediately at her side, with Claire and Alison fast approaching. The two women skidded to a stop and covered their mouths with their hands, their eyes growing larger. Shaeleen rolled back on her back and Cole helped her to sit up. She looked down and saw a green glow enveloping her entire body. She could feel the truth and the light in the room warming her and bringing strength back to her mended body.

Shaeleen put the TruthStone back inside the pouch. But, before anyone could say anything, another woman walked into the room. She seemed to be near the age of Shaeleen's own mother, so Shaeleen thought of her mother and hoped her family was all right. This woman's eyes were pale blue and shone with clarity and truth. Her mouth was open wide in surprise, for she must have seen the fading light of Shaeleen's TruthStone before it had been put back into the pouch.

"Sorry," Shaeleen muttered. "You weren't supposed to see that."

A miniscule smile cracked the newcomer's face. "I didn't have to see it to feel its presence. I am TruthSeer Lana. Welcome to Antioch."

CHAPTER NINE

Later, when she heard a small groan from Orin, Shaeleen jumped out of her bed, and Cole grabbed on to her to keep her from falling. Claire and Alison followed behind him.

"Orin! Orin!" Shaeleen called, putting her hand on Orin's shoulder.

Gradually, Orin's eyes opened: first the left and then the right. They hovered over him. A tiny smile spread across his noticeably dry lips.

"Hello ladies." Orin paused. "And Master Cole. Could someone get me something to eat? I'm starving."

Shaeleen leaned down and hugged Orin. "Oh, Orin. I was so worried for you."

Orin smiled weakly. "I needed a good night's rest. That's all."

"Um, Orin…" Shaeleen paused. "It's been almost nine days. I just woke up earlier today myself."

Orin groaned again. "What happened, Shae?"

"You need to rest, Orin," Alison chided him.

"Can't I eat first?"

Alison nodded her head. "Yes, of course. Claire, come now, and help me get the starving boy some food."

Claire, with a smile for Orin, turned and followed Alison out of the room. Then Lana came back in the room with Shaeleen, Cole, and Orin.

After Orin moved to sit up and got himself rearranged, he said to Shaeleen, "We really slept for over a week?"

"Yes," Shaeleen said.

"It seems you lost a lot of blood," Lana said. "Claire told us most of what had happened, and the king has sent soldiers to secure the compound."

"I have also been out there briefly," Cole said. "I didn't want to leave you two, but I needed to see what was going on there—what had hurt you so badly."

Shaeleen turned to Lana and Cole. "The king's forces are not working well against them. They're trying to use their power of speed. But the compound blocks the use of their powers."

"How would *you* know about their activities?" Lana said sharply.

Shaeleen felt slightly embarrassed. "I just do. That's enough for now." Shaeleen wasn't prepared to discuss her powers with someone she'd barely met. "We need to see the king."

Lana nodded and turned to go. "I will go and set up a meeting."

After Lana was gone, Shaeleen leaned in closer to Orin and said, "Are you really all right, Orin? They took a lot of your blood."

Orin shook his head. "I still feel strange, Shae. I don't know." He closed his eyes briefly. When he opened them again, there were tears at the corners. "I think they took my power of speed—all of it."

"You got us out of there, Orin," Shaeleen said. "You did enough to move us out of danger, and then Claire picked us up in a wagon and brought us here. You saved us again."

"But…?"

Shaeleen nodded. "I know, Orin. It must be hard. I've only had my powers for a little over a month now, and those few days without them were hard—though I didn't miss the stomach pains." Shaeleen paused and then slugged Orin softly on the arm. "Hey, what's this about you being the king's grandson?"

Cole looked down at Orin with Shaeleen. Then Cole turned and looked at her. "Well, it seems that Orin is the son of the king's youngest son." Cole smirked. "Royalty of sorts."

Orin laughed. "Hard for you to believe that, isn't it, Cole?"

Cole just grunted. But Shaeleen knew Orin's actions didn't fit Cole's idea of one of royal blood.

Then Shaeleen's mind whirled, connecting things together. "Orin, in the bakery with Tam, he'd said your uncles were missing, and later, when I spied on the overseer talking to Alain and another founder, the overseer mentioned killing your uncles and going after the remaining son."

"My father may be in danger." Orin's eyes widened.

"Yes, I fear he might be." Shaeleen began to pace back and forth in front of Orin's bed.

"Shae, what's wrong?" Cole asked.

"I… It…" Shaeleen said, stumbling for the right words. Eventually, she stopped pacing and put her hand on Cole's arm while looking back and forth between him and Orin. "Sometimes it's just so much: getting to Verlyn, finding Diamonique, stopping those in the compound, figuring out what to do with Basil, gathering the stones…" Tears filled her eyes. "Oh, Orin. And now we have to find your father."

Shaeleen looked down at the pouch hanging at her side. She brought it closer with one hand and opened the drawstring. Then a green light spread out from the dark pouch.

Orin groaned and put a hand to his head.

"What's the matter?" Shaeleen asked. As she moved closer to him, the green light from the pouch fell upon Orin's arm.

He screamed and moved his arm away. "What are you trying to do to me?"

"What do you mean?" Shaeleen asked, watching the light from the TruthStone. "It's the TruthStone, Orin. You've seen it before."

"But…but…" Orin stumbled with his words. "It feels different to me now. It hurts."

Shaeleen gasped as, across the arm that the light of the stone had just touched, rose a barely visible black tendril of darkness—almost like the dark fog. She moved her other hand and touched Orin's arm. He tried to move it away, but she held it firm. She closed her eyes and pulled the power of the TruthStone into herself. With eyes still closed, she asked him a question with a tone that demanded the truth: "Orin, what did they put into you?"

Orin thrashed on the bed for a moment, but Shaeleen held his arm still.

"Shae!" she heard Cole say in frustration, but she ignored Cole for now. She could feel another presence, deep inside of Orin. *Something dark.* It seemed to struggle to get away from her presence—from the truth—but Shaeleen held firm. She had to know the truth. Then the power of the IntelligenceStone flowed through her, and she knew what to do.

"Tell me!" This was from Shaeleen's voice, but it was the power of the TruthStone that bore the command.

Orin groaned. Then the words poured forth with a voice that wasn't entirely Orin's own: "To rid my blood of the power of the SpeedStone, they gave me new blood—blood tainted with the shadow." Orin gritted his teeth against the TruthSpell.

Then Shaeleen felt the presence of the shadow keeper, Georrod, in Orin's mind. She pushed the power of the TruthStone against this presence, and it receded somewhat.

"Tell me what this ShadowStone is," she commanded. She could faintly remember reading something about it in the *TruthSeers' Journal:* a warning of some sort.

Orin's body seemed to weaken under her touch. His breathing became ragged, and his voice changed to sound like that of the shadow keeper. "The power of the ShadowStone will soon control all. We have been preparing for this. The shadow keepers and their followers are coming."

Shaeleen remembered Melindra, the keeper who had given her the TruthStone. Others had been chasing Melindra, trying to stop her from giving the stone and the books away. *Shadow keepers?* She shivered with the thought.

"Shae," Orin mumbled, thrashing. "Stop. Please stop. You're hurting me."

She felt Cole's hand on her arm, trying to pull her away as he said, "Shaeleen, you have to stop this."

She felt tears streaming down her face. She knew that she was hurting her friend, and this fact hurt her too. But she had to know the truth of it all and rid Orin of the shadow's influence. Pulling more of the TruthStone's power into herself, she reached into Orin's mind and found the influence of the shadow keeper there, trying to hide from her once again. "Shadow, you must leave Orin!" she commanded.

Orin thrashed and then flung the covers off. He strained to pull away from Shaeleen. But, calling on the power of her small StrengthStone, she held on tightly. She had to rid Orin of this evil power. She tried to dig it out of him, but the shadow's power was too elusive and evaded her touch.

Orin roared, an otherworldly sound emanating from his young and weakened body. "Soon all keepers of the stones will fall to the shadow!" Orin yelled and then slumped back in bed, eyes closed.

Shaeleen opened her own eyes as Claire and Alison came running into the room, followed by a half dozen guards. When they saw the scene—Shaeleen standing over Orin's bed, encompassed by green light, and Orin lying still beneath her— they stopped short.

Claire was the first one to rush forward. "Orin! Orin!" Claire said. Then she turned a hard glare at Shaeleen. Shaeleen put the TruthStone back into the pouch, the last glow of its green light fading away.

"What did you do to him?" Claire demanded.

Cole protectively pulled Shaeleen back, nearer to himself.

"Yes, what did you do to him?" Lana said as she came striding into the room. Shaeleen could feel power emanating from Lana. The TruthSeer's face held obvious anger. Motioning toward Shaeleen, Lana ordered, "Guards, take her out of here!"

The sound of a sword being drawn rang through the air as Cole leapt out in front of Shaeleen.

The approaching guards suddenly stopped. Then they drew their own weapons. The air grew tense as Cole stood there, facing the six of them. Shaeleen knew he would defend her to the end, but fighting was not the solution right now.

"Cole!" Shaeleen said and put an arm out and touched his back. He flinched but kept his stance. "Put the sword down. These people are not our enemies."

Cole did as she'd instructed, but he still stood in front of her.

After a moment, she turned and looked down at Orin. "I'm sorry, Orin." Tears flooded her eyes at what she had done to her friend. "I had only been trying to get at the shadow. I'm so sorry that I'm not strong enough—yet."

Alison joined Claire at Orin's bedside, and they arranged him better in the bed. Alison leaned down and listened to his heartbeat and nodded.

"He's still alive," Alison said.

As the guards escorted Shaeleen and Cole out of the room, she saw Claire turn and glare at her. Cole walked stiffly down the hall, as if still ready to defend her if needed. Then they were taken into a room, and the door was locked. She was sure guards would be standing outside the door.

Shaeleen sat down with her head in her hands and tried not to cry. She hadn't wanted to hurt Orin—but she'd needed to find out more about the shadow and needed to rid it from his body.

She felt Cole's hand on her shoulder. "What is it, Shae?"

"Orin has a portion of the shadow in him. Georrod, the shadow keeper in the compound, replaced Orin's blood with some blood tainted with the shadow. I tried to rid Orin of it." Shaeleen choked on her words for a moment and then added, "But I failed."

"You're still weak and tired, Shaeleen," Cole said as if trying to comfort her. "You'll find a way."

Less than an hour later, Lana walked into the room. Her face was stern, but she came over and sat down next to Shaeleen. "The boy is awake once again. I think he will be fine."

Shaeleen shook her head. "No. He won't be fine. I can't touch him with my power without causing him pain. The influence of the ShadowStone is too strong."

"ShadowStone?" Lana's eyes went wide. "What are you talking about? I've never heard of such a thing."

"I read about it briefly in the *TruthSeers' Journal*." Shaeleen sighed.

Lana gave her a look of wonder and suspicion.

"But that's what he told me," Shaeleen continued. "Well, what Orin told me, but it was really the man behind the ShadowStone who was telling me... I know I'm not making sense."

Lana shook her head, clearly not understanding.

"We need to see the king." Shaeleen stood up. She could feel the nearby orange Garnet SpeedStone suddenly calling to her, just as the other stones had. *Maybe with more stones I can cure Orin.*

Lana stood up next to her. "I'm not sure that is a good idea."

"Why not?" Cole asked, his face stern, acting protective of Shaeleen still.

"Because Shaeleen is a very dangerous person," Lana said to Cole, "and I'm not even completely sure what powers you hold. Who are you two?"

"Cole is my wizard guardian and protector," Shaeleen said, and she barely stopped herself from stomping her foot. She had things to do, and Lana was in the way. "And, if you believe the others of nobility that I have talked to, I am the prophesied one," she blurted out.

Lana appeared confused and exasperated. "I don't know what you mean. You shouldn't even have a TruthStone. You escaped the compound somehow, know things you shouldn't know, and almost killed your friend in there."

"My friend in there," Shaeleen said, yelling more loudly than she'd initially intended, "has the taint of a ShadowStone! His father is now being hunted by evil men from Verlyn! And I am on an errand to bring the Gaborian princess, Diamonique, from Verlyn back to Galena to marry—"

She paused here and didn't know what to say next, for her anger had ran ahead of her. She lowered her voice and said, "To marry a prince." *There, that didn't cause any pain.* She looked at Lana, who seemed flabbergasted. "And you would know if I'd lied."

Lana thought for a few moments, as if deciding what to do. Finally, she let out a deep breath and then crooked her slender finger at Shaeleen, saying, "Come. We will see the king, but first we must find you a change of clothes."

Shaeleen tried to smile, but it probably came out as a grimace. She was still wearing the simple gown they had dressed her in for lying in bed. *It will feel good to be dressed properly again.*

Taking a deep breath, to get control of herself once again, Shaeleen followed the TruthSeer of Antioch out of the room, Cole at their heels.

CHAPTER TEN

An hour later, Shaeleen and Cole began to walk with Lana to the king's private chambers. At the doorframe, Shaeleen stopped for a moment to gather her composure. Thoughts of when Keeper Melindra had first given Shaeleen the TruthStone came back to her now. At the time, the words of the old keeper had appeared ridiculous to Shaeleen: *Kings and queens will clamor for your attention, and lords and ladies will want to be your friends. You will know the ones to trust.*

As Shaeleen entered the room, the two men inside stood up. Instantly, she knew she could trust the king but not the other man. She'd seen the king only momentarily in the entryway of the castle when they had first arrived. He stood the closest. His hair and beard had been trimmed short, which made him appear younger. His soft green eyes were kind and considerate but showed a tiredness about them.

"Welcome, TruthSeer." The king bowed his head slightly to Lana and then, turning to Shaeleen, gave a broad smile. "Nice to see you again," he said to Shaeleen. "Thank you for bringing my grandson back to me."

Shaeleen nodded to the king. "Had I known who he is, we may have come earlier and spared ourselves quite a bit of trouble."

The king chuckled. "No doubt."

"Your grandson does have a way of starting mischief around him," Shaeleen responded. "But he has saved my life numerous times."

Then the other man took a step forward and power seemed to ooze off of him. "My lord, I have heard some troubling things about this young lady." The man was tall, and his face was thin. His graying hair hung down past his shoulders, and his pale blue eyes were fixed on Shaeleen. He was obviously TruthSeer Lana's wizard protector.

Cole, as Shaeleen's own protector, visibly stiffened at the man's language and moved up closer to Shaeleen.

"Jarom." The king turned sharply. "Hold your tongue. My grandson has been brought to safety. For all I know, he may be our last hope."

Jarom stood still but glared at Shaeleen.

She took a deep breath and pulled the power of the TruthStone into herself. As intelligence and strength followed, a soft glow swirled around her, making the others in the room take a step back.

"King Eadric," Shaeleen said, her voice commanding attention. "I bring you dire news. I know you have discovered the compound and their intention to eradicate all magic in the land. They are headed by a man from Verlyn that they refer to as their *overseer*. He is actually a very dangerous man named Georrod, who is a shadow keeper and has a ShadowStone in his possession."

"There are no ShadowStones," Jarom said, taking a step closer to Shaeleen. "King Eadric, this woman brings trouble and should be locked up."

Cole took a step toward Jarom, but Shaeleen put her arm out and shook her head at Cole. Then she turned back to the king. "Georrod has created a barrier around the compound that saps anyone's power from the stones. Even at this moment, your forces—strong with the power of speed—are being destroyed while many other people are flocking to the compound through a secret side entrance."

"Bah," Jarom waved his hand in the air. "You surely exaggerate things there. It's been nine days since you arrived here. How can you know of such things?"

"Jarom!" Lana said, censuring him.

Shaeleen turned to Lana and shook her head. "I'm fine. But I am surprised that you missed it, TruthSeer. Another proof that the stones of power are weakening in the kingdoms of Wayland."

The king put his hand on the back of a chair, paled, and took a deep breath. "It is as I suspected. You are correct, Shaeleen. The stones are weakening, for I am getting weaker and am not as fast as I used to be."

"This is also why your two oldest sons are missing," Shaeleen said, softening her words. "I bring you more ill news, then. They are no longer alive."

The king almost fell forward, but Shaeleen jumped to his side before the others had and lowered him down onto a chair. She took that brief moment to whisper to him, "Be careful."

"Once again, you overstep your bounds here," Jarom said, moving closer to Shaeleen. "My king, the only way this woman can know these things is if she is a part of them. I will have her brought to the dungeons to await trial."

The ring of steel filled the air as Cole pulled his sword free. Light crackled along its edges, and he held it out in front of him. "You will respect my sister, Wizard Jarom. She is a TruthSeer."

Shaeleen stood up straight and looked between the king and Jarom. "Eadric," she said and then heard a gasp from Lana at the lack of using his title, and even Cole sent Shaeleen a dark look. "It is your wizard, I am afraid, that is the one to be worried about," Shaeleen said. "I fear he is a traitor to your kingdom."

"I am not a traitor," Jarom blurted out. He must have forgotten about his TruthSeer being in the room, and he clearly didn't yet understand the nature of Shaeleen's powers.

Both Shaeleen and Lana leaned over in pain: Lana keeping hers in better control.

Cole still stood with his sword drawn and now moved closer to Jarom.

"Jarom!" Lana said, recovering more quickly from the pain than Shaeleen. "What have you done?"

Jarom seemed to realize his mistake and began to back away toward the door. "I did what needed to be done. There are too many with magic in our kingdom. The king is weak, and we need a stronger ruler."

Cole moved and then stood in the way of the retreating wizard. "Have reverence for your king, sir."

"We need a stronger king—" Jarom began to say.

"And that ruler was to be you?" Shaeleen said, cutting him off. Then she gasped with understanding. "The overseer promised you that?"

Jarom closed his mouth. His eyes said it all. He had been found out.

Shaeleen laughed, but her voice held no humor in it. "He also promised this power to rule to Alain, one of the founders in the compound. I wonder how many others the overseer has promised this to in his plan to sow discord and weaken us."

"You were part of having my sons killed, Jarom?" King Eadric said, clearly distraught.

Jarom's lips were thin and tight as he tried to move toward the door. But Cole held him at bay.

Then, without warning, Jarom swung his leg around at Cole.

At the same time, Jarom threw up his hands, and Shaeleen realized he intended to attack the king. Without thinking, she drew upon the power of the StrengthStone and pushed the chair that the king sat in just before Jarom shot out a stream of fire toward him. She'd pushed the chair just as the power had flown out of Jarom's fingertips, so she had protected the king from a direct hit. But he had still been struck on the arm.

Lana rushed to the king's side while Cole turned on Jarom, bringing his sword to bear. Jarom pushed his hands at Cole, and Cole went flying on a billow of air, crashing into a nearby couch.

Then Shaeleen jumped at Jarom instead. Calling up her own spell of fire, she shot it forward. But the wizard raced to the door, his speed quicker than her spell, and Shaeleen's fire only blasted the door open, shards of wood flying out into the hallway.

Cole was up by this time, and he took off after Jarom.

"Cole, no," Shaeleen called out, and her brother suddenly stopped. He looked from her to the retreating wizard. "I need you here with me," Shaeleen said.

Cole nodded, understanding duty above all else.

The surprised guards in the hallway moved into the king's room with questioning glances.

"Find Jarom," Lana ordered them. "He is a traitor to the king."

The guards quickly turned and ran off to search for Jarom.

The king groaned, and Shaeleen moved over next to him as Lana and Cole took up guard at the destroyed doorway.

Lana gave Shaeleen an apologetic look. "I'm sorry. I had no idea. I never suspected him."

Shaeleen didn't respond but instead turned back to the king. Jarom's lightning had torn into the king's arm, leaving an ugly gash from his shoulder to his elbow.

"Thank you," he whispered to Shaeleen. "You saved my life. What is it you want from me?"

"Sire, you are losing blood," Lana said. Then she turned behind her and yelled out, "Cole, find a guard to get a doctor!"

Cole looked at Shaeleen for confirmation. She nodded, and then he walked into the hallway, yelling for a guard to attend to them.

"I am fine," the king said, trying to sit up straighter.

Instantly, both Shaeleen and Lana knew it was a lie, but they tried to cover up the pain to respect the king's valor.

Once more the orange Garnet SpeedStone called to Shaeleen. It felt weak, as the others had been, but it was near.

She looked the king in the eye, and his own eyes widened in response to the pleading in hers.

"Lana," the king said softly to his TruthSeer. "Please secure the doorway with Master Cole. Make sure none enter."

"But the doctor…" Lana said, turning from King Eadric back to Shaeleen.

"Will have to wait," the king said. "There are things more important than my health at the moment."

"What could be…?" Lana began to ask.

"Now, TruthSeer!" The king's voice brooked no argument. Lana moved away, and then the king put out his arm to have Shaeleen help him up.

Standing on shaky feet for a moment, King Eadric motioned Shaeleen forward to the far part of the room and then around a small corner, to a bookshelf. Shaeleen's pulse quickened as she felt the power of the SpeedStone reach out to her.

"It's here," Shaeleen whispered.

The king nodded his head. "Yes, at least what is left of it. You are the prophesied one, aren't you? The one to save the stones?"

Shaeleen nodded her head once. "That's what I've been told."

The king chuckled. "Not what you had expected, I am sure."

"Not what you expected either." Shaeleen smiled.

"You do have a sharp tongue for one so young," the king said. "But how do you handle the pain?"

"Truthfully? Sometimes I want to throw the stupid TruthStone out the window or into the sea."

The king laughed hard, but then a coughing fit ensued.

"Sire?" Lana called from the other side of the door at the far corner of the room.

"I am fine, TruthSeer," the king said, getting his voice under control. Moving a few books from a high shelf, he put his palm against a small decorative piece at the back of the shelf. After the king had held it there a brief moment, a slightly orange glow shone from it and a small door popped open.

Shaeleen stood on tiptoe to see it more clearly. She felt her anticipation building as the king pulled out an old, worn, brown leather pouch and held it in front of himself for a moment. His eyes glassed over, and his countenance fell. With obvious resignation, he opened the pouch's drawstring and dropped its contents into his right palm, a brilliant orange stone that was smooth and polished, worn by years of use.

"The Garnet SpeedStone." Shaeleen smiled at the stone. "It's larger than the IntelligenceStone of Galena and the StrengthStone of Gabor." The orange Garnet SpeedStone was the size of a raspberry.

The king nodded his head. "Still, not much left." He rolled it over with his fingers for a moment, and it began to shine—a soft orange glow surrounding his hand. "Given to the rulers of this kingdom, the SpeedStone has helped us to maintain peace, to accomplish great things in a short time. It has been in my family for all this time. Will you protect it for me?"

Shaeleen nodded at hearing the king's solemn words. Then she reached into her own pouch and drew out the TruthStone. It sat in her palm, ten times the size of the SpeedStone.

"I've never seen a stone of power of such size!" the king responded.

A green glow enveloped Shaeleen's palm, reflecting off the nearby walls.

Then Shaeleen heard an unexpected sound—of footsteps, followed by a gasp—at their backs, and they turned around. Lana stood there, gawking at them with her jaw dropped wide open. She stared hard from the TruthStone to Shaeleen and then back at the king.

"My lord," Lana whispered. "Are you sure?"

King Eadric only nodded. "She already has the StrengthStone and IntelligenceStone."

As if on cue, the two smaller stones embedded in the TruthStone sent their small lights of power into the space between them. Now green, red, and blue lights swirled in the air above Shaeleen's hand. The king reached out to her with the SpeedStone, its orange light joining the swirl of other colors. Shaeleen reverently took the stone and placed it next to the TruthStone. A brilliant flashing ensued.

All three turned their heads away from the bright light. When they turned back, the SpeedStone was now embedded in the TruthStone, next to the other stones. The colors swirled for a moment longer and then pulled in on themselves and disappeared into the TruthStone.

The king paled and fell to the floor.

"Cole!" Lana yelled and then ran back to the doorway for help. "The king has collapsed."

Shaeleen put her stone back in the pouch and tied it back to her waist. Then she leaned down by the king.

"My sons," he murmured, fresh tears coming to his eyes. "Is Orin's father, my son Marcus, still alive?"

"Georrod only mentioned the older two sons, so Marcus is all right for now—though Jarom and Georrod will try to find him soon – Georrod hinted at an accident at sea," Shaeleen said.

The king nodded. "Will you find my son for me? Will you find Marcus and keep him safe?"

Shaeleen felt conflicting emotions run through her mind. She needed to get to Verlyn and then back to Stronghaven. She felt bad for this king, but she already had a list of insurmountable tasks ahead of her.

Before she could answer, she heard soft footsteps behind them again.

"Grandfather," Orin said. He had on fresh clothes, but his hair was still uncombed. His eyes were sunken, and his face was pale. He glanced at Shaeleen with a blank expression. Then Orin knelt down next to the king. "I will find him for you. I will bring my father home. I promise."

The king nodded and reached his hand toward Orin. "You're a good boy, Orin. Thank you."

Then others rushed into the room behind Cole—guards, doctors, and maids. All fussed over their king, helping him to his bedroom. Shaeleen remained where she was as everybody left except Cole. Then she stood and walked over to a window and gazed outside. The sky was blue above the castle, but fog had settled into the bay once again.

She took a deep breath and let it out slowly.

"You promised me!" came a tiny voice from behind her.

Both Cole and she spun around, Cole's sword suddenly in front of him. Orin stood in front of them, ignoring Cole altogether. As his eyes bore into Shaeleen's own, she felt guilt and shame.

"You promised you would never use the power on me to compel me," Orin said, his young voice growing louder. Dressed in a simple gown and so pale from his injuries, Orin appeared even younger than his thirteen years.

Shaeleen shuddered and turned away from his stare. "I'm sorry, Orin. I was trying to fix it. It wasn't really even you, you know. It was him, the shadow keeper, Georrod, the man from Verlyn. Somehow he has left some of his shadow power in you." Shaeleen knew she was rambling, but she had to explain herself. Orin had to understand.

"It was still me, Shae." Orin shook his head from side to side. "It was still me in there too. You should have at least asked me."

Cole stood protectively by her side, but he didn't say anything, which was almost as bad as not being there. She knew he hadn't approved of what she had done either.

"Sometimes I have to make hard choices," Shaeleen said and knew it sounded harsher than she'd intended. She didn't know what else to say. She couldn't lie to Orin. She was sorry, but she had done what she thought was right. *Oh, what am I becoming?*

"So we say goodbye, then?" Orin said.

Shaeleen felt her heart breaking, and she rubbed tears from her eyes. "Orin…?" But she couldn't think of what else to say that would make things any better.

"You'll be off to find your father? "Cole asked.

Orin only nodded.

"Where will you find him?" Shaeleen asked.

"In one of the ports, I suppose. He runs the shipping company. Claire will go with me."

"But she doesn't have any powers, Orin and…and…neither do you," Shaeleen said. "You need someone to protect you."

Orin laughed, but it wasn't a laugh of joy. His face had turned dark. "I can fend for myself, Shae. I always have."

Shaeleen nodded and wiped tears away once again.

Then Orin turned to go. He looked at Cole and nodded his head at him, some sort of understanding passing between them. "Take care of her, Cole."

"Orin?" Shaeleen said, calling him back. "Thank you for saving me. Thank you for being my friend. I will make things right again."

"I hope so," Orin mumbled. "I hope so."

As he walked with slow steps out the doorway, Shaeleen could swear that she had seen a tendril of black fog swirling around his arm.

"Orin!" Shaeleen called one last time.

Orin stopped but didn't turn around. Shaeleen needed to let him know how serious the ShadowStone was, for he had to watch out for the evil taint that might be lurking within him now. But she knew he didn't want to hear anything more from her at the moment.

"Take care," was all she could say. Then she watched him go out the broken door and down the hallway of the castle. Wiping fresh tears from her face, she took a deep breath. "Take care, my friend."

With only a brief thought, she pulled on the power of the SpeedStone and grabbed onto Cole's hand, speeding through the castle and out its doors without saying goodbye to anyone else. She was heading toward the docks and hoped to get supplies and catch a ship to Verlyn before the sun could set.

CHAPTER ELEVEN

Shaeleen and Cole hadn't been able to talk their way into any ships sailing from Mistport to Sylvermoor until the next morning. Traveling through the Straits of Mist would be treacherous enough during the day, so no one would want to get caught out there during the dark of night. She had finally found a captain planning to take a cargo of goods there the next morning, and he had allowed them to sleep on his ship that night and then, for a minor fare, had allowed them to ride along with the cargo. There had been one extra bed, in a cabin with the captain's daughter, for Shaeleen, but Cole had slept on the floor on a blanket and would be helping the crew out during the day.

The next day, two hours into the journey, Shaeleen was rethinking her decision to travel on a cargo ship. She was definitely missing the food, lodgings, and smoother ride of the finer passenger ships. She had sailed on those ships when traveling to both North Bay and then, later, down to Mistport—ships she knew now were owned by Orin's father, Prince Marcus, a man who had recently gone from being the carefree youngest prince of the king to the royal heir—if he could be found.

Thinking of Orin made her frown. Plopping down on a crude bench and grabbing its weather-smoothed arms, she held on as the ship lurched to its port and then to its starboard side. The night before, she'd started to write Orin a note and had stopped numerous times. Each time there had been really nothing she could say that seemed to compensate for violating his mind and freewill.

"You might want to get down below, miss." An older sailor with a weathered face walked up to her. "Looks to be a storm coming in."

"Great," Shaeleen mumbled. *Something else to delay my trip to Verlyn.* It seemed there had been one thing after another trying to keep her away. Then she noticed that they didn't ask Cole to go to the cabin—but he was as tall and strong as many of the sailors.

Moving down below, she went into the small cramped cabin.

"Shaeleen!" the captain's daughter, Abby, squealed when Shaeleen came in. "It's going to be a bad storm, my pa said." The girl couldn't be more than nine or ten. Shaeleen wondered why Abby was allowed to travel around on a cargo ship. But this wasn't any of her business—a thought that made her smile, for most things had been having a habit of becoming her business lately.

"Then why do you seem so excited, Abby?" Shaeleen was confused. "Sounds dangerous."

The girl shook her head, short blond hair swishing around her face. "Oh, no. Not dangerous. Think of it as an adventure."

"I've had enough of those." Shaeleen let out a small laugh.

"I've been everywhere—from South Bay to North Bay—but never to Verlyn before," Abby said with a sparkle in her green eyes. "I hear they have magic there."

"All the kingdoms have magic through the stones of power," Shaeleen said.

"Not that kind of magic—real magic!" Abby exclaimed.

As the boat lurched, both girls grabbed a hold of the bolted-down table.

"And what do you know about magic?" Shaeleen asked, knowing her question sounded condescending. But, really, what experiences could Abby have had?

"My mama reads me the stories. You know, about the elves, dragons, wizards, and magic."

Shaeleen laughed. "Oh, the fairy tales, you mean."

Abby frowned. "You're not being very nice, Shaeleen." She paused a moment. "You're afraid, aren't you?"

"No," Shaeleen snapped, but then she regretted it, when a stomach cramp engulfed her.

Abby moved over to Shaeleen's side. "Are you all right?"

Shaeleen started to say yes but instead changed her words. "Just a lot on my mind, Abby. And I need to get to Sylvermoor quickly."

"You're interested in magic too?"

Shaeleen laughed. "You might say that."

Then Abby cocked her head to the side, as if listening to something. "My father's coming," she said with a sparkle in her eye.

"How do you…"

Before Shaeleen could finish her sentence, the captain came in. Shaeleen gave Abby a questioning look.

"Abby, I need you up above," he said.

"But the storm…" Shaeleen said, worried for Abby's safety.

"She'll be all right," the captain said. "You need to stay here, though. Looks like a rough one, and the winds are howling through the strait. We'll be glad to have your brother's help up above."

As the captain left, Abby moved behind Shaeleen to grab a long sailor's coat and hat. Then Abby walked toward the door. Before leaving, she waved at Shaeleen. Then she closed the door.

Shaeleen remained sitting on the nailed-down chair and tried to puzzle things out. She could pull on some of the power of the IntelligenceStone, but she didn't want to waste what was left. *If it works that way.* She wasn't quite sure how it all worked yet. As far as she knew, the only ones who had use of multiple powers were wizards—and, even then, only a few wizards and mostly powers used to protect and fight. At least, until she came along.

The wind howled outside, and the boat wouldn't stay still. Through the small round windows of the cabin, Shaeleen watched bolts of lightning flash across the gray skies. These were followed by rumbles of thunder. She really didn't like being all alone during the storm. So she stood up but almost lost her balance at the next big wave.

Why can Cole be up above but not me?

Opening the cabin's door, she scuttled out into the cramped hallway, where a small set of steps led to a door up above. As she headed toward them, the wind picked up and she was thrown to the floor.

Shaeleen pulled herself upright. What would happen if they were to die at sea? She couldn't imagine not seeing Orin ever again…or the rest of her family…or Prince Basil. Into her mind came the handsome visage of that prince of Galena. Thinking about his dark hair, dark blue eyes, and caring demeanor quickened her breathing. He'd always treated her with such kindness and compassion.

Then she climbed the steps. What would happen in Galena when the truth came out about him and his brother, Prince Calix? The fact that she hadn't told Prince Basil the truth yet gave her a throbbing headache. How long would she be able to live with this pain of not telling that truth?

Reaching for the small door, Shaeleen used all her strength—fighting against the wind—to pull it open. Though it was midday, the sky was dark as night. Waves crashed over the side of the boat, and lightning flashed overhead, highlighting the ripping sails.

Shaeleen held on to a railing as the ship dipped forward, water splashing over its bow. Peering through the relentless deluge, she spied Abby with her father, up in the captain's box, toward the stern of the ship. Shaeleen watched him grab hard on the ship's wheel as his daughter turned her head now and again and then pointed in a certain direction. At her instruction, her father then turned the wheel.

She saw Cole standing with a trio of sailors. They looked to be bringing down the main sail so it wouldn't rip in the wind.

Then, out of the dark sky, a bolt of lightning struck the mast of the main sail, and the ship also suddenly began to spin mercilessly around. Shaeleen saw Cole and the three sailors fall to the deck. Then she noticed that the captain had fallen and was beginning to slide toward the edge of the captain's deck.

"Papa!" Abby screamed. She reached for him but missed. He fell onto the top deck and then slid faster toward its edge.

Shaeleen's instincts took over as she pulled on the power of the SpeedStone. Through the wet and the wind, she sped toward the captain. She was there in moments. Pulling on the StrengthStone, she grabbed the captain's arm, stopping him before he slipped off the side. Then he grabbed a post with his other hand and righted himself.

As he did so, the top of the main mast cracked and began to fall toward the main deck of the ship. Cole tried to pull the other sailors away, but they all were slipping on the wet deck. Then the ship crashed hard against a large wave, and they were all covered in water.

Shaeleen could see that all their deaths were only moments away. Gathering her powers to her once again, she raced around the boat, heedless of her own safety, and grabbed as many sailors as she could out from under the main mast.

"Help!" Abby cried out.

Shaeleen turned in Abby's direction. The mast was still falling now, and Abby was right in its path.

"Abby!" the captain yelled, but he wouldn't reach her in time.

Glowing green in the midst of the dark storm, Shaeleen became a lightning-fast stream of light as she used speed to get to Abby, orange tendrils of light flowing out behind herself. She pushed Abby to safety and then turned to see the mast a dozen feet above herself, falling toward the ship.

Red and blue lights flashed around her body as she used the StrengthStone and IntelligenceStone. Out of the horrendous storm, Cole suddenly appeared at her side. As they both set their feet as firmly as they could on the shifting deck, they put their hands up into the air above themselves. Their muscles bulged as the weight of the plunging mast fell onto their outstretched arms. Shaeleen yelled out into the storm. The muscles in her arms burned, and the strain on her shoulders and back felt like a mountain crushing her.

Looking to one side, she saw Abby lying safely on the deck, her father by her side. They stared in open awe at what she had done. Shaeleen turned to Cole, and he looked to be straining as much as she was.

"Shae! Let it down slowly," Cole said.

Together they lowered the mast to the deck, and it landed with a thud that shook the ship. But everyone was safe from its fall.

Shaeleen moved carefully to the wheel and grabbed it hard, not knowing at first where to steer it. Then she saw a small island looming off their starboard side, scarcely showing through the mist and rain.

"Turn portside," Abby said, who now stood at Shaeleen's side, holding on to Shaeleen's waist.

Shaeleen gave Abby a questioning look. That would move them farther away from land.

"There are rocks on the starboard side," Abby said.

Shaeleen followed her directions. Soon the captain joined Shaeleen and—with an eye that held both fear and awe, as well as gratitude—took the wheel back from her. Cole moved off, to help the sailors with the other sails and try to keep the ship upright.

Soon the lightning and thunder moved on and the wind diminished, but the rain still fell. This continued for another hour. With Abby giving directions to her father, faint traces of land would come and go around them in the darkness.

Shaeleen sat down on a bench, for she didn't want to go down below and leave the others, but she didn't have much strength left.

"Shae, are you all right?" Cole came up next to her. His hair was plastered to his head, and his face looked worn with strain.

Shaeleen nodded. "I'll be all right. Thanks for your help with the mast."

A grim smile covered her brother's face. "I didn't know I had it in me. I can hardly control my powers and have no idea what I can really do."

"I think your powers flare up when I'm in trouble and need your help," Shaeleen said.

The ship lurched then, and Cole fell against Shaeleen on the bench.

"Sorry," Cole said.

"Father!" Abby yelled and pointed her finger. "There is land again on the starboard side. I can hear the waves hitting it hard. It must be Verlyn."

Hearing! Shaeleen thought, berating herself for taking so long to figure out what power Abby was using. Some TruthSeer I am. Abby, the captain's daughter, must be from Althea and had the power of the white Celestite HearingStone. Abby had been listening for how the waves sounded as they'd hit the rocks or land: to know how to steer the ship through the storm.

"We're coming in too fast, Father," Abby yelled into the rain.

"I can't see anything," the captain answered back, trying to wipe the water from his eyes.

"I need to help the crew," Cole yelled out through the rain as he headed to the stern of the ship, where some of the sailors were struggling with another broken mast.

Shaeleen nodded as Cole ran off, and then she stood up and ran in the opposite direction—to the bow of the ship.

"Get back, girl!" the captain bellowed at her. "What are you doing?"

But Shaeleen ignored him and instead wrapped her legs around the railing as firmly as she could. Then, with one hand, she reached into her pouch and pulled out the TruthStone.

What's the use of having powers if I don't use them during times like these?

Raising the stone high up in the air, she instinctively called up a TruthSpell. A bright green light immediately burst out from the stone itself and pushed away the darkness in front of them, lighting the way. Shaeleen held the stone higher and willed its light to go out as far as she could.

Land abruptly rose up in front of them. Waves crashed against the shoreline, and tall trees swayed in the rain above. So the captain turned to port as far as he could, to avoid the brunt of the crash. The starboard side of the ship scraped along sharp rocks lining the shore, the wooden hull creaking and splintering underneath their pressure, the stern of the ship swinging wildly around.

"Shaeleen!" Cole said, his voice soaring through the air above the din of the storm.

Shaeleen turned. Through the wind and rain, she saw her brother fall from the stern of the ship, out into the churning water.

"Cole!" Shaeleen screamed and took a step toward the stern. But, as she did so, the bow of the ship rammed into a rock, and the ship twisted around again. Wood splintering cracked through the air. She and the rest of the crew scrambled to stay on board, and Shaeleen felt torn between needing to light their way forward and helping her brother. Her tears mixed with the rain as she remained where she was while the captain tried to guide the ship into a small inlet, between two giant outcroppings of rock.

"Hold on!" the captain yelled out as he pulled hard to starboard, the hull of the ship scraping on rocks and sand underneath them. Then, lurching forward, both the port and starboard sides were crunched between large, jagged rocks. They stopped with a jolt, throwing everyone to the deck of the ship.

"Off the ship," the captain bellowed. Shaeleen was slumped over the railing. Her light had diminished, and she felt so exhausted she could hardly move. It was all she could do to shove the TruthStone back into its pouch. Then she saw the captain grabbing Abby's hand in his as he ran toward the bow of the ship. The captain and Abby pulled Shaeleen along as they climbed over the railing, moving toward the rocks.

"My brother," she mumbled. "Find Cole, please!"

Then Shaeleen fell to the ground, somehow hitting the sand. A wave crashed over her head, and she sputtered and coughed, trying to stand back up. But another wave knocked her back down again, and the water began pulling her back out to sea. She tried using her powers, but there was nothing left. As she went under again, she tried once more to regain her footing, but she slid out even farther.

"Don't let that girl die!" she heard the captain yell to his men. "Or I'll have your heads. Get her!"

Then strong arms grabbed Shaeleen out of the water and dragged her up to the shore. Another pair joined the first, and they carried her farther away from the rocks and waves. She rolled to the side and coughed out a lungful of water.

"Where's my brother?" Shaeleen groaned.

The captain shook his head at her. "I don't know, miss. I sent two men to walk the coast, but…"

Her brother couldn't be gone. She closed her eyes and tried to find Cole through their magic connection. But she was so weak and found her mind drifting. For a moment, she thought she felt something, but she wasn't sure.

"Where are we?" Shaeleen said a few moments later. Her throat felt sore and raw.

The captain, sitting on the ground next to her, grimaced and waved an arm around as he said, "Welcome to Verlyn, miss. Though I'm sure this was not the way you had intended to arrive. From what I can tell, we are at the north end of Verlyn, at the edge the Eyvindr Jungle."

CHAPTER TWELVE

Of the past few hours, all Shaeleen could remember was rain and being carried around. In a few lucid moments, she had tried to reach out to Cole, but she had then drifted back into unconsciousness. Her body had been so exhausted that she couldn't keep track of what had been going on or how much time had passed. Finally succumbing, she had fallen into a deep sleep.

But now she could hear voices from far away. As these came closer, Shaeleen's mind gradually became more aware of her surroundings once again. With eyes still closed, she could hear that it was the captain talking to some of his men. They seemed to be trying to find something to light a fire with, something that wasn't drenched in water. Eventually, Shaeleen did open her eyes. Abby was sitting next to her, hair wet and plastered to her head.

"Shaeleen!" Abby exclaimed upon seeing Shaeleen's open eyes.

Shaeleen turned her head to look around a bit. They seemed to be in a small cave. Through the opening, she could see what she presumed was the jungle of Eyvindr.

"How are you feeling?" Abby asked her.

Shaeleen thought about Abby's question for a moment. Then she grimaced and felt at her side—to make sure her pouch was still there. When she felt it, relief flooded through her, but then she remembered her brother.

"Cole?" Shaeleen asked instead.

Abby shook her head. "The men looked, but they didn't find anything. I'm sure he survived, though."

Shaeleen appreciated the girl's attitude, but tears came to Shaeleen's eyes nonetheless. *Why do we always get separated?*

Abby helped Shaeleen sit up, and she wiped the tears away. Then she realized she hadn't felt any pain with Abby's hope about Cole surviving. That must mean he was still alive at least!

The captain was quickly at her side, and he knelt down next to her. "Miss, you saved us all. I didn't lose even one member of my crew." He ran his fingers through his beard. "A few scrapes and bruises, but that's all. I've never seen anything like that in my life!" His excitement quickly soured as he seemed to realize what she must have been thinking about. "I'm sorry about your brother," the captain added. "His strength saved many of my men from harm. I'm sure he has survived. He was a strong man. We'll meet up with him again."

Shaeleen nodded her head, but she couldn't quite bring herself to speak yet. So she looked around a bit more. The rest of the crew stood further back within the cave. They seemed to be trying not to stare at her—but they did so nonetheless.

What must they think of me after my display of magic?

Abby continued to sit next to Shaeleen with concern in her young eyes.

Clearing her throat, Shaeleen spoke softly to the captain. "Your daughter was quite amazing. I presume now that you are from the kingdom of Althea?"

The captain studied his daughter with adoring eyes. "Yes, she does have a good dose of the HearingStone flowing in her blood. Helps us out quite a bit at sea. But you…?"

"Me?" Shaeleen shrugged her shoulders. "You want to know what I am?"

She could see the rest of the crew lean in closer, as if trying to hear what she would say next. She would bet they had never seen anything like what had happened on the ship in all their lives. If she hadn't been the one doing it, it would be hard for her to even believe it.

"I am the holder of a stone of power," Shaeleen said. She owed these brave men the truth—at least some of it. And the statement definitely was true.

"And a bit more, I would surmise," the captain added.

"Yes." Shaeleen nodded her head. "And a bit more." *But not enough to save Orin or to save my brother.*

Shaeleen stood up and walked to the opening of the cave. Her body ached, and she was still exhausted. She gazed out on her first look at the island of Verlyn. The rain had stopped, and the sky was darkening as evening approached. She could still hear the waves crashing against the shore, telling her they hadn't moved too far inland.

Cole! she called out with her mind, barely able to feel any of her powers. A flicker in her mind caused her to close her eyes and concentrate harder. He was still alive; she was sure of it. She couldn't tell anything further than that at the moment. But it was enough for now.

"Quite an amazing sight, isn't it?" the captain asked as he walked up next to her.

Shaeleen opened her eyes and took a deep breath. She hadn't really been looking at the jungle just now.

"I've been to the port at Sylvermoor before but never to the jungle," the captain said. "Our best estimate is that we are on the northwest part of the island."

"And the ship?" Shaeleen asked.

The captain shook his head. "Not much left."

Shaeleen continued surveying the area, but plants with leaves larger than her own head blocked much of the view in front of her. Up above, on some taller trees, hung vines that were as thick as her arm. Colorful flowers poked their ways through here and there, both on the ground and in the trees.

Soon the storm began to blow over, and the sounds of birds squawking and of a few ground animals flitting by filled the air around them. The jungle would be quite a beautiful sight if it wasn't for the fact that they were marooned there with little provisions and her brother, Cole, was missing.

"Now what?" Shaeleen asked.

Abby came out and joined the captain and Shaeleen. She grabbed her father's hand and looked up at him, awaiting his answer.

"We stay here tonight," the captain said. "Storms are hard to predict in this area, and we don't want to be caught out there in the middle of the night in one. Then, tomorrow, we explore the area, look for your brother, and see if there are any paths or people around here."

"Magic people?" Abby said, her eyes as round as saucers.

The captain laughed. "Haven't you seen enough magic today, Abby?"

"Never," Abby answered. "I want to see a Verlynian. I hear they all have magic."

"Well, I wouldn't know about that," the captain said with a questioning glance at Shaeleen.

"Me neither," Shaeleen said. "But I really do need to find my brother and get to Sylvermoor. I am on an errand—from the prince of Galena and the queen of Gabor—to find Princess Diamonique."

"A real princess?" Abby smiled up at her father. "Oh, Papa, we really need to help Shaeleen. I want to meet a real princess."

Both Shaeleen and the captain laughed and then headed back inside. Then the captain gave directions to some of his crew to "find something to eat and maybe some wood that would burn for us."

And an hour or so later, they finally had a somewhat efficient, though very smoky fire burning at the edge of the cave. Shaeleen stood in front of it, trying to dry out her clothes and hair.

As darkness began to fall outside, the sounds of the jungle grew louder. Then the captain placed rotating guards at the entrance of the cave and ordered the rest to get some sleep.

* * *

Early the next day, their group of thirteen got up and came out of the cave as daylight approached. As Shaeleen stood at the mouth of the cave, she marveled at the multitude of colors spread out in front of her. She had never realized there were so many shades of green.

The sky was still cloudy, and the rain the previous day had allowed the morning to start off cooler. But Shaeleen knew that, when the heat of the day hit, the humidity would make things very unpleasant.

When she saw the captain sending a few men off to look for her brother, she ran up to him.

"I will go with them too, Captain," Shaeleen insisted.

The captain shook his head. "You are not well enough yet, miss. This is rugged terrain."

"He's my brother," Shaeleen pushed harder to go. She suddenly felt dizzy and put her hand against the entrance of the cave to steady herself.

The captain gave her a knowing look, and she reluctantly agreed with him. She thought about using her powers, as she could feel the TruthStone, but she still had hardly any strength to pull on its power.

"Fine." Shaeleen watched the searchers leave the area and then joined the others walking further inland to find help.

She watched the back of the captain as he directed the rest of them forward. A few of the sailors found strong sticks and then walked in front of the group to clear a trail for them to walk.

After a while, they found a small game trail and used that to cover ground more quickly. At midday, they foraged for fruits and other edible plants, and then they continued walking. But everyone seemed tired and weak, and the going was slow.

Shaeleen noticed that it was becoming darker as they began to enter the thickest part of the jungle so far, and Shaeleen felt relieved each time they passed through a thinning that would allow the light of day in. She thought many times of trying to use that light to find her brother, but the sun kept hiding behind the clouds, and she still wasn't sure she'd have the strength for it.

* * *

Later in the day, the men that had been out looking for Cole came back.

"I'm sorry, miss," one said to Shaeleen. "We couldn't find him."

Shaeleen held back the sudden tears—for she knew inside that he was still out there somewhere.

"Any signs?" she asked.

Another sailor said, "We found a few indents in the sand that could have been his footprints. Hard to tell. But, if he made it off the beach, Cole could have found help somewhere."

As they resumed their journey, Shaeleen took a deep breath. For now, she would hold on to that hope.

A few moments later, one of the men in the front, blazing the trail, turned around and motioned for the group to stop moving.

"I hear voices ahead, Captain," the sailor said.

"Let me see," the captain said. With his daughter in tow, he pushed to the front of the group. Then he motioned for

Abby to listen, to see what she could hear. Abby nodded and motioned for them to all retreat back down the trail. After a few dozen feet, the group turned and looked at Abby.

"I can hear a few of them talking. Men and women," Abby said, mostly to her father. "They are on some kind of annual trek, to Sylvermoor and Mount Eyvindr."

"Anything else?" her father prodded.

"Something about a keeper." Abby scrunched up her nose. "But I don't know what that means."

Shaeleen sighed, and the men and Abby turned in her direction. So she tried to remember what her books had said.

"A keeper is chosen in each village and town," she explained, "to keep guard or control over any of the stones of power or other magical artifacts." She thought about what she had learned from Shadow Keeper Georrod in Mistport. Did the people ahead of them have a keeper with them? And, if so, a true keeper of the stones or of the shadow?

"We must take our chances," the captain said. "We don't have the means or supplies to take care of ourselves out here for long. And we all need rest."

The men nodded and began to move forward, the captain taking his place in front.

"Captain," Shaeleen said, calling the man back. He looked annoyed at allowing the delay, but he did so anyway.

"Make sure your men don't say anything about me." Shaeleen said. "Don't tell them what I can do. Lie if you have to." Her stomach clenched in discomfort at the thought, but she really didn't have any other choice for the time being.

The captain nodded and then made sure each of his crew had heard the request. Then they also nodded their understandings.

"And, Abby," Shaeleen said in a whisper, "try not to use your hearing either—we don't know who these people are or what they can detect."

"Are you expecting trouble?" the captain asked as he furrowed his big brow at Shaeleen.

Shaeleen shrugged. "We all just need to be careful."

The captain motioned for Abby to stay in the back with Shaeleen. And then the group slowly moved forward, with the captain in the lead.

CHAPTER THIRTEEN

The trail was narrow here. Branches and leaves scraped against Shaeleen's legs and arms as she tried to keep stray branches out of her face. She couldn't help but be excited about being on Verlyn, despite their circumstances. This is where the stones of power all originated from.

Maybe I'll get some more answers here.

After a short time, she heard voices from ahead. The front of her group had apparently come upon the group of local people Abby had heard earlier.

"We were on our way to Sylvermoor," the captain explained. "But then we got caught in a storm and our ship crashed."

"We are escorting our young keeper here," a woman with a full, rich voice answered, "to his first annual gathering of keepers, along with his uncle, Keeper Dunstun. You are welcome to join us. We were just stopping for a short midday-meal break. We have extra food if your men are hungry."

Shaeleen and Abby followed the captain and the crew out into a small clearing. The ground was green here, a mixture of grass, clover, and small plants. And ferns encircled most of the clearing.

Shaeleen surveyed the group of local people. There were about fifteen men and women. Off in a corner, next to a large rock, sat two of the men. They were dressed differently than the others: dark cloaks covered them, whereas most of the rest of the Verlynian group had cloaks of lighter, softer colors.

One of the two men faced the group. He was older and seemed to have a perpetual scowl on his face. He was clean-shaven, as were most men in Verlyn, and had long, dark hair and light blue eyes. The man that he sat talking to had dark blond hair but sat with his back to the group. So Shaeleen could not ascertain his age.

"Oh!" Abby said, sounding excited. "They are the most wonderful people. They all have such long, silky hair: blond, white, and brown."

* * *

Shaeleen had laughed at Abby's earlier excitement. But she too was soon enamored with the group. They had seemed pleasant and had talked to the crew, sharing their food with them. She'd tried to observe them and stay in the shadows with Abby. But, like most things on this errand, her luck didn't hold out very long. For, while Shaeleen had been looking one direction, someone else had come up behind her.

"Hello," said a rich, musical voice.

Shaeleen turned and had to stop herself from gasping. Standing before her was a man that could only be described as the most beautiful man she had ever seen. Then she recognized him as the man she had seen talking, off in the corner, to the older man. He appeared a year or two older than Shaeleen herself. His long, blond hair framed a thin but pleasant-looking face. And, as he moved his hand through the side of his hair, she saw his upturned ears. His light blue eyes—a shade darker than Shaeleen's own—looked at her intently.

"My name is Taegen. May I be of assistance to you?" he asked, his voice carrying a light tone. "You must be hungry."

"No, no," Shaeleen said and took a step back from him and his intense gaze. "I'm fine."

This lie brought a cringe to Shaeleen's face, and she tried to smooth it over with a cough while covering her mouth.

"Are you all right?" Taegen asked as he touched her arm lightly with his fingers.

Even through her long-sleeved shirt—if you could call the dirty thing a shirt anymore, Shaeleen could feel power in his touch—a power of the stones, but one that also worried her. *Something darker.*

He lifted his hand off of her arm. "I meant no offense." His voice felt comforting. "You two were with the captain's crew when they crashed?" he asked Shaeleen and Abby.

Shaeleen felt as if he were fishing for answers as to why two young women were on a cargo ship.

"The captain is my father," Abby said. "And Shaeleen is my friend."

Shaeleen let out a deep breath that she hadn't realized she'd been holding. *No pain.* She smiled at Abby.

"My brother was also on the ship, but he was lost overboard." Shaeleen wanted to reach out now and see if she could feel Cole again, but something from within the TruthStone gave her a warning not to.

Taegen's face fell, and he looked genuinely concerned for her loss. "I am sorry to hear that. I will see if my uncle will allow a few of the men to search for him."

Shaeleen breathed a sigh of relief. If he'd had bad intentions, why would Taegen offer to help her, when she hadn't even asked him to?

"Thank you," she whispered to him.

Taegen continued to look at her eyes—light blue like his own. Although this color of eyes was not common on Wayland, it was normal for those on the island of Verlyn.

"And what are you doing here, Taegen?" she asked as the TruthStone guided her questions. "It seems that everyone else is much older than you."

Taegen took a moment to gather his words. "I am a keeper, and they are escorting me to the gathering of keepers, along with my uncle," he finally said.

Shaeleen could tell that these words were true.

"Oh, you have magic?" Abby almost purred next to Shaeleen.

Shaeleen rolled her eyes at Abby and shrugged her shoulders to Taegen with a small smile. The girl was obsessed with magic.

"Yes," Taegen responded. "I have been blessed to have some of the power of the island's stones in my blood." He paused for a moment, looking at Shaeleen as if he were trying to determine her real reason for being there.

Shaeleen knew that his words were true, but a tingling in her head told her there was something he wasn't saying.

Then Taegen turned to Abby. "And I see you have a power of the stone also."

Shaeleen coughed and shook her head slightly at Abby, to tell her to not say anything.

The girl frowned, obviously excited to be talking about magic.

How did Taegen know this? Shaeleen wondered.

Taegen only laughed and clapped his hands lightly. "I see we're keeping secrets," he said. "Well, that's fine. But you look like you could be from Althea, where the HearingStone resides." He leaned in close to them and whispered, "I won't tell anyone." His eyes sparkled at Abby, and Shaeleen had to turn away to keep from being pulled in by their beauty. Then Taegen turned to Shaeleen and asked, "And you?"

Shaeleen panicked, and her body swayed with worry. "What do you mean?" *There is no way he could tell if I have any stones.* The pouch where the TruthStone resided had always protected her stone. *But, would it work differently on Verlyn?*

Taegen reached his hand over, as if to steady her.

She backed away from him, but some part of her had wanted to stay near him.

"I am from Galena," Shaeleen said firmly. She knew that wasn't what he had been asking, but that was all she was going to answer. She could almost feel his displeasure at hearing her answer.

"My uncle tells me the power of the stones are diminishing in Wayland," Taegen said.

"Oh really?" Shaeleen said with a smile. "And how would your uncle know about these things?"

"He's also a longtime keeper of stones—he is my mentor," Taegen said.

Suddenly, a new voice spoke, this one more deep and sinister. "Taegen, you should leave these girls alone."

Shaeleen turned to find the man that had been sitting with Taegen earlier. He had somehow snuck up next to their small group. Shaeleen could instantly feel something was wrong about the man; he gave her the creeps.

"This is my uncle, Keeper Dunstun," Taegen said, introducing him to Shaeleen and Abby. "This is Abby. I think she has the power from Althea," Taegen added and then winked at Abby.

Shaeleen stepped between the two. "Leave her alone, Taegen," Shaeleen said.

Taegen chuckled and said, "And this one, Uncle, is Shaeleen. She is from Galena and, I suspect, is hiding something."

Shaeleen fumed at Taegen's inference. But before she could open her mouth to protest, Dunstun, Taegen's uncle, spoke.

"The power of the stones is not something to be trifled with by young girls from Wayland," Dunstun warned.

"Dunstun," Shaeleen said, purposefully leaving off the man's title. She found a measure of joy at the look both Taegen and Dunstun gave her in response. "I have always been taught that the stones of power were given freely to King Wayland, as a sign of friendship, from your people to ours." Shaeleen decided to put a question forward to see if Dunstun would lie or not. "The powers of the stones are to be shared by all people. Do you not agree?"

Dunstun stood silent for a moment, glaring at her, before he spoke. "Magic should not be in the hands of those that don't understand its true power."

Shaeleen was impressed by the way Dunstun had been able to avoid lying. He must have had some interactions with a TruthSeer.

"So, you're saying if someone, even a young girl like me," she said, using his own words against him, "understood the true power of magic and how to use it appropriately, then it would be all right for me to have it?"

"That's a preposterous question," Dunstun said and then turned to his nephew. "Taegen, let's leave these two alone for now. We have much more important things to do than discuss superfluous questions with young girls from Wayland."

Without warning, truth flowed through Shaeleen, and she took a dangerous step forward. It was not *physically* dangerous, but she knew her words would have a threatening tone to them as she said, "Like discussing taking magic away from Wayland?"

She heard Dunstun suck in a breath of air, and Taegen cleared his throat and then coughed.

"They would never do that!" Abby said at Shaeleen's side.

"You have no idea what you are talking about, young lady," Dunstun said.

Pain hit her in the gut, but this time she relished it because feeling it meant that through his lie she *had* learned the truth. She gritted her teeth and breathed deeply, doing all she could to stay standing. But she still swayed a bit, and Abby grabbed on to her.

"You're upsetting Shaeleen," Abby said to the two men. Abby held tightly on to Shaeleen's hand and helped her back up a few feet, lowering her down onto a large rock. "The captain will not stand for this," Abby added.

"The captain will not stand for what?" Abby's father said from a few feet away, walking up to the group.

"These men are upsetting Shaeleen with their talk and warnings about magic," Abby said as she left Shaeleen's side and walked closer to her father.

Sometimes Shaeleen wondered if Abby was really older than she seemed. Of course she wasn't. But Abby was acting much more mature in dealing with people and events than Shaeleen herself had many times.

"Is that so?" the captain said. "I was just assured we would be treated kindly and escorted to Sylvermoor on your way to the gathering."

The captain was a big man, and Shaeleen heard Dunstun breathing more heavily now. Her TruthStone grew warm against her thigh in response to this man, who she now assumed was another shadow keeper. *Which means he could take the captain down with barely a thought.* Her heart sped up as she realized that she would have to be extra careful now. *I may have pushed him a little too hard.*

Both Dunstun and the captain glared at each other a moment.

Then a female voice sounded from across the small open area. "Keeper Dunstun, are we ready to move out?"

"Yes, yes, it is past time…" Dunstun said, his voice trailing away as he spoke.

"And you, young man?" the captain said to Taegen, who hadn't moved yet. "Same for you. I expect you to treat these young women with respect."

"Yes, sir." Taegen seemed to struggle to find his words. But somehow he added a graceful bow as he said, "Of course."

"Then let's go," the captain said.

As the captain and Keeper Dunstun moved away, Shaeleen stood and began walking forward with Abby. But Taegen remained where he was.

"Keeper Taegen?" Shaeleen said, purposefully emphasizing his title.

"Yes?" he answered as he joined them.

"Do you believe in your uncle's sentiments: that those in Wayland should not have the use of the power of the stones?"

"That's not what he said," Taegen said carefully.

Shaeleen felt the stirrings of a barely missed lie in her gut and wondered if Taegen was also a shadow keeper. "But that's what he meant. So, do you hold fast to those beliefs also?"

Taegen sighed and said softly, "It's complicated. That's all I'm going to say. Now, no more questions. I will do as I promised, however, and send a few men to look for your brother."

Shaeleen was surprised that Taegen had remembered his promise, after all that had happened since then. "Thank you," Shaeleen said. As she felt her cheeks warm up, she tried not to let Taegen notice.

Taegen leaned in closer and whispered, "I don't know who you are or what you want, but you must have a death wish to taunt my uncle so." As he drew closer, Shaeleen noticed that his breath held a touch of sweetness to it, although she could also smell traces of the nearby plants, dirt, and humidity lingering on his slender body.

"Who are you really, Taegen?" Shaeleen stopped and looked him in the eye, trying to decipher the truth. "And don't just tell me *A young keeper.*"

"I am not your enemy."

"That's not what I asked," Shaeleen said as she and Taegen began walking forward once again.

"But it's all I can tell you without causing you either pain or alarm," Taegen whispered.

Shaeleen stopped walking again and glared at him. There was no way he could know she had a TruthStone, was there? Were things different here on Verlyn? Lies and secrets seemed to be the way of things. *Not so unlike politics in the kingdoms of Wayland.*

"Taegen!" Dunstun yelled from up ahead. "You belong in the front of the procession, not in the back with those girls from Wayland. Show some respect for your people. You are a keeper."

"I have to go," Taegen said softly as he touched her arm briefly with his hand.

Unexpectedly, she missed his touch as soon as he let go. "Just tell me, Keeper Taegen, do you think the same as your uncle?" Shaeleen tried asking one more time.

"What do you think?" he whispered while raising his full, slanted brows at her. Then he jogged up ahead and joined his uncle.

"Shaeleen!" Abby called from up ahead. "You're falling behind. What were you two whispering about back here?"

"Boys!" Shaeleen stomped forward, almost dragging Abby along. "They are so infuriating."

CHAPTER FOURTEEN

Over the past three days, the group Shaeleen had been traveling with had grown. Each night they had stayed in a new village, and each morning they had headed out with an additional keeper and a few more Verlynians.

Taegen had only talked to Shaeleen once during that time.

"The two men I had sent to look for your brother have returned without finding him," he had informed her. "But they were told about a weakened and bruised young man in another procession of keepers moving through this area, and they said there was talk that he was from Wayland and had light blue eyes."

"Thank you," Shaeleen said as she let out a breath she hadn't realized she was holding during his sharing of information. Now Shaeleen wanted so badly to try and find Cole herself, but she knew she wouldn't have any idea of where to even start to go.

On the morning of the fourth day after joining the group of locals, a morning storm cleared away and the sun came out. She was tempted to travel through its light and find Cole. But it seemed as if either Taegen or Dunstun always had an eye on her. Even as night approached and they'd stopped at an inn in a small town south of Sylvermoor, she could sense them close by. She didn't know what the two keepers could or couldn't do with their powers, and so she comforted herself with knowing that her brother was alive and was traveling in the same direction her group was.

"I heard my father tell the crew we should be close to Sylvermoor by tomorrow evening," Abby said to Shaeleen at dusk.

Shaeleen and Abby were now sitting in their room on the second floor of the inn. Its wooden walls were smooth and had been polished in a way that showed off the wood's beautiful grain. A small dresser with a basin of water and a table with two chairs filled one end of the room, while the large bed the two were sitting on filled the room's other end.

Thinking, Shaeleen stood and walked to the table. Its carpentry was exquisite—even surpassing her father's. The most amazing thing was that the top of the table flowed down into the legs, as if they were from one piece of wood. She ran her hand over it and then shook her head, trying to figure out how they had done it.

"Magic," Abby whispered. "All the buildings seem to be natural outgrowths of the trees and land around us. It's quite amazing."

"Amazing or not, Abby, some of these people are trying to take magic away from us."

Shaeleen peeked out of their room's small window. It was dark outside, but each window over the small village's main street seemed to hold a light, which gave an almost twilight glow to the small village. Tall trees formed a canopy over the town, blocking the stars and the moon from sending their light down to the ground.

"I'm tired of sitting here every night," Shaeleen said, turning to Abby. "Let's go out."

"But…" Abby said, looking at Shaeleen.

"We'll be fine." Shaeleen pulled gently on Abby's arm, lifting her up from the bed.

"Are you sure?"

"The town looks peaceful enough." Shaeleen smiled. "What could happen?"

What could happen indeed! was the next thought that came to Shaeleen's mind. Two young women from Wayland, alone and out at night on the foreign island of Verlyn, a mysterious land known for its secretive people and strange magic.

"We can protect ourselves if we need to," Shaeleen said, dragging Abby toward the door.

"But my father—" Abby began to plead and tried to stop Shaeleen from pulling her along.

But Shaeleen interrupted her. "Your father and the other sailors will be in the common room for hours. The Verlynians' ale and fine singing will keep them busy." As Shaeleen opened the door and stuck her head out, she added, "We won't be gone for long."

Seeing the stairs leading to the common room, Shaeleen took Abby in the opposite direction. Soon they found the back stairs.

Running out into the night, Shaeleen held her hands out to her sides and turned in circles until her head began to get dizzy. "Oh, it feels so good to be away from everyone."

Abby smiled at Shaeleen, giving her the feeling that Abby wanted to ask Shaeleen more about her magic. Abby clearly wondered how much power Shaeleen really did have.

Shaeleen wondered that also!

She walked with Abby down the village's main street, keeping primarily to the darker parts so they wouldn't be spotted. After a short distance, Shaeleen stopped and turned around. She could smell something sweet.

"Is something wrong?" Abby asked, moving closer to Shaeleen.

Shaeleen laughed. "Oh? No, Abby, something is definitely right. Do you smell that?"

"Smell what?" Abby seemed perplexed.

"Sweets." Shaeleen smiled broadly. "Sweet pastries, to be exact. Somewhere over there?" Shaeleen pointed a finger across the street at a small, nondescript building with no name, which sat at the end of town. Its doors were closed, but its brightly lit windows indicated something was going on inside.

"We can't go in there!" Abby's eyes opened wide.

"But we can go in through the back," Shaeleen said mischievously. "Come on." She grabbed Abby's hand and pulled her across the road and around the side of the building. At a small window, they ducked down and crawled. While still underneath it, Abby froze and didn't move forward any farther.

"What?" Shaeleen asked.

But Abby shushed her. Turning her head to the side of the building, Abby seemed to be listening. After a few moments, she motioned Shaeleen to keep moving.

Soon they were at the back of the building, and Abby pulled Shaeleen into the shadows of a large tree. Shaeleen turned her face up and saw that its leaves were twice as big as her head. The plants she'd seen so far on the island were incredible, and Shaeleen had hardly been able to see much of the island so far.

"The keepers are in there," Abby said.

That brought Shaeleen's attention back to Abby. "The keepers?"

Abby nodded her head. "I didn't understand what they were saying."

"You mean you couldn't hear their words?"

"No, I didn't understand the meaning of their words."

"What words were they saying?" Shaeleen asked, looking at the back door of the building. There was a small window in the door, and she could see a small kitchen inside. *That's where the wonderful smells are coming from.* She tried to pay attention to Abby, but it was hard. It had been so long since she'd had something sweet. Fruits and vegetables and very little meat were all she'd been having since they'd crashed on Verlyn.

"Shaeleen! Are you listening to me?" Abby tugged on her arm.

"Yes, yes. Of course," Shaeleen said. Then she pushed the pain away. "Tell me what you heard."

Abby scrunched up her face for a moment. "They were talking about a big meeting."

"The annual gathering of keepers?"

Abby nodded her head. "That must be it. But they were discussing having enough votes or not."

"Enough votes for what?" Shaeleen looked around them. She didn't like staying in one place, like this, for too long. Someone could find them.

"Then something about the five stones of Wayland." Abby pushed the heels of her hands against her eyes. "I don't know, Shaeleen. There were many people talking in small groups. It was hard to pick up all of it."

Shaeleen motioned Abby forward, closer to the back door, and said, "Let's find out more."

Abby opened her eyes wide. "But, Shaeleen, this could be dangerous. Those men and women have magic. Real magic."

"And so do we," Shaeleen said, feeling confident enough. "This is important."

Coming closer to the back entrance, they walked up a few steps and then shrank down under the window in the door. Shaeleen peeked inside. The kitchen seemed empty—except for a tray of sweet pastries, sitting on a counter. Shaeleen's mouth watered at the thought. She put her hand on the door handle and turned it, pushing the door open slowly. It gave a small creak and both girls froze for a moment.

Shaeleen ushered Abby inside and then closed the door behind them. They moved quickly and quietly to a door at the far end. Shaeleen pushed on it carefully and then peered through the crack. There was a small hallway on the other side of it that was dark, its only light coming from the few kitchen candles. Moving through the hallway, Shaeleen began to hear voices.

"Are we close enough?" Shaeleen asked.

"Yes." Abby nodded her head, but she appeared frightened.

"It'll be all right," Shaeleen said to try to comfort her. "Just listen for a bit, and tell me what you hear."

Abby turned her head and closed her eyes. After a few moments, she started to repeat to Shaeleen the snippets of conversations she was hearing. "Kingdoms in chaos, as planned. Galena almost at war. Antioch founders disrupting things. Lightfort closed off from the rest of Shema. Princess of Gabor removed from training in Sylvermoor—"Shaeleen nudged Abby. "Is there more about Diamonique?"

"Who?" Abby opened her eyes.

"The princess," Shaeleen said. "Find out more about her."

Abby nodded her head and closed her eyes again. "I hear more talk on the voting at that gathering," Abby said. "It seems most of these keepers want to take magic away from Wayland. Something about a ShadowStone."

Shaeleen gasped as she started to put things together. These were the keepers of the shadow, all gathered here together.

"Is Taegen in there? Anything else about the princess? What about the ShadowStone?" Shaeleen asked, firing questions rapidly at Abby.

"Shaeleen—" Abby turned to her, eyes opened wide. "I can't hear if you keep asking questions. It's too much." Tears formed at the corners of Abby's eyes.

Shaeleen put her hand on Abby's arm. "I'm sorry. Let's just find out about the princess, then."

After listening for a moment, Abby turned to Shaeleen. "Someone knows where she is, but they won't tell the others."

"I've got to find out where." Shaeleen pushed lightly on the door, gazing into the room as far as she could.

All of a sudden she knew someone was looking at the door.

"Taegen," Shaeleen whispered loudly to Abby while closing the door. "I think he saw me."

Abby put her head to the door. "Someone's coming."

"Hold on to my hand," Shaeleen said and then, without thinking of any consequences, pulled upon the power of the SpeedStone. They raced through the darkened hallway and into the kitchen. But, as Shaeleen glanced at the sweet pastries on the counter, she lost her concentration.

Falling out of the speed and onto the wooden floor, the two of them crashed into a table and knocked utensils and pans off it and onto them and the floor. As they scrambled to get up, the hallway door opened behind them.

Into the light of the small kitchen came Taegen.

Abby squealed, and Shaeleen's hands reflexively grabbed Abby's.

"What are you two doing here?" he said, his voice firm. His eyes flashed dangerously. "Did you hear anything?"

Shaeleen took a few steps toward the pan of sweets and then swiped one. "Just looking for something sweet to eat, Taegen."

Taegen glared at her for a moment, as if waiting for something. But Shaeleen just took a big bite of the pastry. Sugar and cinnamon met her taste buds. It was delicious.

"Do you think I'm lying?" Shaeleen challenged him.

Taegen shook his head. "I can see you are not."

Shaeleen looked up at him in surprise. Did he know what she was, or only guessing from her actions? *Verlyn was a dangerous place.*

"Keeper Taegen!" came a voice from the other room. "Everything all right in there? I felt someone using a power of the stones."

Shaeleen heard some shuffling in the other room.

"Everything is fine," Taegen said. He put his finger to his lips for Shaeleen and Abby to be quiet. "What are you doing here?" Taegen whispered, moving to within mere inches from her.

His proximity took her breath away. *Get a grip and stop staring at his beauty,* Shaeleen told herself.

"What do you know about Diamonique?" Shaeleen asked.

This question was obviously not what Taegen had expected her to say.

"Did you take her somewhere?" Shaeleen prodded.

His eyes opened wide. "No, why would you think that? I—"

"Someone's coming," Abby said.

Shaeleen heard the door on the other end of the hallway open.

"Taegen?" called out his uncle, Dunstun. "What did you find?"

"Go!" Taegen told Shaeleen and Abby.

"But, did you?" Shaeleen tried to ask.

"Go now!" he said. "We'll talk later."

As the door to the kitchen began to open, Shaeleen grabbed onto Abby's hand once more. In a matter of moments they'd gone through the back door, around the building, down the street, into their inn, up the back stairs, and into their room. As the door closed, both young women fell onto the bed, breathing hard.

It was silent for a few moments.

Then a knock came to their door.

"Abby?"

It was the captain.

"Yes, Father?"

"Everything all right? There were noises up here."

"We're fine, Father. Everything is fine."

Shaeleen heard the captain walk away, and she and Abby lay back on the bed and started laughing with relief.

Their laughter eventually died down.

"I hope that Dunstun didn't know it was me who had used magic," Shaeleen said.

"Is there any power you don't have?" Abby asked as she turned to Shaeleen, her voice serious.

Shaeleen felt safe answering her innocent question. "Only healing and hearing. Before all this is over, I will have them as well."

Abby's eyes opened wide, and she looked fearful for a moment, but then took a deep breath and just stared intently at Shaeleen.

"Are you afraid of me, Abby?"

Abby shook her head, but Shaeleen didn't want to be looked at as if she were a monster.

I haven't asked for any of this.

Sometimes Shaeleen cursed Melindra, the keeper who had given her the TruthStone. Before, she'd thought that maybe she could give the stone back when she arrived on Verlyn. But now Shaeleen knew she couldn't do that. There was more at stake than she'd ever supposed. With the number of shadow keepers she'd seen tonight, it appeared that Verlyn was as much in trouble as Wayland was.

Abby continued to gape at Shaeleen.

"Don't hate me, Abby," Shaeleen pleaded. "Please?"

Then Abby smiled broadly and leaned up on her elbows, resting her head on her hands. "I don't hate you, Shaeleen. I think you're the most amazing person I have ever met!"

CHAPTER FIFTEEN

The next morning, as the party left the small village and continued their trek to Sylvermoor, on their way to Mount Eyvindr, Shaeleen noticed that the group now numbered close to one hundred. Shaeleen was once again walking with Abby and was enjoying the scenery around them. However, Shaeleen was getting more and more nervous and jumpy the closer they got to Sylvermoor. She'd hoped to be close enough to find Cole by later that night, and then they could find Princess Diamonique and get back to Galena. The princes' birthday, the day of crowning and betrothal, was coming close.

"The jungle is getting thinner, and the trees are shorter," Abby said. "Look, I think that's Mount Eyvindr." She pointed over the tops of the trees up ahead.

As Shaeleen glimpsed the snowy peak, she was amazed by how big it must seem up close. She had seen Great Mountain Divide, east of Mistport, when they had been there. But the large, volcanic peak of Mount Eyvindr had a splendor in its own category.

She wondered, *Among all the travelers with us, how many are shadow keepers? And what type of keeper is Taegen?*

"Greetings, ladies," Taegen said from beside Shaeleen, making her jump.

She hadn't seen him coming back toward them through the crowds, but thinking of the young man seemed to have attracted him to her side.

"I thought you were special and had to stay up front?" Shaeleen said to him with a smile.

"No, not special." Taegen smiled back and tilted his head slightly to one side. "Just more powerful than most of them."

Shaeleen knew it for the truth, and she shuddered, wondering who was the more powerful one out of the two of them.

"Shae, it looks like we are stopping for the midday meal," Abby said from her other side. "I'm going to go and find my father. I'll be back soon."

"But…" Shaeleen felt torn between a desire to stay with Taegen and a worry about what he really wanted with her. His eyes seemed to hold a pool of mysterious secrets in them whenever he looked at her, and she didn't know if she could trust him or not.

"I will stay with her," Taegen offered to Abby. "You go and see your father. On my word as a keeper, I will keep Shaeleen safe."

"Do keepers lie?" Abby asked Shaeleen, suddenly seeming hesitant to leave her now.

"Yes, they can," Shaeleen said.

"But you will know if I do, won't you?" Taegen said with a touch to Shaeleen's arm.

Even through her long sleeves, she felt an electric spark as he touched her. She jerked her arm away involuntarily. "Shae?" Abby asked.

"I will be fine, Abby," Shaeleen said more confidently than she felt. "Go eat with your father and the crew. There are plenty of others here around us."

"I won't be gone long," Abby said as she took off in a run down the dirt road toward her father.

For a moment there was only silence.

Shaeleen thought that soon Abby's father and his crew would be back at the port in Sylvermoor, and she wondered what he would do about a new ship.

"You're quite jumpy," Taegen said close to her ear. Taegen's presence so close to her made Shaeleen jittery, but his smooth voice and earthy scent had a calming influence.

Shaeleen's heart pounded. "You seem to have that effect on me."

"You have a sharp tongue for one so young," Taegen said with a laugh.

"I've heard that before," Shaeleen mumbled. Trying to regain control of the situation, she added, "But you aren't much older than me, I would guess."

"No, I wouldn't think so." He paused a moment and then put his arm around her shoulders. "I want to take you somewhere," Taegen said as he began to lead Shaeleen down a path off to the side. "There is something really amazing close by that I think you should see."

"What about the others?" Shaeleen tried to pull away from him, but his arms were strong.

"Everyone is busy. They won't miss us for a few moments."

The sounds of the group receded into the distance as Shaeleen was led down another, smaller path that moved farther inland, into the jungle. She stumbled on a root, but Taegen kept her standing.

Readying her powers if they were needed, Shaeleen's curiosity overruled her senses and she continued forward with Taegen.

"Tell me what you know of me," Taegen said while they continued walking.

"You have long, blond hair; you're taller than me—well, most people are, at that—"

Taegen laughed. It did not seem to be a teasing laugh, but one of joy.

"You have the normal characteristics of one from Verlyn," she continued. "Your face is thin, with fine features, and is quite…" She stopped as soon as she realized she was going to tell him he was quite handsome. Her cheeks grew hot. *What is happening to me?*

"Not just about how I look," Taegen said. "I meant what do you really know about me?"

"That's about it," Shaeleen said, not wanting to say out loud what she'd guessed about his uncle's powers and had presumed about Taegen also. And then the pain hit. She stopped and pushed her hands into her gut, trying to rein in the pain.

Stupid stone!

"You're a bad liar," Taegen said matter-of-factly.

As they began walking down a slight slope, Shaeleen heard the sounds of water becoming louder and felt the warm air growing cooler.

"So, how does one become a keeper?" Shaeleen asked to change the subject.

They took a few more steps before Taegen answered, "Part of it is desire; but the potential to tap into the stones of power and of course the will of the people are also factors. My uncle has been a keeper since before I was born. He is getting older now, and the people have chosen me as his successor."

"But the others seem to already give you deference."

"Oh, so you *have* been watching me?" Taegen teased.

Shaeleen felt her cheeks growing hot again, and she cursed her own words. *I need to be more careful with how I answer. Taegen is quick.*

"I have to watch those who may get in the way of my mission," Shaeleen said, growing more serious.

"And you think I may get in the way?" Taegen asked.

The ground became steeper, and they stopped talking for a moment while Taegen helped lead Shaeleen down a small set of rough rock steps. Water now roared louder just ahead of them, around a bend. Shaeleen didn't know how to answer Taegen's question. His mind was quick and she was afraid he was fishing for answers that she wasn't sure she wanted to divulge.

Taegen stopped and moved around behind her. He placed his hands around on her cheeks then slid them up over her eyes.

Shaeleen flinched at his touch and felt her heartbeat begin to race, but she didn't move away. Part of her screamed to do so, but she also found herself drawn to him for some reason.

"I have to cover your eyes for the surprise," Taegen said with amusement in his smooth voice. Shaeleen could feel his breaths, his lips mere inches from her ear. A racing excitement inside of her battled with bells of warning. She took a deep breath and tried not to show how his presence affected her.

"Walk forward slowly," he directed.

She felt him place one of his hands on her back, applying gentle pressure to one side or the other to direct her forward. The warmth of the sun hit her face, signaling they'd entered a clearing. Soon she heard the roar of water closer now, and then felt a slight spray wet her face. It felt good in the growing warmth of the sun.

He moved around in front of her and slowly removed his hand from her eyes. "What do you think?" he asked.

Shaeleen peered up into his eyes—just a shade darker than hers—and her pulse quickened. *What do I think of him?*

Taegen seemed to have the good sense to not say anything right then. He only took a step to the side and turned, waving his arm in front of him. Shaeleen followed his arm to where he was pointing, and then she gasped.

"I meant what do you think of *this?*"

"It's beautiful!"

She looked down into an iridescent glen of color, where a beautiful waterfall fell gracefully, sparkling in the sunlight, down into a deep, clear pool.

There was a walkway behind the falls, and Taegen lead her there now. The ground was slippery, and the path was narrow. Pushing the spray of water out of her eyes with one hand, she let Taegen hold her other hand as he led her around the falls. The rock wall fell back behind them into a narrow cavern that grew darker.

Shaeleen turned and stood facing the back of the waterfall, seeing the jungle distorted through its sheets of water. A small stream led out from the pool below the falls, winding its way through green patches of ferns, vines, and trees. Near the base of the falls, she could see small flowers blooming at the edges of the stream.

Then Taegen pulled on her hand once again, leading her out from behind the falls. Now the pool of water was directly below them. As she noticed he hadn't let go of her hand, she found that she didn't mind.

He turned to her and smiled. Then he waved his other hand, with a smooth motion, out over the clear water. At the same time, he'd uttered strange words, and Shaeleen would swear she had seen a slight swirl of black fog around his hand. But before she could think on this too much, a new sight in front of her took her thoughts away.

"Stones of power!" Shaeleen exclaimed while peering down into the pool.

Sparkles of color—red, blue, orange, pink, and even clear white—glittered throughout the water, breaking into smaller flickers as the water was agitated by the falls.

"What are those?" She pointed to other, smaller colors that flickered in between the larger ones.

"Other stones of power," Taegen said. "Besides the major stones, there are many other stones of power—stones of seeing, compassion, caring, leadership, and growing—that make up the life we have in Verlyn."

In front of all these stones, Shaeleen felt a tugging from her own stone of power and was tempted to bring it out. It wanted to feel the power that was here. But a small thought in the back of her mind stopped her, and she let go of Taegen's hand.

Glancing over at Taegen, she saw that his eyes had turned gray and were now turning back to their usual light blue. She stepped backward as previous internal warnings came finally to the forefront.

As he turned to look at her, his face seemed warm with tenderness. "Isn't it beautiful, Shaeleen? Aren't the stones of power so beautiful!"

Shaeleen took another step backward, farther away from the falls, with a sudden foreboding in her heart. The power of the TruthStone drove her to discover the answers.

"What did you do, Taegen?"

"I summoned the stones as all keepers can do. Pools like this all over Verlyn are where the stones live. Stones like those that were given to your King Wayland many years ago. Stones that are now failing in your land." His face became more stern and his eyes grew harder.

"Taegen!" Shaeleen was becoming afraid, but she pulled on the power of her TruthStone for support. "What power did you just use?"

Taegen seemed to come out of a daze. His eyes returned fully to their normal lightness, and his countenance seemed brighter. "Shaeleen," he said and then took a step toward her.

"Stay where are you are, Taegen," Shaeleen said. "Don't come any closer."

"Shaeleen! What has gotten in to you?" Taegen said. "I brought you here, where few from outside of Verlyn have ever been. I thought you would appreciate it."

Taegen put his hands out in front of him and beckoned Shaeleen closer.

Maybe I misunderstood.

He stood in front of her, smiling and pleading for her to come near him.

Shaeleen shook her head a few times to clear her thoughts. Then she remembered that she still held the power of the TruthStone. "Tell me, Taegen, what stone of power did you use to clear the waters?"

Confusion flickered across Taegen's face. He brushed a few strands of his blond hair out of his eyes and wiped water off his brow.

"I don't think that matters," Taegen said. "Please, Shaeleen, you are frightening me."

Shaeleen took a step closer to him, and he smiled. But then she looked deep into his eyes and poured the power into her words. "Tell me now!"

She hated forcing people to tell the truth. *But sometimes using this type of TruthSpell is the only way.* She thought briefly of Orin and cringed inside. *Have I lost his friendship for good? And, will I now lose Taegen's also?*

Taegen's face grew stiff, his mouth held tight. But Shaeleen directed the power of the TruthStone directly at him. And, finally, his shoulders fell, and he dropped his head down. With confusion still written across his face, he reached into his pocket and drew out something. Holding it in front of him, he opened his hand. A dark stone sat on his palm, small swirls of black fog circling around it.

Shaeleen glanced up at his eyes. They had once again turned dark gray.

"A ShadowStone. Taegen, put it away."

He did, and his face became clear again. Tears filled the corners of his now light blue eyes. But Shaeleen kept her powers ready to use.

"You are a keeper of the shadow," Shaeleen whispered.

Taegen nodded. "Please, Shaeleen, help me into the light!"

His words felt convincing, and her heart broke. Tears dripped down his face, marring its perfection but adding to her attraction for him.

Is he telling the truth? Of course he is, or I would have known. Or, does the presence of the ShadowStone alter my powers?

Taegen fell to his knees, mud splattering his dark blue pants and tunic. Bits of water sprayed onto him from the nearby falls. His face turned down in shame.

Shaeleen took another step closer to Taegen, but then a new voice broke into the conversation.

"Taegen!" his uncle roared. "What have you done?"

CHAPTER SIXTEEN

Shaeleen twisted her head around, searching for Dunstun. She spotted him on the path, near the other side of the falls, the direction they had just come from. His black hair hung down over his dark green cloak. His eyes were dark, and his look was threatening.

Taegen, still on his knees, gazed up at his uncle but spoke to Shaeleen. "Shaeleen," he whispered, so softly she could barely hear the words over the sound of the falls, "please help me."

"You!" Dunstun roared at Shaeleen. "What are you doing to my nephew? Stay away from him!"

Shaeleen shook her head. "I can't do that. Taegen needs my help."

"I knew you were more than you had seemed to be," Dunstun said, hands on his hips. "You are here to sabotage the gathering of keepers."

"Don't flatter yourself so," Shaeleen answered back, trying to think of how she and Taegen were going to get out of there. "I was on the ship heading to Sylvermoor, and we *did* crash. I'd never intended to go to the gathering. But, now that you mentioned it…"

"You are trifling with things beyond your control, girl. This is why the powers need to be pulled back from Wayland,"

Dunstun said as he put a hand out in front of him. As Shaeleen watched, swirls of darkness extended from Dunstun's hand, similar to what Georrod had tried to use on her in Mistport.

"Where is Diamonique?" Shaeleen asked.

This question seemed to catch Dunstun by surprise, and he laughed. "That's who you came for? That pathetic girl? She hardly holds a modicum of strength, compared to us. The StrengthStone is so weak in her it might as well not even be there."

"I am here on her mother's and Basil's requests. She is to marry the prince." Shaeleen felt a slight pounding in her head. That lie had been small—even though she hadn't said which prince, she knew in her heart that what she wanted was not currently the truth.

Dunstun took a step closer down the path, but he still had not used his power. Taegen stood up next to Shaeleen. She glanced at Taegen briefly, and he gave her a quick smile.

"Go back, Uncle," Taegen said. "I can handle this. Shaeleen will help me."

"You don't get to choose this now!" Dunstun yelled over the roar of the falls at Taegen. "The ShadowStone has already chosen us—you and me—to usher in the new order of things in Verlyn and Wayland. We will hold all the power of the stones. We will be as gods."

Wisps of black fog flew from his hand, out over the water, and hovered there. The pool of water roiled and seemed to be boiling, turning darker and darker.

"Where is the princess?" Shaeleen asked again—pushing the power of the TruthStone through her voice.

Dunstun shook his head as if he were trying to clear it. "Get out of my head, girl!" Then a flash of black and yellow fire shot from his fingertips and raced toward Shaeleen and Taegen.

Taegen pulled Shaeleen down, onto the ground, as the bolt of lightning exploded above them on the hillside, sending shards of rock and dirt flying into the air. Shaeleen quickly covered her head with her hands.

"Why do you care about our doings on Wayland?" Shaeleen yelled to Dunstun.

Dunstun laughed, and the sound echoed off the walls around the falls. "We only care to sow discord among its kingdoms. I care nothing for the girl or for any of you who think you hold some semblance of power. You are all pathetic. Now, Taegen…come, and I will forgive you for chasing after that attractive young woman. Don't let her become your downfall."

Taegen stood and took an obedient step toward his uncle.

"No, Taegen. Don't go," Shaeleen pleaded, standing up herself. "We have to get out of here."

Taegen turned and held her eyes. Pain tortured his face. "You don't know how hard this is," he pleaded in a loud whisper. "The constant fight between light and shadow. It just might be easier to go. I'll convince Dunstun to let you go free. You don't need to get mixed up in this."

"Too late." *I'm already up to my neck in this because of the TruthStone.*

Shaeleen looked over at Dunstun. He held his hand out toward Taegen. Between them, down in the churning pool,

Shaeleen saw colorful stones of power rising to the top of the shadowy water. Then their lights dimmed in the murkiness.

At the same time, a ray of sunlight pushed through the trees and came down through the waterfall. Dunstun and Taegen didn't seem to notice this, but Shaeleen followed the path of light with her eyes as it went from the falls into the small cavern behind them. It was as if the light was showing her the way.

Taegen still stood, looking longingly at his uncle's outstretched hand. A look of desire to please Dunstun began to fill Taegen's face. Shaeleen pulled Taegen with her across the path and into the cavern, following the path the light had taken. As Taegen stumbled along behind her, toward the back of the cavern, Shaeleen glanced back and saw him turning to look toward his uncle. Dunstun had pointed his hand out toward the water, and the stones of power began to be lifted up out of the blackness. But Shaeleen noticed they had hesitated, as if they were fighting against the shadow.

"Come to me!" Dunstun ordered the stones, and an increased amount of black fog flew from his fingertips and encased the stones in a wall of blackness.

Shaeleen drew upon the power of the TruthStone and brought along with it the powers of the StrengthStone, IntelligenceStone, and SpeedStone. She moved over a few feet and stepped into the sunlight there more fully. The power of the light met with the power of truth and fueled her capacity.

So much power!

It gathered around her—green, red, blue, and orange. She spun her arms in the air and gathered it all into one ball of fire, which hovered in pulsating brilliance just above the palm of her hand.

Dunstun yelled, and his voice filled the beautiful glen with a gruesome and dark roar. He shot out tendrils of shadow from the fingertips of both his hands, the darkness racing toward Shaeleen.

But she was ready. Forming the TruthSpell in her mind, she had focused all the stones of power she held. But instead of shooting it out toward Dunstun's dark shadows, she focused it on the stones rising out of the dark pool of water. Her ball of fire hit them in the center, breaking them free from Dunstun's ShadowStone. The stones of power from the pool of water gathered into one, and a brilliant white light shot forward and met the dark tendrils of power from the shadow keeper's hands.

These two forces of power stood against one another for a few brief moments, neither one giving way. And Shaeleen took that moment to run over to Taegen. The young keeper stood in confusion, watching the fight between the two forces—light and shadow.

Shaeleen grabbed his arm and pulled him with her into the sunlight behind the falls, power still filling her body. Taegen roared, and Shaeleen knew her power must be hurting his. Then she pressed him ahead of her anyway.

"Go!" she ordered, power filling her voice.

After Taegen was on his way, she turned back around and went out of the cavern opening onto the path behind the waterfall once more. She gathered another TruthSpell and shot a bright green stream of light into Dunstun.

This new attack caught him by surprise, and he dropped his previous spell, allowing the brilliant power of light to consume the dark shadow and shatter the remains of his spell. The pool of water turned clear, and the stones dropped back down beneath its rippled surface.

Shadow Keeper Dunstun was kneeling on the ground, his considerable power seemed almost spent. Then he brought his hand up again and pointed at Shaeleen, saying, "Now you die!"

Shaeleen dove back into the cavern opening just as a stream of fire hit the rocks around her. The power exploded behind her, and she jumped back up and moved farther away. Turning around, she watched as the cavern's entrance collapsed, sealing her and Taegen in with the darkness.

Once the rumbling had stopped, Shaeleen turned around. A soft green glow still emanated from her body as her powers receded back into her. It was enough to see Taegen sitting on the ground, knees pulled up to his chin. His long, blond hair hung straight down both sides of his head.

"Don't hurt me," Taegen said, eyes wild and afraid.

Shaeleen walked slowly over to him and reached her hand down.

"Taegen, come with me."

"It hurts, Shaeleen," he said.

"I'm sorry," she answered back. Then Shaeleen drew the power back into her TruthStone before reaching out again. "It should be all right now."

He nodded and stood, reaching out tentatively to her, looking broken and troubled, but trusting her nonetheless. He held on to Shaeleen's hand.

"So much power." Taegen shivered.

Shaeleen looked at him and then brought up a small light in her other hand, to light their way. She hoped it wouldn't hurt him too much.

Taegen grunted but kept a hold of her hand. Together, they turned and began to walk down a narrow tunnel inside the cavern that led them deeper underground.

CHAPTER SEVENTEEN

Shaeleen moved on ahead of Taegen trying to figure out where to go. After many minutes of apparently mindless walking, Taegen called up to Shaeleen and finally broke his silence.

"Thank you, Shaeleen," he said, his voice soft.

Shaeleen stopped for a moment, turned around and smiled. "Thought you were gone there for a bit."

"Me too." Taegen stood up straighter, the fire returning to his gaze. "I thought I felt something powerful within you these past few days, but I had no idea what you could really do."

"I did what I had to," Shaeleen said. "I'm just glad we got away from your uncle." She had not wanted to show Taegen the extent of her abilities—she still didn't know if she could fully trust him or not. Her heart said to, but her mind—and she reluctantly admitted, the TruthStone—both said for her to be careful.

"I thought I was powerful. But you, Shaeleen…" Taegen paused, taking her hand in his, and gazed deep into her eyes. "You have powers that I can't even comprehend. Who are you? What are you?"

Shaeleen was uncomfortable with his intense—and covetous—look, and she dropped his hand. Then she began walking again more quickly down the tunnel, making Taegen almost have to run to keep up as she continued again in silence.

Shaeleen herself didn't know what she really was. She did know something about the prophecy. That she was supposed to gather all the stones and restore strength and balance to the kingdoms of Wayland. But the powers she'd exhibited against Dunstun and his ShadowStone had terrified even her. *And I still have to gather the HealingStone and the HearingStone. What then?* With two more stones of power, what would she *not* be able to do?

Shaeleen slowed a bit and let Taegen walk next to her. "As I began this errand," Shaeleen finally said softly, "I told my brother, Cole, I would become so powerful that I could do whatever I wanted to do. I told him I would become all-powerful and make anything I wanted happen. I could ensure Basil takes the throne, I could crush Commander Kerr's army, and I could destroy Calix if need be. Now, I also have to restore peace in Antioch, take care of the shadow keepers, and still find Diamonique."

Taegen flinched when she mentioned the shadow keepers, but stayed listening without interrupting her.

They turned a corner, and daylight came from a small opening a dozen yards ahead of them. They walked to the opening and peered out. They were on a small ledge, about twenty-five feet above the sea.

The day was still bright, though the sun had moved considerably further west. Shaeleen blinked a few times and had to shield her eyes to look out over the Straits of Mist. Off to their left, the domes and peaks of Sylvermoor shone in the distance and Mt. Eyvindr's snow-capped peak sat in the haze, even further to the south

Shaeleen took a deep breath and tried to calm herself. "And, do you know what terrifies me the most about all of these seemingly insurmountable tasks?" Shaeleen looked over at Taegen.

He shook his head, still not speaking.

Tears filled Shaeleen's eyes. "I am frightened that I might accomplish them all—the good and the bad—and that I might become a bigger monster than those I'd have vanquished."

She dropped her head, tears dripping slowly down her face. Then she felt a light touch on her shoulder. She lifted her head up and found herself looking directly into Taegen's eyes. Just that touch and his look brought comfort. Then he leaned his head down and kissed her softly on the lips. After this one gentle kiss, he pulled back and gazed into her eyes again.

Shaeleen wrapped her arms around him and stood in this embrace until her tears had stopped. She could feel the battle raging within Taegen—the light versus the shadow.

"We're quite the pair, aren't we?" Taegen said. "Me, a keeper of the shadow, and you, the most powerful magic user in Wayland and Verlyn. Did fate throw us together to kill or to save one another, I wonder?"

Shaeleen laughed and wiped tears from her face. "Quite the poet, Taegen."

Taegen snorted, and then they both laughed, the tension of the day flowing out of them. They turned and stared out at the Straits of Mist, standing side by side. A colorful bird sailed over their heads and landed on a leafy palm tree that was growing at the edge of the cliff. It squawked at them, as if it were telling them that they were intruding in its home.

And maybe we are.

Shaeleen wondered at Taegen's words. *Am I destined to save or destroy him? He still holds a ShadowStone!*

Taegen moved to the edge and glanced down. "There seems to be a way down, if we are careful. We may be able to make Sylvermoor by nightfall."

* * *

With the sun directly on them, the late afternoon grew hot as they began walking along the western coastline of Verlyn. Within the idyllic beauty of the island, it was hard for Shaeleen to imagine the chaos that was rampaging through her world.

"It's beautiful here." Shaeleen sighed. "Have you ever been to Wayland?"

Taegen shook his head. "Never been to Wayland. I've hardly even been off the north side of this island, where I grew up. I did go to the gathering of keepers last year. It was quite a mess."

Shaeleen had plenty of questions about that, but she needed to focus in on what really mattered.

"How were you introduced to the power of the ShadowStone?"

"Well, I…um…" Taegen seemed to stumble over his words for a moment before finally answering. "My powers manifested themselves about seven years ago, when I was ten. I was out playing by a small stream, and a few stones of power called to me. My uncle, Dunstun, was the keeper of stones in our village at the time. He was a good man and took care of all the magic in the area. He took me in, became my mentor, and kindly taught me how to use magic."

Shaeleen raised her eyebrows in a questioning pose, and Taegen laughed.

"Yes, I know it's hard to believe, at this point," Taegen continued. "But he was a good man. A little over a year ago, he went to Sylvermoor to meet someone. I'm not sure who it was, but it had to be someone very important. When my uncle returned, he had changed. His countenance was darker, and he was short-tempered. He began to meet secretly with others often. Then, a year ago at the gathering, a group of keepers tried to vote against allowing magic on Wayland. Someone had warned the keepers of the stones of the ShadowStone, so they were prepared, and the motion did not pass. On the way back from there, my uncle and another keeper brought me and the other man's son to a pool and offered us the power of a ShadowStone."

The conversation stopped now, as they met with a broad rock outcropping blocking their path. Finding handholds and footholds, Taegen climbed up first and then leaned down and offered his hand to Shaeleen. For the hundredth time in her life, she wished she was taller. She stretched as far as she could, standing on her toes, and grabbed his wrist. Then he pulled her up.

Climbing to the top of the rock, they then had to turn inland, back into the edge of the jungle. A small flock of colorful birds took off out of a tree above them, and Shaeleen jumped, at first, and then squealed with delight.

"Are all your birds so colorful?" she asked.

Taegen smiled and nodded. "Yes. Aren't yours?"

Shaeleen laughed. "Oh no. Seagulls, pigeons, sparrows, blackbirds—all fairly boring compared to these."

"I would like to visit Wayland someday," Taegen said. "Maybe I could come and visit you."

The direct look he gave Shaeleen brought heat again to her cheeks. She put it down to exertion from climbing, but she knew it for what it was. She wondered if he might have put a spell on her with the ShadowStone, but she dismissed that idea at once. *I care for Taegen, but…* Unbidden images of Prince Basil came to her mind now.

Taegen is only trouble for me.

But she looked up and found him looking into her eyes with his beautiful eyes, and she felt herself blush again.

Ah, boys! I need to concentrate on finding Cole and getting Princess Diamonique.

"Did I embarrass you, Shaeleen?" Taegen laughed and then turned down a small gaming trail that paralleled the coast from just inside the jungle. "No quick barb from your tongue?"

Shaeleen glared at his back. "I wasn't embarrassed, just caught by surprise." She paused for a moment. "Taegen?" She waited until he stopped and turned around. "I just need to concentrate on finding Diamonique and my brother for now, and we will worry about you visiting Wayland later."

Shaeleen caught a slight sigh escaping his lips, but outwardly he smiled and nodded.

The trail descended slightly, and soon they were able to walk along the shore once again. As the sun began to set, they came into the bay with Sylvermoor on its southeast side. The coastline curved inland quite a bit, and Shaeleen could see the city from here. Its white-domed rooftops sparkled pink and orange as they picked up the rays of the setting sun. She could also see the outlines of dozens of tall ships between here and the city, ships from Wayland that brought goods and people back and forth.

With these ships in her line of sight, Shaeleen thought of Abby and Abby's father and his crew. She hoped they were all right.

"What do we do about the others?" Shaeleen asked.

"My uncle will be looking for you, Shaeleen," Taegen said. "It's not safe for you to go back."

"What about the captain and his men and Abby?" Shaeleen said as she followed Taegen. "They will be worried about me."

"I'll try and get word to them," Taegen said. "What about your brother?"

Shaeleen closed her eyes and reached out. Almost immediately she felt Cole. He wasn't too far away, but it was starting to get dark. "He's not far." Taegen's stomach growled, and Shaeleen laughed. "I guess we can wait a few minutes. I don't sense him in any danger."

"There are small villages here, among the ships," Taegen explained. "We can eat here and then go into Sylvermoor later."

* * *

They had found a small inn, whose owner didn't ask any questions about a boy from Verlyn traveling with a girl from Wayland. As long as he got paid, he would keep quiet—some things were the same everywhere. The clientele of the inn had seemed to cater to rough sailors, most of which were actually from Wayland. For some reason, many of them had been giving hard looks at Taegen, but he seemed to be ignoring it fairly well.

"I wonder what's going on?" Taegen said while they waited for their food.

Shaeleen shrugged. But, as Cole had said once, trouble seemed to follow her wherever she went. She sighed deeply and wished that for once things would go her way.

Soon their food came, and she ate a bowl of vegetable stew. Then Shaeleen was itching for something sweet. She excused herself from the table and went toward the kitchen, in search of the cook.

"Shae?" Taegen called after her. "You can't go back there."

Shaeleen just smiled. She had been going into kitchens of friends and at inns most of her life. *That's where they make the sweets.*

"We'll see," she called back to him.

She poked her head into the kitchen and saw an older woman, wearing an apron and barking orders to her underlings. Shaeleen listened to this for a moment while her eyes roamed the room. On a small, black stove in the back sat a pot with steam coming out of it. A girl about Abby's age continually stirred it, as if mesmerized by its contents.

Breathing in deeply and narrowing her focus on the pot, Shaeleen tried to figure out what its sweet scent was.

"Looking for something, miss?" The cook came up next to her with hands on her hips. "This is no place for bystanders."

Then Shaeleen realized that her own clothes looked quite poor. After the crash, their walk through the jungle, and her run-in and escape from Dunstun, she must look a mess.

"Either you help or you leave," the cook said.

"Help? Can I taste whatever is cooking in that pot back there?" Shaeleen asked.

The woman huffed, but Shaeleen could see a sparkle in the woman's eyes. "Ahh, it's my chocolate you crave?"

Shaeleen's eyes went wide. "Chocolate?" Besides sweet rolls and breads, chocolate was her biggest weakness.

Now the woman did laugh and pointed Shaeleen to the back. "Give Lyssa a break there, and stir it for a while. Five more minutes of boiling, and then we can pour it into the molds."

As she stirred the chocolate, she decided it was one of the most wonderful things she had ever done in her life. Then her mind went to the bigger tasks at hand. She thought of Prince Basil and Prince Calix. But her stomach cramped up at those thoughts, so she moved on to thinking about her brother. Cole was close, and they would meet up again that night. She hoped Cole wasn't hurt still.

The sweet smell of the chocolate was becoming heady, and to know that she was actually part of making something so tasty was unexpectedly thrilling.

After Shaeleen had spent a few minutes stirring, Taegen poked his head into the kitchen. A moment of searching, and then his eyes locked onto hers. He furrowed his brow in a questioning look, and Shaeleen laughed.

He was worried about me.

"I'm helping to make chocolate," Shaeleen called out to him.

The cook turned and saw Taegen. Then she moved over to him and shooed him back out. Shaeleen giggled and mouthed to Taegen that she would be out soon.

Stirring the chocolate, she closed her eyes and resumed thinking—this time about her errand to find Princess Diamonique. She wondered if Cole might have heard anything of her whereabouts. *Who will she marry?* Shaeleen thought. Prince Basil and Princess Diamonique would do well ruling Galena, but Shaeleen didn't know how to make that happen. The TruthStone constantly implied, with pain, that Prince Calix was to be the next king. *Poor Basil!*

"Girl!" The cook came over and swatted her on the bottom. "Stop daydreaming of princes and princesses."

"What?" Shaeleen almost dropped the wooden spoon into the pot.

How could the cook know what I was thinking about?

"How…?" Shaeleen began to ask.

But the cook laughed. "I know what young common girls dream about. I was one once, you know?"

"One what?" said a man about the cook's own age. He must have just walked into the room. His hair was graying, but his arms were muscled and tight, and he walked with a sailor's sway.

"A young girl, with fancies of meeting a prince," the cook replied, an amused smile on her face.

The man leaned over and gave the cook a kiss. "Well, I'm no prince, but I guess you're stuck with me anyway."

"Ah, you're *my prince*, Ned."

The girls and boys in the kitchen snickered and laughed.

"Back to work now, you no-good kids," the cook shouted, but her eyes never left her husband, Ned.

The cook moved away from Ned and took the pot from Shaeleen and set it on a counter next to the molds. Then the cook began pouring the chocolate into the molds—ships, serpents, swords, horses, and other wonderful shapes.

"Something strange is going on in the city." Ned had spoken this softly to his wife, but since Shaeleen was the closest, she'd overheard him. "There's more guards than normal around the old merchant district. The old Verlynian buildings—that have been vacant for decades—now have something going on in them. Rumors are that Prince Brevin is spending more time there than in the castle."

"Hmmm," the cook said. "Glad to be out here, away from the city. Too many Verlynians there, for my taste. They don't appreciate good food either. They're not a bad bunch, just always so secretive. I'm fine here, cooking for Wayland's sailors—they know a good meal when they get one."

Ned wrapped his arm around the cook once more and kissed her on the forehead. "Speaking of good food, I'm going to join the men and get me some."

Ned headed out as the cook finished pouring the last mold. Shaeleen stood there, watching and thinking about what she'd heard.

"Don't worry yourself about those things, young miss," the cook said, turning to face Shaeleen. "Just stay this side of the city, and you'll be all right." She reached back, behind herself, and brought out a small piece of chocolate for Shaeleen. It was molded into the shape of a dragon.

"Oh, it's beautiful!" Shaeleen cooed. "It seems hardly fair to eat it."

The cook laughed. "You are a mighty strange one. Now get out of my kitchen, and eat your dragon—before a real one comes and eats you."

Shaeleen knew there were no such things as dragons. But, when she was little, she did enjoy the old stories brought from the East by King Wayland's ancestors. Dragons and magic horses and wizards—it had all seemed so wonderful. Now she wondered about all of it. So far, having magic hadn't been so wonderful at all.

Just a lot of running, hiding, and being afraid.

She took a bite from its tail and then bit the head off the chocolate dragon for good measure as she walked back into the common room. The chocolate was smooth—and a bit bitter— but tasted oh so good.

She stood on her toes, to search for Taegen, and suddenly spotted him in a corner with two other men—Verlynians by the look of their long hair. They seemed older than Taegen, and stood close and talked in whispers.

Taegen turned around, as if looking to make sure they weren't being overheard, and saw Shaeleen. She gave him a questioning glare, but all he did was turn his head back around as if he hadn't seen her. Then he waved his hand at her behind his back.

What is he trying to tell me?

The other two men began to turn in her direction, but she moved behind a small group of taller soldiers. Sometimes her lack of height was an advantage.

Taking another bite of her chocolate, Shaeleen peered around one of the tall men to get a better look at Taegen's companions. Then the one man, whose back had been to her turned sideways, and Shaeleen froze mid-bite, the rest of the chocolate dragon sliding out of her hand and onto the floor.

The Verlynian that Taegen was speaking with was Georrod, a shadow keeper, the overseer from the compound in Mistport, the one who had tried to cleanse and then kill Shaeleen and Orin.

CHAPTER EIGHTEEN

Without thinking, Shaeleen drew upon the power of the SpeedStone and sped through the crowded room and out the front door. She almost ran into a group of sailors that were walking in, but she skidded around them just in time. Then she raced around to the side of the building and stopped there.

Breathing in deeply, she tried to quiet her beating heart. What was Taegen doing by talking to that man? Was Taegen leading her into a trap? And, had he been playing a game with her all along?

Staying in the shadows of the settling darkness of the night, Shaeleen stood listening for a moment and moved further back into the shadows. Then Shaeleen heard the door of the inn open. She wished she had Abby by her side right now. Abby's hearing ability would have been very beneficial. Sliding against the building, she moved farther toward the back. With her left hand, she felt the back corner of the inn and had slithered around it just as voices floated her direction from the front corner.

"Taegen," said a deep voice that Shaeleen recognized as belonging to the overseer. "Did you see someone in the back of the inn that looked out of place?"

"I'm not sure what you mean, Keeper," Taegen said.

"A girl—not much younger than you, but quite a bit shorter—from Wayland," the overseer explained.

There was silence for a moment, and Shaeleen imagined Taegen shaking his head—at least, she hoped that was what was happening. And, if nothing else, the lack of words did not cause her any pain.

"Who is this girl?" Taegen finally said.

"A magic user from Wayland that could cause us trouble."

Shaeleen smiled at the unintended compliment.

"How can someone from Wayland cause us problems, Keeper?" Taegen said. "I thought the shadow was more powerful than their stones."

"Don't try and preach to me about the powers of the stones, young keeper," Georrod said. "The ShadowStones must be protected. You are still true to the shadow, aren't you, Taegen?"

Shaeleen held her breath, awaiting his answer. She would know if it was a truth or a lie.

"I still hold the power of the ShadowStone," Taegen sputtered, seemingly trying to not answer the question fully.

Shaeleen's head began to pound, but not as hard as Shaeleen would have liked, given Taegen's words. She still couldn't tell if he could be trusted or not.

"Where is your uncle?" the third man asked. "I thought you were traveling together."

"We were unfortunately separated," Taegen said. "We will meet up at the gathering, I am sure."

"You can travel with us," the third man said.

Shaeleen risked a peek around the corner. It was dark, but there was a glow from the inn's windows on the three men talking—this light would hopefully blind them from seeing someone in her direction. Taegen and the overseer were standing with their faces toward her, but she couldn't see the face of the third man.

As she watched, Taegen moved his weight from his left foot to his right and glanced around in the night air. "I fear I have other business on my way. I will have to meet you gentlemen at the gathering."

Georrod put his arm around Taegen, and, even in the darkness of night, Shaeleen thought she saw tendrils of his shadow power brush up against Taegen's skin. Involuntarily she gasped, and then she stepped quickly back behind the corner of the building.

"What was that?" Georrod said. "Keeper Hutchin, go and see what's there. I'll take our young keeper inside so he is safe."

"No need, Keeper, I am fine," Taegen said, but he sounded afraid. "I can help Keeper Hutchin look."

Shaeleen heard heavy footsteps coming in her direction. She thought about using the considerable power at her disposal, but there were at least two shadow keepers here—not counting Taegen, who she still wasn't sure about—so she didn't want to draw attention to herself quite yet.

She still wanted to find out what was going on. She'd sensed that Taegen was still trying to protect her, but she didn't know how much sway the others would have over him. As the footsteps came closer, Shaeleen began to back away without watching where she was going. Then she tripped—apparently on an old crate left lying on the ground in the alley behind the inn—and fell hard onto her right knee. Pain shot down her leg, and she winced, trying to stand back up.

"Who's there?" came a gruff voice from around the corner.

Shaeleen put a hand on the wall of the building and steadied herself. Then the man Taegen had called Keeper Hutchin came around the corner and looked right at her. Hutchin smiled wickedly and brought his hands out in front of him. Black fog emerged from his fingertips and raced across the short distance toward Shaeleen.

Speed! Shaeleen pulled upon the power of the SpeedStone once again and moved quickly, only to find herself on the ground again, less than ten feet away. She grabbed her knee in agony and tried to stand back up, but Hutchin was in front of her once again.

Hutchin laughed. "So you are what causes the great overseer problems. You don't look like much to me!"

Shaeleen used the precious seconds of his amusement to think of what to do. She drew upon the power of the StrengthStone and picked up a rusty metal can she saw next to her on the ground. Still sitting, she lifted the can over her head and threw it at Hutchin. He tried to move, but her unexpected throw had caught him unaware, and he instead tripped over his own legs, falling down onto the hard ground.

Forcing herself to stand up again, Shaeleen realized that, in her injured condition, she couldn't use the power of the SpeedStone. Instead, she gathered the power of the TruthStone and formed a small ball of green fire in her hands. When

Hutchin stood back up and saw what she was doing, he thrust his own considerable power at her.

In the middle of the alley, black and green fire met in a clashing glow.

The back door of the inn opened, and an apparently drunk man stumbled outside, leaned over, and vomited. This distracted the shadow keeper for a brief moment, but that was long enough for Shaeleen. Using strength once again, she turned one hand toward the drunk, lifted him off the ground, swirled him in the air, and then threw him at Hutchin with such force it threw the shadow keeper back ten feet. Hutchin's power winked out immediately, and he struggled to get the limp drunkard off of himself.

Shaeleen kept to the shadows of the alley and moved as fast as her injury would allow her. Soon she limped past the last inn at the west side of the docks and, moving farther away from the shore, came to the edge of the jungle.

Glancing back behind herself, to make sure no one was following, she entered the jungle. Quickly, all the light from the inns, lamps, and stars disappeared, and she was plunged into deep darkness. Her knee throbbed, hurting more and more with each step.

Taking a few moments to rest, Shaeleen leaned against a tree and took a few deep breaths. Bringing her hand up in front of her, she created a small light in the palm of her hand. Holding her hand up in front of her, she looked around for any clues of where she should go.

Shaeleen closed her eyes for a moment and drew upon the power of the IntelligenceStone. *Where should I go?* she asked herself. Opening her eyes, she noticed a faint trail running parallel to the edge of the jungle and not going in too much farther. It moved south, closer to the city of Sylvermoor. She felt drawn to it and moved farther in that direction.

Keeping the light in front of her, she limped along, regretting moving farther away from Taegen. *But I have to get somewhere to rest. Once I have rested, I can think about going back to help him.* Although, as thoughts of Cole swirled around her, she realized she needed to get to her brother first.

After an hour, the trees thickened around her, and she noticed a flicker of light through the trees in front of her. Dousing her own light, so as not to be caught using magic, she stumbled forward. A small grouping of what looked like homes seemed to have grown out of the trees themselves. Vines wrapped around their smooth wood, leaving spaces for windows and a door. The porches held containers of brightly colored flowers.

Shaeleen toppled forward onto the porch of one and called out, "Help me!"

She heard voices that grew louder inside, and soon someone opened the door. Shaeleen looked up at a woman about twenty years older than herself. This woman and the others had such soft skin and hair that it was hard to tell the Verlynians' ages with any certainty. The woman ran a few fingers through her long, straight, blond hair and smiled with compassion down at Shaeleen.

"I'm hurt," Shaeleen said. "I hurt my knee and can't walk any farther."

The woman turned to the people behind her and called out for someone to help. A good-looking man, about the same age as the woman, walked out. His hair was brown, and he had classic Verlynian features.

"Let me help you up," the man said, his voice smooth. He reached down a hand, and Shaeleen grabbed on to pull herself up.

"Thank you," Shaeleen said with a nod of her head. Grasping the man's arm with her two hands, she hobbled forward with him, up a step to the porch and then through the front door.

Inside were three children, ranging in age from toddler to a young teen. The oldest, a boy, offered Shaeleen his seat, and the man led her to that chair.

Shaeleen sat down in the simple rocker and ran her hands over its carved armrests. "What fine craftsmanship," she murmured, totally enthralled with the intricate curves and the grain of the wood. Her father would have been proud of this piece.

"Thank you," the man said as he bowed. "I took great care in forming it."

Shaeleen turned to the man. "You did this? The workmanship is quite marvelous."

The man blushed slightly as he and the woman sat back down together in a large chair. The boy that had given Shaeleen his chair dropped himself smoothly to the floor.

"She's got our eyes, Mama," said a young girl—about six, if Shaeleen had to guess.

"Shh, Grace," the woman said. "That's not polite." Then, turning to Shaeleen, the woman smiled broadly, and it was as if the light in the room had grown brighter. "And where are my manners? I am Lorelei, my husband is Ruven, and our children, from youngest to oldest, are Amara, Grace, and Cameron. Welcome to our home."

"My name is Shaeleen. I'm sorry to have bothered you, but I couldn't go any farther," Shaeleen said.

Lorelei stood up from the chair she was sharing with her husband, walked over to Shaeleen, and kneeled down on the floor. She took a moment to examine Shaeleen's knee. It was bruised and swollen and hurt Shaeleen when the woman prodded it softly with her finger.

"Ouch," Shaeleen said and automatically pulled her knee back.

"You are from Wayland, I can tell," Lorelei said. She looked up into Shaeleen's eyes. "But you have the soul of one from Verlyn."

Shaeleen didn't know what to say at the moment. After meeting so many shadow keepers, she was becoming more guarded with her words. So she nodded her head and kept quiet. Shaeleen watched as Lorelei placed both her hands over her injured knee. Then Lorelei closed her eyes. A warmth spread from Shaeleen's thigh to her shin. It was not uncomfortable but tickled slightly.

Lorelei opened her eyes, her bright red lips parting into a smile. "That should feel better."

Shaeleen was shocked. It did feel better. She looked at her knee and moved it up and down. There was no bruise now and no pain—only a slight stiffness, as if she had been sitting for too long.

"How did you do that?" Shaeleen asked. "You must hold a HealingStone."

Lorelei returned to her seat next to her husband. He reached over and held her hand.

"Being a healer is one of her many talents," Ruven said. "My wife is a powerful keeper of some renown."

"My mother is a master keeper," piped up Cameron. "She protects many stones of power."

Shaeleen had another question, but she didn't know if she should ask it. Could she trust these people she had just met?

I don't feel any taint of the shadow here.

Shaeleen opened her mouth a few times but then closed it again, trying to think of the best way to ask it.

"Go on, Shaeleen," Ruven said. "You have a question for my wife?"

Shaeleen nodded—not quite sure how to word her question—so she just plowed ahead. "Well, what do you know of the ShadowStone?"

CHAPTER NINETEEN

After Shaeleen had asked the question, the room had gone quiet, and everyone looked back and forth at each other. All except young Amara, who had fallen asleep in the nook of one of Ruven's arms.

Then Ruven stood up briskly, still holding onto Amara, and motioned to Grace and Cameron. "Come with me, children. Your mother and our visitor have something to discuss."

"B-but…the shadow…" Cameron stuttered as he shifted his attention between Shaeleen and his father.

"Now!" Ruven said, and the children followed him out of the room. They closed a dark wooden door behind them, and the room fell quiet once again.

Shaeleen shifted in her seat, waiting for Lorelei to speak. So far, the master keeper had kept her head down and her eyes closed. *What is she doing?* Shaeleen felt the house grow noticeably cooler for a few moments. Then the candles in the home brightened, and the room grew so bright Shaeleen had to shade her eyes.

At the same time as the room had brightened, Shaeleen had felt warmth on her leg where the TruthStone sat in her pouch. Her mind seemed to lose focus, and the power of the

TruthStone sent her soul into the light within the room, scattering her thoughts wide and making it hard to concentrate.

What is happening to me?

Shaeleen tried to regain control over herself as another power pulled her farther into the light. The force moving her was not evil, but it was doing this against her will. And, in that way, it was not *good* either.

Leave me alone! she yelled out in her mind and pulled upon all the stones in her possession. She gathered the strength to resist from the StrengthStone—which, up until now, she had thought was only good for physical strength. She called upon the IntelligenceStone to figure out what was happening. With that intellect, she drew upon the power of speed and pushed away the power pulling on her and tried to send it far away.

It began to budge, but she still felt trapped.

Is this what others feel when I force the truth from them? Is this how Orin had felt?

A new stream of guilt flooded through Shaeleen, and she gritted her teeth against the power. Finally, she wrapped all the power she possessed within the vast potency of the TruthStone, which was hers and hers alone. The stones next to her pulsed with power, and Shaeleen pulled this all in—truth wrapping itself around speed, intelligence, and strength—and then she pushed this all out against the other power with a quick jab.

Within Shaeleen's mind, the light shattered as a glass lamp falling on stone. Shards flew through her mind, and she heard a scream. Opening her eyes, she found the room enveloped in the green glow of her TruthStone. Lorelei was slumped sideways in her chair, her pale blue eyes open but unfocused.

Shaeleen stood up slowly, stepping gingerly on her knee, until she remembered the healing that had taken place. She strolled the rest of the way to Lorelei's side and knelt down next to her. Putting her hand on the keeper's arm, she called her name.

"Lorelei. Lorelei."

The master keeper stirred and blinked a few times. Shaeleen stood up and helped Lorelei to sit up straighter. Lorelei smoothed down the soft skirts she wore and then turned her head up to Shaeleen. Her expression looked neutral, neither angry nor happy. If anything, Shaeleen thought she saw a spark of fear, mixed in with pride.

"Melindra chose well," Lorelei said.

Shaeleen was surprised to hear Lorelei speak the name of the woman who had given Shaeleen the TruthStone in the first place.

"What did you do to me?" Shaeleen asked, not feeling very happy about being pulled against her will.

"I was testing you to see how strong you are," Lorelei said, taking a drink of something from a nearby cup.

"Well, you could have asked me first." Shaeleen bristled as she turned around and headed back to the chair she'd been in, for those were the same words that Orin had used on herself afterward. Plopping down in the chair, she let out a long breath. "Fighting the shadow is hard enough—without having to worry about those with the light also."

Lorelei pursed her lips, and her face grew dark. "Do you even know the power you possess, Shaeleen? This is not a game you are playing. There are real forces at work here, forces for the control of all you and I hold dear."

Shaeleen was tired and hungry, and she had missed eating most of her chocolate dragon—which had made her cranky as well. "Then maybe you should have chosen someone else. Maybe Melindra should have been clearer with what she'd wanted from me." She drew the TruthStone from her pouch and held it in front of herself. It immediately flashed light around the room. "Is this what you want, Lorelei? Do you want my power also?"

Lorelei froze but had leaned forward in her chair just enough that Shaeleen could see a glimmer of desire in her eyes. "No, no. Of course not," she said, almost as if trying to convince herself.

Shaeleen's stomach cramped, and she glared at the woman sitting across from her. "Liar!" she screamed. "Everyone wants my power!" Shaeleen's head throbbed from the absurdity of what she had just screamed. She closed her eyes and took a few deep breaths. Opening them once again, she put the TruthStone away.

"Shaeleen." Lorelei's voice had grown softer. "Of course many want your power. But there is a difference between the shadow keepers and the true keepers of the stones. The shadow keepers will take your power if they can—make no mistake about that—but we won't. You are the only one who can save us, for you may be the only person able to keep the shadow at bay."

"Great," Shaeleen mumbled and then slouched in her chair.

Lorelei laughed, a light musical sound that immediately lifted Shaeleen's heart. "You must be hungry and tired."

"Maybe a little," Shaeleen said, biting back a harsher retort. "Do you have anything sweet to eat around here?"

"Oh, my dear child," Lorelei said and then laughed once again. "You are a complicated one, aren't you?" She stood up and walked over to a small kitchen area.

After rummaging around for a few minutes, Lorelei returned with a bowl full of small, round pastries.

Shaeleen raised her eyebrows at the Verlynian woman and then looked back into the bowl at the pastry. She had never seen its like before. A small round ball, about the size of a large walnut, dusted in a white powder of some sort. She picked one up in her fingers and bit into it. Then, with a big smile and no hesitation, she popped the rest of it into her mouth. There was a sweet pudding inside the pastry—with sugar powdered on the outside.

"Mmmm," Shaeleen said while popping a second one into her mouth. "Thank you, Lorelei. These are delicious. What are they called?"

"Cream puffs."

Neither woman said anything else for the next few minutes as Shaeleen ate the entire bowl. After she was done, she licked her fingers clean and then grinned broadly.

Lorelei retrieved the bowl, put it back in the kitchen, and then returned to the living area and sat back down. She drew Shaeleen's attention as her face grew deadly solemn.

"Now, you need to listen to me, Shaeleen. This is serious."

Shaeleen gulped and stared at the master keeper. The stones were telling Shaeleen that she needed to pay attention.

"You must be very careful about using your magic anywhere, but especially here on Verlyn," Lorelei began.

"But—" Shaeleen said, trying to ask a question. But she was shut down with a wave of Lorelei's hand.

"Not now," Lorelei said. "Just listen. The stones here, on the island of Verlyn, were found shortly after a remnant of elves arrived from the Eastern Kingdoms. That was over five hundred years ago now. These stones of power were found in streams and waterfalls and helped the exiled people to reclaim some of the magic they had previously lost in the great wizard wars."

Shaeleen nodded her head. She had seen those stones just recently, in the pool below the waterfall, with Taegen. *Taegen!* She wondered how he was. She needed to help him get away from the power of the ShadowStone.

"Shaeleen!" Lorelei called, bringing her back from her musings. "You must pay attention."

"Sorry, just thinking about my friend."

Lorelei nodded her head in apparent understanding, but she continued in her previous vein of speaking. "For hundreds of years, we in Verlyn had used the magic for good, and it became part of our everyday lives. The stones, nature, and our people had existed together peacefully. Then other people came and settled in Wayland—though it wasn't called Wayland at first. You are probably familiar with the history from then on:

of King Wayland and of us giving him the stones of power, as appreciation for his friendship and loyalty."

Shaeleen nodded. She did indeed know about all of this already and wondered why she had to listen to it again now, when so much needed to be done. But she sat still and endured it.

"What you do not know," Lorelei continued, "is how the ShadowStones were created." Lorelei paused, apparently to make sure Shaeleen was listening.

"I have seen it mentioned in the *TruthSeers' Journal*," Shaeleen said softly. "But I read from it only briefly."

"Yes." Lorelei nodded her head. "Anciently, the TruthSeers of Wayland would have been aware of the danger of the shadow. When the stones were given to King Wayland, there were some people on Verlyn who disagreed with sharing magic with others. This caused a rift among the keepers of Verlyn."

"Like now," Shaeleen added.

Lorelei frowned. "So, you have found that out already." This was a statement, not a question. "The keepers of the stones almost two hundred years ago gathered the best stones they could find and prepared to give them to King Wayland. What they didn't know was that, by finding the biggest and best stones and taking them away from Verlyn, an imbalance in the magic on Verlyn had occurred."

"And caused a backlash of magic—a shadow of the real stones formed," Shaeleen said in awe.

"I see you do have a portion of the IntelligenceStone in you." Lorelei nodded her head in agreement, but then her demeanor fell. "It was us, the keepers of the stones—in our desire to show appreciation for King Wayland—that created the ShadowStones, stones that came into existence to fill the void of magic on Verlyn."

Lorelei sighed and then said, "At first, we didn't even know they existed. Then small things happened that didn't make sense. Fear and greed grew slowly but surely among our people, something that hadn't occurred before that time. The first large division within the keepers occurred a little over a year ago, before the gathering of keepers last year: between those who'd decided to leave things as they were and those who'd wanted to bring the magic back to Verlyn—to strip King Wayland and his heirs of the powers we had given them."

Shaeleen felt enthralled. None of that was in their history books in Wayland. But it made sense, and she knew it was all true.

Shaeleen could understand now what had happened. "And so, these keepers of the shadow have risen up now—when the stones are so small—to try and rein the magic back in by taking it away from us?"

Lorelei's face grew even more grim, and she nodded.

"So, do the keepers of the stones and the shadow keepers both want magic to disappear from Wayland?" Shaeleen asked, growing worried.

Have I misjudged Lorelei? Does she indeed want my powers?

"It's more complicated than that, I am afraid." Lorelei sighed. "But you are correct, to some degree. The shadow keepers have swayed many of the other keepers to their side— or, if not altogether swayed to the shadow, then at least swayed to look away, with the excuse of bringing magic back to Verlyn."

"But, where does that leave me?" Shaeleen prepared to defend herself should Lorelei try to take her powers from her. "And you? Whose side are you on?"

Lorelei reached a hand out toward Shaeleen. But Shaeleen pulled herself back further into the chair.

"I am a master keeper, as is Melindra. She traveled in Wayland for a year, until she found you. We have stayed true to the power of the stones. We have awaited the one that will bring the fulfillment of prophecy spoken by an ancient master keeper. That person is you, Shaeleen."

Shaeleen nodded her head slowly and scooted up to the edge of the chair. The TruthStone told her it was indeed true. "So, in the end, do you expect me to give all the power back to Verlyn? To leave Wayland without any magic?"

Lorelei shrugged her shoulders. "We don't really know how it will end. That is up to you."

Shaeleen leaned her head back against the chair and sat in silence for a moment. It was all really too much to comprehend. *How am I going to gather all the stones back to me and defeat the ShadowStone all by myself?*

She smiled at Lorelei. "Got any more of those cream puffs?"

A laugh burst from Lorelei's lips, and she stood back up. Then she called her husband and children back into the room.

Ruven looked from Lorelei to Shaeleen and back again.

"Is everything all right, dear?" Ruven asked.

Lorelei started laughing as she grabbed a plate of the remainder of the cream puffs. Nodding her head, she blurted out between laughs, "I think it might be. I think it just might be."

CHAPTER TWENTY

Over the past hour, Shaeleen had eaten more of the delicious cream puffs and had been fed a delicious meal of fried vegetables and tasty bread. Conversation had been lighter during the meal, and Shaeleen had learned more about Lorelei and Ruven and their life in Verlyn. They had decided to live away from Sylvermoor, and the other homes nearby were filled with their brothers' and sisters' families.

"The politics in Sylvermoor are getting worse by the day," Ruven said. "I'm afraid many are calling for a ban that would even keep those from Wayland out of the city."

"What about near the docks?" Shaeleen said. "There are people from Wayland living there. I was at an inn ran by people from Wayland. It seemed mostly Wayland sailors were there, but I did see some from Verlyn as well."

Ruven nodded his head. "Yes, that is the problem. We have many from Wayland living among us now, primarily near the docks—and our trade with Wayland is important. We are a small island and need to import other things."

"But some Verlynians want to shut us off from the world altogether—and not just those who follow the ShadowStone," Lorelei said. "For others, wizards and those that possess the powers of the stones on Wayland aren't the only problem anymore, it seems."

Cole!

"My brother is a wizard," Shaeleen said. "He fell off the ship I was on but is somewhere in Sylvermoor now—I can feel him not too far away."

"Is he a powerful wizard?" Cameron asked. "I want to see a true wizard."

Confused, Shaeleen frowned for a moment and glanced around at the family. "You mean you don't have wizards here on Verlyn?"

Lorelei shook her head. "No, we don't. In the old world, in the East, we had powerful wizards. But their magic was lost in the great wizard wars. We now have the power of the stones, and our blood has a propensity for the magic of nature. The power of wizards only arose on Wayland *after* the power of the stones began to spread throughout its population. Over time, wizards usually became associated with guarding each TruthSeer. But there have been other wizards, as well."

Shaeleen put a hand to her head and said, "This is a lot to take in." She took a deep breath and called upon the powers of her stones to help her relax. "I need to find my brother, and then he and I need to find Princess Diamonique and bring her back to Galena."

"I'd heard the princess was here; she has been training in our great library," Ruven said as he rubbed his hand back and forth on his smooth chin. "But I haven't heard about her in a few days."

"The shadow keepers have taken her," Shaeleen said.

Lorelei seemed to shiver. "The shadow keepers have grown more bold leading up to the gathering this year."

Shaeleen felt things continually becoming more clear to her. "Right now, the heirs of Gabor, Galena, and Antioch are in trouble. I've heard that Lightfort has closed itself off and that trouble is brewing in South Bay also. The shadow keepers are definitely causing havoc throughout the kingdoms."

As they sat in silence for a few moments after Shaeleen had spoken, she thought about Taegen. *He needs help.* But she felt more strongly compelled to find her brother and Princess Diamonique. She worried about Taegen, though. He was very fragile at the moment and could still be swayed either way. And she remembered the way he had pleaded with her to help him.

"I have a favor to ask," Shaeleen finally said.

Lorelei helped Amara down off a chair, and the young girl scooted off to a corner where a few toys were on the floor. The rest of the family, including the other children, looked at Shaeleen.

"I have a friend who needs help," Shaeleen began. "But it could be dangerous."

"Of course, Shaeleen," Lorelei said with a smile. "I am a true keeper of the stones, and our only hope is you. A friend of yours is a friend of ours."

Shaeleen grimaced. "Well, it may not be that easy. You might have heard of him."

"Go on. We will help." Ruven waved his hand for her to continue.

"Have you heard of Keeper Taegen?" Shaeleen said, bracing for their reaction.

But nothing came.

Lorelei shook her head. "I haven't. There are many keepers spread throughout Verlyn. But, he is your friend. Like we said before, we will help him. If he is in trouble, we will do what we can to help. Where is this keeper from?"

Shaeleen took a deep breath. She knew they wouldn't like her answer. "He is from the north part of the island. He is the nephew of Keeper Dunstun."

This answer did bring a reaction. Little Grace even growled. Cameron stood up, his fists balled, and Ruven's eyes grew dark. But it was Lorelei who finally spoke.

"We have suspected that Keeper Dunstun is a keeper of the shadow—and one of their most powerful keepers?" She'd spat out his name.

"He is," Shaeleen said. "I fought him."

Ruven stood up in surprise. "You fought Keeper Dunstun?" He shook his head. "You must be powerful indeed to escape his grasp."

"He is surely one of their leaders," Lorelei added. "If Taegen is his nephew, Taegen is surely tainted by the shadow."

"I told you this would be difficult," Shaeleen said, plowing forward. "Taegen told me he wants to change. He wants to get away from the shadow."

Lorelei directed her husband to sit back down. She pursed her lips for a moment before saying, "Shaeleen, as the holder of a TruthStone, I trust what you have said. But…" She paused. "This may be an impossible task. Once someone has gone over to the shadow, it is very difficult for them to come back. Is Taegen with his uncle now?"

Shaeleen shook her head. "No."

"That may make things easier," Lorelei said.

Shaeleen grimaced and sat back. "Well, not really."

"Where is he, then?"

"The last I saw of him was at an inn in the sailors' district," Shaeleen said. "He was with another shadow keeper named Hutchin and a man referred to as *the overseer* in Mistport—Shadow Keeper Georrod."

Ruven jumped out of his seat again. "You are crazy!" He turned to his wife, who sat with her head in her hands. "She is crazy, Lorelei. There is no way you are going up against him! There are not enough master keepers left. I will not allow this! We must leave here immediately and go to the east side of the island."

Shaeleen looked from Ruven to Lorelei. She didn't understand the strength of the outburst. She knew how powerful Georrod was. But she had bested Georrod once. Surely a group of master keepers and others true to the power of the stones could get Taegen away from Georrod and his men. It didn't make sense.

"Mother?" Cameron begged, appearing older than he was. "Father is right. If Georrod is close by again, we need to leave."

Grace came over to her mother and put her head against Lorelei's arm. Only Amara, off playing in the corner of the room, didn't appear affected by what Shaeleen had shared.

"I don't understand," Shaeleen began to say slowly. "Surely Georrod is not all that powerful, for I—"

Ruven cut Shaeleen off with a loud roar and said to Lorelei, "No. We pack and leave tonight. If Georrod is as close as you say, Shaeleen, he will feel your power. I'm surprised you didn't lead him here already. Maybe that was his plan all along."

"He can't feel my power," Shaeleen said and then patted her pouch. "No one can as long as I keep the stones hidden in here. Please. You must help me!"

Ruven began moving around the room, gathering their things together. His lips were tight with concern. "I'm sorry, Shaeleen. We can't."

Pain roared through Shaeleen's body and she took a moment before she could speak. "*You* can't?" Shaeleen slammed her hand down on the table. "I'm putting my life on the line every day—you even look to me to save your precious stones and island—and you can't help me with this one thing? What am I missing here?" Shaeleen tried to think through all the reasons—she used everything she knew—but their reactions still didn't make sense.

"Please, Shaeleen, you don't understand," Ruven said. He moved over behind Lorelei, who still had not spoken a word since Shaeleen had mentioned who Taegen had been with. "If Taegen is with Georrod, there is no hope." He put his hands on his wife's shoulders.

"But why?" Shaeleen pleaded once more.

Slowly, almost as if pushing it through thick mud, Lorelei raised her head up and faced Shaeleen. The master keeper's eyes were rimmed red; her face was ashen and worn to exhaustion. She moved to stand, her shoulders still drooping under some invisible weight. She finally stood and put her hands on the table in front of herself.

"Georrod is my father," Lorelei whispered.

Shaeleen's hand flew to her mouth, letting only a small cry escape her lips. Then she sucked in a deep breath and let it out again. Even little Amara now knew something was wrong and came running back to her family, all of whom stood together across from Shaeleen.

Shaeleen didn't know what to say. She knew how powerful Georrod was, for she had barely escaped with her life, and Orin had been stripped of his powers by Georrod's magic.

But Georrod still has to be stopped.

Shaeleen took another breath and brought her hands back down to her sides. "I am terribly sorry, Lorelei. I truly am, but—"

"There is nothing else to say," Ruven said. "We need to leave. And you need to leave. We are sorry."

Shaeleen dug inside herself for strength. "But…I can't do this myself. I need your help."

Lorelei took a step forward. "We can't help you."

Pain erupted inside of Shaeleen once again. *Their stupid lies!* Her gut tightened, causing her to bend over in excruciating torment. Her chest heaved, and she felt like fire had spread through her organs. Stabbing needles of pain hit her temples and then multiplied and expanded to her entire head.

Shaeleen screamed from the overwhelming agony of it all and fell to the floor. A soft rug there did nothing to lessen the additional pain of hitting the floor. In the midst of this torture, a well of anger arose inside her. She steered the pain to her anger and fueled its fire with the power of the StrengthStone.

Both Lorelei and Ruven had knelt down beside Shaeleen, but the children were standing behind them and took a few steps back in fear. As the two adults put their hands on Shaeleen's arms, the lie they had spoken burned like fire with their touch.

She pulled her hands back and gradually got up onto her knees. Shaeleen could feel the burning of power in her own eyes. And then, before either Lorelei or Ruven could back away, she snapped her hands out and grabbed onto an arm of each of them.

"You lie!" she screamed. "You all lie! The keepers of the shadow and of the light! Why do you torture me so?"

Why does everyone abandon me or try to stop me from doing what needs to be done?

Part of her mind knew her reaction to their words was more explosive than it should be, but something had finally snapped inside of her.

"We—" Whatever Lorelei was about to say froze on her lips.

"You say you *can't* help me," Shaeleen bellowed, bringing the full force of her powers to bear. "But, what you mean is you *won't* help me, isn't it? You all want *me* to help you, but no one wants to help me!"

I can't save the world by myself!

"Shaeleen!" Lorelei pleaded. "Stop. Your powers are too strong. Georrod will find you."

"You mean he will find your family!" Shaeleen said. Color sizzled and flowed from Shaeleen's fingertips and wrapped around Lorelei's and Ruven's arms.

"You're hurting us, Shaeleen," Ruven said. "Please stop this. We can discuss things more."

"I thought you said there was nothing else to say and that you wanted to run and hide away, Ruven." Shaeleen let the anger coarse through her veins. At this point, she knew she could use a TruthSpell and compel them to do anything she wanted them to do. She could force them to help her, to confront the overseer, to join with her to banish the shadow. She knew she could do all this.

But, at what cost? a small voice whispered within her mind. She was remembering hearing the angry voice of Orin after she had TruthSpelled him to tell her what she wanted. His voice, his face—these brought fresh tears to her eyes.

No one should have this much power!

But she could feel that the power inside of her wanted a release to avenge her anger. It wanted to make Lorelei and Ruven do her bidding. But she held the power at bay—just barely—and glared deep into their eyes—and saw fear!

What kind of monster am I that they would fear me so?

Then she heard a sniffle and turned her head and regarded Amara and Grace. Tears streamed down their small faces. *Where is Cameron?* She turned her head the other way but didn't see him there either.

Pain, anger, fear, and power were barely balanced by her own power of will. Any moment, one could tip the scales, and her power would be let loose into Lorelei and Ruven. She then imagined another voice joining Orin's in the back of Shaeleen's head—it was the calm and reasonable influence of her brother, Cole.

He is near and needs me. She could feel it. She had to get to Cole.

Pain erupted in the back of her head—not magical pain but physical pain. *Someone must have hit me with something. Cameron!* Her power receded, and stars appeared in front of her eyes. Her grip loosened on Lorelei and Ruven, and they pulled back, but Shaeleen's power still trailed from her fingertips.

Pain came again. *Another hit.* She screamed and fell forward, onto her face. She'd intended to put her hands out to break her fall, but blackness had been closing in. Sounds around her began to fade as her vision blackened.

"Cameron," Lorelei's voice said in what seemed a faded whisper. "What did you do?"

"I couldn't let her hurt you…" the boy said, his next words becoming jumbled in her mind.

I wouldn't have really hurt them, would I? What was I thinking before I'd been hit?

Cole! she screamed in her mind and out toward her brother.

Then Shaeleen sank down all the way, and the darkness took over fully. She almost grunted with the ridiculousness of it, but she didn't have the strength to.

CHAPTER TWENTY-ONE

Shaeleen opened her eyes to find herself in a dimly lit room. The very early makings of dawn seeped through nearby windows, but not with enough light to see clearly. The early chirpings of birds hung in the air. Looking around, she noticed that she had been laid on a blanket on the floor and that her head rested now on a soft pillow. She had apparently slept the entire night there, on the floor. Blinking a few times, she moved to sit up.

Cole! I was supposed to find him last night!

Next to the door in the room, Ruven stood with his three children. These four were shrouded in darkness, but Shaeleen could see that they all had packs on their backs. They gave Shaeleen grim looks. Then Lorelei stepped in from the kitchen area and gave Ruven a small kiss, and he and the children opened the door and left.

Shaeleen put a hand to the back of her head. "Ouch," she said involuntarily. There were two goose-egg-sized bumps there, and part of her hair was matted with blood.

Lorelei moved next to her and sat down. "You took quite a hit to your head. You might be dizzy for a while."

"Cameron?" Shaeleen asked, knowing the truth as soon as she spoke this.

"He did what he thought was right, to protect us," Lorelei said, her voice subdued and even. A lone candle burned on a table nearby, giving her a ghostly appearance. "I won't apologize for him. The amount of power you used was a beacon to everyone with power on Verlyn—for good or bad."

"I'm sorry." Shaeleen hung her head low. "I'm sorry for almost losing control but not for the words I said. Those were all true," she said now, not out of anger but with a factual tone.

Lorelei nodded her head, her own eyes looking as if she hadn't slept at all during the night. "I know. That is why I am still here." She pulled Shaeleen to her feet and gave her a small bundle of clothes. "Hurry and change clothes. Then we must be on our way," Lorelei said.

Shaeleen took the clothes with one hand and put her other hand on the back of a wooden chair to steady herself. Then she walked into the other room, but she only partially shut the door so they could continue to talk.

"I have sent my husband and children off to safety," Lorelei said. "You were right that we have put too much on you without being willing to sacrifice enough ourselves. We are a proud people and are not used to giving or needing help from others."

Shaeleen knew these words must have been hard for the proud Verlynian keeper to admit.

Shaeleen finished dressing herself. The black leather pants fit well enough, though she had to roll the cuffs up a bit. A light blouse and darker cloak covered the top of her. She stepped back out into the room. Shaeleen closed her eyes for a moment and felt another presence flare up in the back of her mind.

"My brother is nearby," Shaeleen said as she came back out.

Lorelei blinked in surprise. "I can't have him here, Shaeleen. There is already too much power here. The only thing that may keep us safe is that the shadow keepers are moving toward the gathering. Hopefully, they're too busy to spend time coming here right now—though, after last night's display, they will know someone of extreme power is on Verlyn."

"I will go and meet my brother," Shaeleen said with a nod. "I truly do not want to bring harm to you or your family."

"I know. I know." Lorelei put a soft hand on Shaeleen's shoulder. "But you must learn to curb your powers, Shaeleen. Every time you use them, you bring the ShadowStone closer to yourself. You are not ready yet to confront them head-on."

Shaeleen tried to protest Lorelei's last words. She remembered how powerful she had been the night before. It had surprised her—and, admittedly, had made her more afraid of her own self. *What will the future really hold for me?*

"You must still gather the remaining two stones—the pink Azeztulite HealingStone from Shema and the white Celestite HearingStone from Althea. Stay away from the shadow keepers until you are ready."

Shaeleen knew Lorelei was right. She took a deep breath. "I need to find my brother, then get Diamonique back to Galena, and hopefully stop a civil war from happening."

"I will try and help Keeper Taegen, but if he is truly tainted by the shadow…" Lorelei let the rest of the sentence go.

"I know he can be a strong ally for us, Lorelei. He knows a lot and wants to be good. He could tell us who else has a ShadowStone."

Lorelei turned her head and seemed to be thinking about something else for a few moments. "There was a boy who could tell if someone held a stone of power or not."

"He could be helpful," Shaeleen said. "I can't even tell until they use their power or I touch them. I felt Dunstun's power by being close to him, but I think that is rare."

"Feyn had the remarkable ability to tell what stone or power anyone held. But he left last year, after the gathering, and we haven't been able to find him."

Shaeleen nodded. "Someone needs to."

Lorelei nodded her head. "I will send someone out, and I will do what I can for Taegen. But I am not powerful enough to face my father either." Lorelei's face fell, and she almost appeared ready to cry. "You must understand that."

Shaeleen nodded. "I do. Taegen is smart. He will find a way to play along with them until an opportunity to escape provides itself. If you are there, then you can help get him to safety."

"I will try, but I too must get to the gathering. The vote will be taken in the next few days, and my fellow keepers and I must be there." Lorelei walked to the table and grabbed a small burlap sack. "I have packed some food for you, and there are some extra coins in there also." She handed the sack to Shaeleen. Then Lorelei cocked her head to the side a moment, as if she were listening to something. "We must go now!" Lorelei said as she grabbed a bag of her own and pushed Shaeleen out the door.

Shaeleen paused on the doorstep. Looking up through a break in the thick trees, she was greeted with a pink and orange dawn. The door closed behind her, and Lorelei pulled Shaeleen down a path behind the small group of homes.

Then Shaeleen noticed the birds had stopped singing.

"A shadow keeper approaches," Lorelei whispered. "I will steer him away from you. Head toward Sylvermoor."

Shaeleen's heartbeats quickened as she heard rustling in the trees. "Will you be all right?" Shaeleen asked Lorelei. "I can stay and help."

"No, Shaeleen," Lorelei said forcefully. "And you must remember what I said about using your magic. The ShadowStone will be drawn to you and your brother whenever you use the stones of power. Remember it is a reflection of them."

But Shaeleen didn't know if it would be possible to curb her powers. The magic was such a part of her now she didn't even really think before using it anymore. "Take care, then, Lorelei. I will do my part, but you make sure the keepers do theirs."

"It will take all of us to banish the ShadowStone," Lorelei said fiercely. Then she turned, going the opposite way than she had pointed Shaeleen in.

"Keeper!" a deep voice said from around a short curve in the path. "I know you are there."

Shaeleen knew that voice. It was Shadow Keeper Hutchin—the one who had chased her behind the inn. *At least it isn't Georrod, Lorelei's father.* Shaeleen hesitated briefly, wondering if Taegen was with Hutchin.

Lorelei moved down the path, toward the voice, while waving a hand at Shaeleen to get moving. Shaeleen felt tempted to draw upon the SpeedStone's power to get herself away safely, but then she remembered Lorelei's warning. With a grunt of frustration, Shaeleen took off running with the softest steps she could manage.

A flash of light and the sounds of fighting erupted behind her. But Shaeleen stayed focused on the path ahead, and she prayed Lorelei would get away safely. Within a dozen yards, the path narrowed, and the jungle grew thick around her.

She headed toward Sylvermoor with thoughts of Princess Diamonique and Cole in her mind. She could feel Cole's presence not too far away to the south. Now that she was close to meeting up with her brother again, she ran with a renewed sense of confidence.

* * *

Less than an hour later, the city of Sylvermoor rose up in front of Shaeleen. She had stopped running some time before now, so as not to draw attention to herself. She pulled her cloak up over her head, but her short stature would give her away as one not from Sylvermoor.

Unless…

An idea began to form in her mind now. With a cowl up over her head, most of her hair and both of her ears were covered. Her eyes were the color of those from Verlyn, and maybe she could use her small size to pretend she was younger than she really was: only a child. She smiled at her plan and began to walk straight up to the gates of the city.

The gate she was approaching stood in the middle of a tall rock wall. The sounds of the sea, lapping against the shore, sounded off to her right, and faint sounds from the docks and the cries of gulls filled the background. A line of people stood in front of the gate as two guards questioned each visitor.

Shaeleen watched as, time and time again, people were turned away, preventing them from entering the city, and were told to go back down by the docks. She noticed that none of the people who were turned away were from Verlyn—all were from the kingdoms of Wayland.

Coming closer to the front of the line, she hunched over even smaller and then started to dart through the crowd.

"Mama," she yelled out and then pushed her way through. One of the two guards turned away from the man he had been questioning and hooked an arm around the running Shaeleen.

"No, hold on there, little girl," the guard said.

Shaeleen smiled inside at this greeting. She opened her eyes wide with an innocent look. The man seemed to relax upon seeing her light blue eyes.

"Where are you going in such a hurry?" he asked, his eyes watching the others around him rather than Shaeleen.

"Just trying to catch up with my parents, sir," Shaeleen said, speaking softer and slower than normal. Pain gripped her insides, but she gritted her teeth and pushed though. "I was watching the ships and lost them." She dropped her head and brought tears to bear. She surely had said enough things that would cause her to cry.

The line surged forward with another influx of people.

"Hey, you can't keep us out of your city," said a man from behind Shaeleen. "I have contracts here."

"They're searching for magic users," said another man. "They mean to take our magic away."

The guard holding Shaeleen watched the restless crowd carefully. Then he turned back to Shaeleen again.

"That man has magic." Shaeleen pointed at the second man who had spoken. He looked to be from Althea, and, although the magic of healing should not be intimidating to anyone, she thought it would be a way to get the attention off of herself.

The guard gave her a quizzical look.

"My mother is a keeper," Shaeleen said, the lie coming easily from her lips. But then she had to do all she could to keep from bending over in pain. She should have been smarter than that.

She cursed herself and shrugged at the guard. "Feeling a little sick is all."

The guard waved a hand toward the city. "Fine. Go find your parents. These are not good times to get lost, little one." He then turned toward the man Shaeleen had pointed out and pulled him to the side.

Shaeleen left the gate behind and walked into the crowds of Sylvermoor. After getting far enough away from the gate, she moved off into the shadows of a building and then looked out at the gleaming city for the first time in her life.

The ancient city of Sylvermoor was said to be the first settlement upon the nearby islands. The city seemed to be a combination of new and old—but in a way that was breathtaking to Shaeleen. There was not one piece of trash on the ground. Blooming flowers lined the walkways of every street. And giant trees hung over the parts of the city closest to the jungle, while the clear blue morning sky shined above the portion closest to the coast.

Most of the buildings were no more than two stories tall and held colorful roofs. Off in the distance, she could see the domes and turrets of the castle of Sylvermoor, built up against one of the slopes of Mount Eyvindr, with its snow-capped peak rising thousands of feet above the city. Next to the castle, a waterfall fell down a cliff, turning into a picturesque wide river that wound its way through the city, eventually emptying into the ocean. Parks with green grasses, flowers, and trees lined its banks.

Shaeleen walked slowly, taking it all in. She examined the people of Sylvermoor—all strikingly beautiful and tall. Their skin was smooth and youthful, and they had long, silky hair—blond, brown, and black—hanging down their backs. Small children, not any bigger than herself, played in the park along the riverbank. Their laughs lent a whimsical quality to the air.

Everything seemed so peaceful—almost too peaceful for Shaeleen. Where was all the division she had been led to believe was here—keepers fighting for the shadow against those for the light? All seemed perfectly serene at first glance.

Walking into a park, Shaeleen climbed a small hill and looked farther out in the city. She drew upon a bit of the power within her TruthStone, and her eyes widened at what she really saw before her. The TruthStone had revealed to her signs of a people under strict control, torn apart by their divisive government. Looking more intently at each person in the park down below her, she now noticed a sadness in their eyes—a resignation of some sort.

Farther off in the distance, toward the castle, a shadow had settled over the land, making the colors there more muted and the trees less healthy. Thinking it was a cloud or fog of some sort, Shaeleen looked up. All that greeted her was a blue, cloudless sky.

The ShadowStone.

The shadow must have begun to take over the government here, and so the people would hardly know what was happening to them. The shadow's influence was altering the land as well.

"Mama, look!" a young child along the banks of the creek yelled out, her finger pointing toward Shaeleen. Others followed suit, and soon a crowd stood pointing at her.

Cursing her lack of intelligence again, Shaeleen saw that she now held a slight glow around herself from using the TruthStone. *The ShadowStone must be influencing my own mind also. I should have been smarter than to use magic in the center of the city.*

Off to the side of the park, a small contingent of guards turned in her direction. They wore long gray robes and carried black bows on their shoulders and swords at their sides.

"Oh no, not again," Shaeleen muttered. Glancing around, she took off, running down the hill, away from the shadow guards and toward the stream. The guards picked up their pace behind her, and a crowd gathered behind them.

Soon Shaeleen realized she would be trapped between the river and the guards. Turning to her left and right, she saw no way out, so she did the one thing she had been told not to do. She pulled upon a stone of power, the StrengthStone.

Shaeleen's legs strengthened—the power burning through her body—and she leapt up into the air and flew across the river. Landing in a crouch on the other side, she turned her head and faced a sea of questioning eyes—some held hope, while others held fear.

In one smooth motion, the guards knelt on the ground, pulled their tall bows off their shoulders, and drew arrows. Three arrows zipped across the river toward her—their aim true. But their arrows were nowhere as fast as the power of the SpeedStone made Shaeleen.

Pulling upon that power, she moved in a blur away from the river and down into another part of town. She slowed her speed behind an older building and then stopped to look around. Breathing hard, she noticed it was darker here. Then she realized the ShadowStone had drawn her right into its quarters.

So much for not using my powers.

They knew she was there now.

CHAPTER TWENTY-TWO

The streets were less populated in this quarter of the city, and the few people Shaeleen did see walked with stooped shoulders and hollow eyes. There was even a dullness to the buildings and their grounds that almost made Shaeleen weep. The beauty of Verlyn and her people was renowned throughout Wayland, but the shadow was taking all that away.

Cole was here somewhere, she could tell.

Hearing footsteps coming closer, she ducked behind a large bush in a grouping of trees. On her knees, she peered through its thinning branches. From around a corner came a group of ten shadow guards—their march was exactly in rhythm, and their eyes were clouded over with deception. A man at the back was dressed differently than the others. His eyes seemed more alert but held a hardness to them that Shaeleen could hardly bear. *A shadow keeper.*

He and the others passed by her without a moment's notice. Once they were farther down the street, she let out a deep breath and stood up. But, just as the guards turned a corner, the shadow keeper in the back stopped and turned around. Even at a block's distance, his eyes burned into hers, and she gasped.

Calling the guards to stop, the shadow keeper motioned them back toward Shaeleen. She was tempted to pull upon her powers again, but that's what the shadow wanted. So she resisted this and let her natural instincts take over. She bolted off toward an alleyway.

Quickening footsteps sounded behind her as she wound her way through a maze of buildings. Doorways stood open and bare beside crumbled stone, and the cobblestone streets were now more dirt than rock. Shaeleen wondered how long the shadow had been growing in Sylvermoor without the people knowing. *Years? Decades?*

The sounds of boots behind her faded as she scrambled through unknown passages and alleys. She wondered how she had outrun the guards, but she was happy to have done so. She stopped at a darkened recessed doorway and leaned against the decrepit building, allowing her heartbeats and breathing to slow. Then she turned her mind inward, being careful to not access any of her powers. But a soft presence still remained. *Cole!*

He was so close by. She tentatively moved out of the doorway and turned down another street. And jumped back instantly. The guards that had been following her were now ahead of her.

How had that happened?

Peeking carefully around the corner, she saw that the shadow grew thicker the farther she looked. The guards were walking away from her toward a sizeable stone building. Through what seemed almost a thick fog, Shaeleen glimpsed its freshly painted doors and its glass windows. Seeing that in the midst of this run-down neighborhood, Shaeleen knew something definitely was going on there.

Must be what the cook's husband had been talking about—the prince's old home.

Shaeleen moved down the street, holding herself tight against the side of another decrepit building. The ten guards that had been chasing her were now at the large stone building, where they'd been stopped by other guards in front.

After a moment, they were let in.

Shaeleen knew she shouldn't use her powers, but she really wanted to know what was going on. The TruthStone seemed to grow warm against her leg, and her hand went to her pouch.

No! came a prevailing voice from the back of her mind, and she pulled her hand away from this temptation. A ShadowStone must be close, for it seemed to be interfering with her ability to think clearly.

Then she slipped and cried out. She had stepped on a loose piece of stone, and a chunk had slid out from under her foot. The last man into the building turned around—the shadow keeper—and scowled at the sound. Then he saw her, and his eyes widened. She held his gaze for a moment, trying to think of what to do. Then he smiled, turned, and headed back into the building.

Shaeleen thought that was a strange thing to do, and she breathed a sigh of relief.

Then, unexpectedly, a loud sound of running footsteps came from her left, across the street. Five men raced toward her—all dressed in the shadow garb she had seen earlier. She gasped and turned, to run around a corner, but instead she ran into someone, and both of them fell to the ground.

Untangling herself from the other person, she flung out her hands and prepared a quick TruthSpell.

"Shaeleen!" came a voice she recognized as her brother's from inside the dark hood.

"Cole!" Her heart leapt with joy.

He pushed her to the side and drew his blade at the approaching guards. "Nice to see you again, but you have to get out of here," he tried to order her.

"Not on your life," Shaeleen said. "I'm not going to lose you again." Even with the pending danger coming at them, she couldn't help grinning. She felt better just being close to Cole once again.

"I thought you were gone at first," she whispered. "We tried to find you, but we couldn't…"

"Shaeleen, I'm really glad to see you too. But let's discuss this later," Cole said with a grim smile. "We have trouble to deal with right now."

Shaeleen nodded her head. *He is right.* Then she noticed a small scar down one side of his face and the evidence of other scrapes and bruises.

"Then stand back." Cole waved his swordless arm toward Shaeleen, to push her back behind him. "I can take care of them."

Shaeleen took a few steps back and watched as her brother plowed into the guards with relentless fury. Sparks flew from the tip of his sword and then sizzled down the blade. Using the sword in one hand and his wizard powers in the other, Cole made quick work of the first three guards. The last two came at him at the same time. Both were clearly expert swordsmen, and they pushed Cole back, almost squishing Shaeleen between him and a building.

She was tempted to draw on her own powers once again. But Cole's uses of power would be beacon enough to draw the shadow.

"Cole, hurry," Shaeleen encouraged him. "They can sense your uses of power."

"Who can?" Cole leaned back to let the tip of one sword barely miss his neck. Then he stepped forward and slammed his fist into that guard.

One more down.

"The shadow keepers can sense when we use our powers," Shaeleen said.

"Shadow keepers?" Cole questioned. "That doesn't sound good."

"It's not," Shaeleen said, ducking as a ball of fire flying down the street hit above her head. Shards of rock tumbled down onto her, pelting her head, leaving it covered with small cuts.

"We have to go, Cole," Shaeleen screamed. "You can't take them all on."

"But Princess Diamonique is somewhere around here," Cole answered back. "I heard a guard talking about her." Cole's face grew dark. "Crude mouths they have."

"We need a plan," Shaeleen said. "Come on, Cole, let's go. We'll come back."

"We were both drawn here for a reason, Shae," Cole argued. "We have to get her out."

Another blast of fire sizzled past their heads, along with three arrows. Shaeleen looked down the street and saw another group of shadow guards—at least twenty strong—marching toward her and Cole. At this group's head walked Hutchin and another younger man—about the age of Cole, hands out in front of themselves, sizzling with dark powers.

Shaeleen groaned at seeing Hutchin here and hoped Lorelei had gotten away from him safely.

But Cole pushed forward in a fury of unyielding strikes until the guard in front of him fell to the ground. Cole turned toward Shaeleen and then roared with pain. An arrow had hit Cole in the top of the shoulder blade of his sword arm.

"Do something, Shae!" Cole screamed.

So much for not using my powers in Sylvermoor!

Shaeleen pulled upon all her powers at once. They came much easier now. She drew upon the power of the SpeedStone and headed off, directly into the oncoming guards. She flew between them and, with the power of the StrengthStone, punched half of them. At the same time, she drew upon the significant powers of the TruthStone and struck out with waves of green fireballs. To the guards, she was a blur of danger.

All the keepers on Verlyn will feel this.

Guards fell around her until only the two shadow keepers stood there. They brought their hands out in front of themselves and sent out a fog of shadow that took the speed away from her. She fell forward and scraped her hands on the rough stone as she tried to break her fall.

More guards emerged from the stone building and came down the street toward Shaeleen and her brother. Shaeleen wasn't going to be taken by them again. The sounds of these new guards took the shadow keepers' attention away from Shaeleen for a brief moment. That time was all she'd need. She brought up her hands in front of herself and formed a TruthSpell against the two shadow keepers. A green glow flew from her hands and surrounded the two.

"Where is Diamonique?" Shaeleen yelled at them. She'd only have a few more moments until the others would show up.

The two shadow keepers struggled to not say anything, pushing back against Shaeleen's power.

"Tell me now!" Shaeleen demanded of the younger one, feeling his resolve breaking down quicker than Hutchin's.

The younger man gritted his teeth, fighting against her power. "She is—"

"No, Tanyth." Hutchin forced the words out. "Resist her."

Tanyth shook his head, and Shaeleen pushed harder. "Tell me what you know."

"In the basement," Tanyth said as he slumped to the ground.

"Shae!" Cole yelled from down the street. "Let's go!"

Shaeleen looked up. A dozen more shadow guards had kneeled down on the ground, and another dozen stood behind them. Those on the ground drew arrows and nocked them.

Then Shaeleen heard the sound of arrows leaving their strings as they raced toward her. Letting go of the TruthSpell, she drew upon the SpeedStone and moved away. The arrows raced past where she had just stood, near the shadow keepers, and barely missed her back and legs as she sped away, dropping with a rattle on the stone walkway.

Speeding back to Cole, she grabbed his hand, and they continued on down the street. Whizzing through alleyways and empty streets, she brought them to the edge of the district being held in the shadow, and then she collapsed to the ground, sending both of them rolling forward into a grouping of small bushes.

Cole yelled out in pain, the arrow's shaft having broken off a few inches from his shoulder. Then Shaeleen noticed that a small group of men and women stood over them, apparently wondering where she and Cole had come from.

Shaeleen stood and helped Cole back to his feet. She was so exhausted. The extreme use of her powers had worn her out.

"Where do we go now, Shae?" Cole asked.

Shaeleen didn't know. She didn't know Sylvermoor or anyone in the city.

Then a man pushed through the crowd. His long, dark hair was graying, but he moved with a quick step. A pale blue robe—the same color as his eyes—hung on his tall, thin frame.

"Come with me," he said as he motioned to her and Cole.

Shaeleen backed away. "Who are you?"

"Melindra sent me," the man said curtly. "I am Aeron, her husband."

Melindra! She was the keeper that had given Shaeleen the TruthStone originally.

"How—?" Shaeleen started to ask.

But Aeron interrupted her words. "The use of your powers was a beacon to all keepers," he said, apparently anticipating her question. "Now, come quickly, before the shadow keepers find you again."

Shaeleen nodded and pulled Cole along with her. Cole stumbled once but stayed on his feet as they moved closer to the castle. They walked down a few more streets, until Aeron brought them around to the back of a house.

He took out a key and unlocked the back gate. Then he led them inside and past a fountain. A flower garden and a large tree grew near the back door of the modest-sized residence. Opening the door, Aeron led them inside. Bright candlelight greeted them as they moved down a short hallway.

There was a sense of power in the home that Shaeleen had felt once before. She glanced around the small but tidy living area. Stuffed chairs and a wooden table filled the room, but what drew Shaeleen's attention was the woman in a smaller chair in the corner.

Melindra.

"Hello, Shaeleen," Melindra said. Her mouth was set in a frown, but there was a sparkle of pride in her eyes. "I see you have alerted the entire city—if not all of Verlyn—to your presence. You have grown strong since our last meeting."

Shaeleen felt her cheeks blush slightly. "Melindra, I would say it's nice to see you again, but that would probably cause me pain right now."

Melindra smiled and nodded her understanding.

"Almost every day, I curse the day you gave me the TruthStone," Shaeleen said.

"A heavy burden indeed...to be the fulfillment of prophecy."

"Shae?" Cole whispered behind her and then collapsed onto a chair. "Could we talk about this later?"

Remembering the arrow, Shaeleen jumped to Cole's side to help him, calling out to Melindra's husband for help.

CHAPTER TWENTY-THREE

Later that day, as the sun sat low on the western horizon, Shaeleen took Cole into the small garden area behind Melindra's home. Giant bird-of-paradise plants grew around the fountain, and smaller flowers grew around the walkways—the names of which Shaeleen couldn't possibly know—but they spread their sweet scents into the evening air.

Melindra and Aeron had supplied them with a clean change of clothes. Shaeleen now wore a white shirt under a light burgundy cloak that hung down to below her waist. The leather pants underneath had needed to be hemmed up a bit to fit her. Aeron had gone out to find some clothes for Cole, for his broad shoulders were bigger than most Verlynians. He now wore a white shirt, brown leather vest and pants, and a dark cloak that Aeron had found for him.

The day was growing warm, so both Shaeleen and Cole shed their cloaks.

"Cole, I'm so sorry that we couldn't find you after the ship crashed," Shaeleen said.

"I know you tried," Cole said. "You had to worry about your own survival. Another group of keepers—not shadow keepers, mind you—found me, fed me, and took care of me until we arrived in Sylvermoor last night."

"I could feel you close by," Shaeleen said.

"Me too," Cole agreed. "I just couldn't figure out which direction you were in for sure."

"Until we bumped into each other." Shaeleen laughed, and Cole joined in. She had told him earlier about her ordeal in getting there: her confrontation with Dunstun, running off with Taegen, and avoiding the shadow keepers.

"And you said earlier that they can track us when we are using our powers?" Cole asked.

"That's what the keepers say," Shaeleen said and hung her head down a bit. "But I haven't been very good at following their directions."

Cole tried to stifle his obvious amusement, but it came out as a barking laugh anyways. "Shae, you have never been very good at following directions. Admit it."

Shaeleen raised her brows at her brother and put her hand to her chest, in mock innocence. "Me? You must be mistaken. I always follow…"

"Shae!" Cole jumped up and then grimaced and grabbed his arm. "Don't lie, even in fun. It'll cause too much pain."

"I don't know why I can't remember that," Shaeleen mumbled under her breath.

"Maybe because you have been used to lying your entire life," Cole said.

"That's not nice," Shaeleen said. "But it is true. I never thought a little lie would hurt anyone."

"I guess you know that now." Cole smiled.

Shaeleen grunted. "Says the man who is always honorable and truthful."

Cole shrugged. "It does make things easier."

"We'll see," Shaeleen said in a low voice. "We still have Basil and Calix to deal with. Any news from Galena?"

Cole shook his head. "All they talk about here is the gathering of the keepers and the new law to limit those from Wayland from entering Sylvermoor."

"Great." Shaeleen slapped her hand in the fountain's water without thinking.

"Hey!" Cole jumped up, water dripping off his face. "What'd you do that for?"

"Sorry," Shaeleen said and then laughed at the water dripping off Cole's shaggy hair. Then she grew serious. "Their birthday is at the end of the week."

"And the announcement of the betrothal," Cole added.

They both sat in silence for a few more minutes. Then Aeron came out and invited them inside to eat. During the meal, they began to discuss a way to rescue Princess Diamonique.

"Shaeleen, you are a TruthSeer," Melindra reminded her at a break in the conversation. "Why are you so worried about one lost princess? You need to be preparing to fight the ShadowStone. That is your destiny."

"My sister made a promise to Prince Basil," Cole said, "and to the princess's mother, Queen Victoria, to bring back the princess safely."

Still looking at Shaeleen, Melindra spoke to her again. "But you hold no allegiance to any one kingdom. Neither of you do."

"We made a promise," Cole said.

Shaeleen smiled. It was that simple for her brother. To Cole, a promise held importance over anything else that might come along—ShadowStones, evil keepers, anarchy in the kingdoms—all else paling compared to honor and integrity.

But she didn't say anything and let Cole answer for her because she had her own reasons for helping Princess Diamonique, and she wasn't quite sure they were as honorable as her brother's. The princess had an important part to play—in the gathering of stones and in the future of Wayland—and, although she didn't understand how yet, it was the truth of things.

Melindra let out a puff of air and looked at Shaeleen for confirmation.

Shaeleen just shrugged her shoulders in response.

"We are thankful for any help you give us, Shaeleen," Aeron said. Turning to Cole, Aeron said, "Honor is indeed a noble attribute. Not enough of it around in the world anymore. Even now, our leaders are giving way to the ShadowStone and its keepers."

"Any idea of how to get into the shadow keepers' building without being seen?" Shaeleen asked.

"That building used to be Prince Brevin's home," Melindra said. "And I've never been inside."

"But," Aeron said, "I know someone who might know. She works at the city archives and is one of the smartest people I know on Verlyn. She has the most amazing ability to remember things."

"Ah, Solanna." Melindra nodded her head. "She and I have not spoken in a while—not since I came back from Wayland." The old keeper looked concerned.

"We can trust her," Aeron said to Melindra.

Melindra nodded. "She has always been a friend to the keepers of the stones."

"That she has," Aeron said. "I will go and bring her to us."

As Aeron left the room, Melindra got up from the table and began to clean up. Then they waited for Aeron to return. As it grew darker outside, Shaeleen began pacing the room.

"Shae, what's wrong?" Cole asked.

"I'm feeling anxious," Shaeleen answered. "I need to get back to Basil. I want to know what's going on."

"*Prince* Basil," Cole said, emphasizing the word *prince*. "He and Prince Calix will work things out. They will do the honorable thing for our kingdom."

"You really think Calix is honorable?" Shaeleen stopped pacing and faced her brother.

Cole's lips went tight, and his face grew harder. "Shaeleen, they have been raised as princes of our kingdom. We've gone over this before. Prince Calix, as the oldest heir, will become king and will rule for a long time. He will want to do what's good for the kingdom."

Shaeleen bent over with pain, and Cole jumped up and ran to her side.

"Shae, what did I say?"

Shaeleen groaned and slammed down her fist on the back of a nearby chair. "Stupid TruthStone. I hurt whenever talk of

Basil or Calix occurs. It's like nothing is ever the truth when talking about those two. Maybe the stone's broken."

"The TruthStone cannot be broken," Melindra said, walking into the room. "My forebears and I held that stone in secret for two hundred years, waiting for the right person."

"Then maybe I'm broken." Sudden tears came to Shaeleen's eyes. It really was quite infuriating—dealing with the kingship of her own kingdom.

"Oh no, dear," Melindra said, wrapping a warm arm around Shaeleen's shoulders. "You are not broken, just learning."

Shaeleen laughed as she wiped her tears away. "It's still stupid sometimes."

"Shae!" Cole said. "Have respect for the stone."

Shaeleen stuck her tongue out at her brother for his relentless decorum, and they all laughed.

Then the door opened as Aeron returned. Walking in front of him was a middle-aged woman of average looks. Solanna had medium brown hair and wore glasses under her arched brows, and a long, flowing white robe hung over her slender body.

Solanna stopped mid-step when she saw Shaeleen and Cole standing in the middle of the room. She turned abruptly to Aeron and said, "You told me you had visitors wanting to know about the history of some of the older buildings in the city."

Melindra stepped forward. "This is Shaeleen and Cole, Solanna. They need your help."

Solanna shook her head and took a step back toward the door. "No, no. They are magic users from Wayland."

Aeron moved to block the doorway. "You can trust them, Solanna. They are here to help us." He tried to motion Solanna toward a seat.

"I am surprised at both of you," Solanna said to Aeron and Melindra. "Don't you know a law was passed today by the council, outlawing magic in all of Wayland? The gathering of keepers is expected to confirm the law by later this week."

"I am a keeper of the stones." Melindra stood up straighter, though she was not much taller than Shaeleen. "I will not vote that way."

Solanna turned to Melindra. "Ever since you went to Wayland, you have changed, Melindra. Who did you see there?" Then Solanna turned from Melindra to Cole and Shaeleen. Her eyes went wide. "You didn't bring a stone to Wayland, did you? That wasn't you, was it? Tell me, Melindra!" Solanna put her hand on Melindra's arm and held it tightly.

Melindra pulled her arm away. "I don't answer to you, Solanna. What has gotten into you since I left Verlyn last year?"

With the TruthStone guiding her, Shaeleen asked softly, "Solanna, who do you serve?"

No one else in the room seemed to follow Shaeleen's line of reasoning.

"I don't know what you mean." Solanna looked from Melindra to Shaeleen. "I work at the city archives for Prince Brevin."

For Shaeleen's mind, it was as if the tumblers of its lock all fell into place now—the IntelligenceStone and the TruthStone working together. She had wondered who was behind all the shadow keepers, and now she suspected it was this prince, Prince Brevin. But for now, she'd keep her thoughts to herself. They first had to find Princess Diamonique.

"I need to know about an old building in the north part of town that has recently been used again," Shaeleen said to Solanna, jumping back to the original reason for Solanna being there. "How can we get into Brevin's old house without being noticed?"

Solanna had put a hand over her mouth at the mention of Brevin's name without his title, and she shook her head. "Girls and boys from Wayland should not be here, in Verlyn." Turning to Aeron and Melindra, Solanna continued, "You are messing with things that are beyond your control."

"Please, Solanna." Melindra was trying to be polite, but Shaeleen could tell the old woman was quickly losing her patience. "I am a keeper of the stones. We would not be asking for this information if it wasn't important."

"I don't understand," Solanna said, still looking like she might bolt any minute. "Why do you need to know about that building?" Then Solanna put her hand over her mouth, and her eyes went wide. "You're not going to kill the empress? I can't allow that." She shook her head and moved to get up.

Melindra motioned for Solanna to sit back down. "I promise you, they are not here to harm the empress or her family."

Shaeleen raised her eyebrows at that. She couldn't make any promises herself, as she didn't know who was under the shadow's influence or who belonged to the empress's family.

"Why do you ask that?" Shaeleen said, the IntelligenceStone driving her forward at a pace that was hard for her to keep up. "Is there a way from that building to the palace?"

Solanna nodded her head. "Old tunnels run under the city. They are not used much anymore. They used to be used by nobility to move from one part of town to another without being noticed."

"But what is special about that building?" Shaeleen asked.

Solanna squeezed her eyes closed and took a few deep breaths. When she opened them again, her eyes were watery and looked pained. "Historically, that building housed the emperor's or empress's family when they were not in the castle. The last person to use it full-time was the son of Empress Veronia. He died in an accident while visiting Wayland, and his son, Prince Brevin, the empress's grandson, took up residence there for a short time, as he was grieving. He blamed the continent of Wayland for his father's demise. He was young and brash—still in his teens—and the building fell into disrepair during that time."

Solanna turned her eyes to one side as if thinking about something. "That would have been almost twenty years ago. About a year ago, Prince Brevin began using the building once again."

"Melindra," Shaeleen said. "When did the most recent uprising of shadow keepers begin?" Shaeleen's mind took a leap in logic.

Melindra's pale blue eyes opened wide. "About a year ago."

"You can't possibly be saying the empress's grandson, Prince Brevin, is a shadow keeper?" Solanna slumped into her seat. "I won't believe it. Prince Brevin spends much of his time in the archives, reading about our heritage. He was never named a keeper. I would know that."

Shaeleen thought through this explanation.

But before she could say anything, Cole jumped in. "But Prince Brevin could be the holder of a ShadowStone."

Aeron stood up and paced back and forth. "This makes things much more dangerous for you, Shaeleen." He glanced around the room. "For all of us. We need to leave for the gathering at Mount Eyvindr soon. We hope the keepers can find a solution for our current problems."

"I work for Prince Brevin." Solanna's eyes filled with tears. "He is cruel sometimes to the others. I—I've seen it," she stuttered. "But he has always been nice to me, so I won't believe this."

"He's nice because you bring him books from the archives," Shaeleen said. "Books which taught him about the ShadowStone and the power of the shadow."

Solanna gasped. "N-no. You are wrong," she stuttered again. "I thought Prince Bevin was interested in learning—like a scholar—to prepare himself to be emperor."

"Emperor?" Shaeleen stood up now and put a hand on her head. "One more kingdom under the shadow's influence? I'm getting tired of this! So, there is a tunnel from the palace into Brevin's old residence?"

Solanna could only nod her head.

Cole stood up to join Shaeleen, and he said, "That's where we need to go, then."

"You can't just go into the castle of Sylvermoor." Solanna stood up, disgust and surprise mixing on her face. "The empress doesn't see just anyone. She is old, and there is protocol, and you—you are from Wayland."

"Yes, we are," Shaeleen said, feeling proud of it. Turning to Cole, she motioned to him. "Let's go, Cole. We have an empress to meet."

Melindra and Aeron stood up with them, and Melindra said, "Solanna is correct. Seeing the empress is difficult. She is strong in the powers of the stones but is old and has many people protecting her."

"We have a few tricks of our own," Shaeleen said to Melindra, without giving away too much in front of Solanna. "And I have a feeling your empress is not running things in your kingdom as much as you might think she is."

The three Verlynians stood with their mouths agape.

"You don't think…?" Aeron left the sentence unfinished.

"Think of the law that was passed today by the council," Shaeleen said. "Prince Brevin is already in charge, and the shadow has control of the throne of Verlyn."

Melindra's hand went to her mouth. Solanna put her hand up against the wall, to keep from falling. And Aeron's eyes flashed in pain.

As Shaeleen and Cole moved to the door, she turned around one last time. "If Wayland falls, Verlyn might survive— but, if Verlyn falls to the shadow, we are all doomed. We need to find Diamonique and return to Galena to stop a war, but then I will return to Verlyn."

Cole opened the door and led Shaeleen through it and out into the gardens. The sky was now dark. Pinpricks of stars and a waning moon shone down brightly, reflecting in tiny sparkles off the water of the fountain. Aeron hurried out after them, bringing the key to unlock the back gate.

Walking out of the back gate, Cole turned to Shaeleen and said, "So, what's your plan for getting into the castle and finding the tunnel entrance, Shae?"

Shaeleen looked up at Cole, his light blue eyes reflecting hope in the moonlight. Then she shook her head and said with a grim smile, "I have no idea."

CHAPTER TWENTY-FOUR

On their way to the castle, Cole and Shaeleen had needed to stop and hide from patrolling guards a few times. Luckily, the city was full of trees, bushes, and large flowering plants, which had given them enough places to easily conceal themselves.

After the patrol had left this time, Shaeleen turned to Cole and said, "Not all the patrols are shadow guards. This, at least, gives me hope that we still have a chance—and that the Verlynian government hasn't turned totally to the shadow yet."

"Can you tell—when you first meet people—if they are tainted by the shadow or not?" Cole asked as they started walking again.

Shaeleen thought for a moment. The castle loomed up in front of them. The only visible thing taller than the castle was the faintly glowing, snow-capped Mount Eyvindr overhead.

Then she shook her head and said, "Not always at first. But if they speak, then I can usually tell—the TruthStone tells me."

"But that may be too late." Cole smiled grimly.

Shaeleen cocked her head and smiled back. "Might be. That's why you're here as my protector."

Cole chuckled. "Glad to be of service. And it's nice to be back together, Shae. But why do we always seem to get into trouble when you're around?"

"Me?" Shaeleen joined him in his laughter. *It is true. Trouble does seem to follow me around.* She shook her head. "We're getting close. What now?"

"You're the one with the IntelligenceStone," Cole said.

"But you were always the smarter one," Shaeleen shot back.

She motioned for Cole to follow her behind a side of the wall surrounding the castle complex. Tall palm trees and ten-foot ferns concealed the wall for most of the way, from what they could see in the dark. Thick vines hung down from even taller trees, which Shaeleen could not see the tops of.

"Well, I see two options," Cole whispered a few minutes later. "One, we storm the castle with all our combined powers, or two, we sneak in and try to find the tunnels on our own."

Shaeleen pursed her lips. She loved the idea of storming the castle, flashing their powers wide around them. But, without knowing who supported the shadow, it probably wasn't a good idea. She had been warned by Lorelei against using her powers too much. And, she had to admit, each time she had used them, it had indeed attracted the ShadowStone to her.

"I think we'll use stealth." Shaeleen closed her eyes to think better. *Don't know why, but it helps me to concentrate.* She could feel the powers of the TruthStone and its embedded stones pulsating. Without pulling on their powers, she let a bit of them seep into her.

Opening her eyes, she continued her previous train of thought by saying, "But, for some reason, I feel I need to see the empress and warn her."

Cole sighed. "Nothing's easy anymore, is it?"

Shaeleen shared a grim smile. "Nope."

Shaeleen stood next to Cole in the cover of the trees and watched the rotation of guards around the castle's perimeter. She was anxious to get inside and then to Diamonique. There wasn't much time left. But in watching the guards, something didn't seem right. They continued to watch for over an hour.

Then Cole said, "I see a pattern. Shae, see those guards there?" Cole pointed to a group they had seen a few times in the past hour. "They're here not to keep people out but to hold people in."

"You're right, Cole," Shaeleen said. "That's what I was missing." To make sure of what they had concluded, they watched those guards' marched formation for another half an hour.

"Do you think they are shadow guards?" Cole asked.

Shaeleen had already come to that conclusion and nodded. "Definitely, and they are keeping Veronia and others as prisoners in the castle, while Brevin rules behind the shadow."

"Then we must find *Empress* Veronia," Cole said, emphasizing her title to Shaeleen.

Shaeleen rolled her eyes at her brother for his propriety. "Yes, you are correct, *Wizard* Cole, we must find and protect *Empress* Veronia."

Cole tsked his tongue. "You're mocking me, Shae."

"Only a bit." Shaeleen laughed. "Come on, they don't seem to be watching the side walls much."

Moving farther back, down the side of the castle complex, Shaeleen and Cole found a thick vine hanging over the wall. It was as thick as Shaeleen's arm and ended a few feet above her head. She motioned for Cole to lift her up. She grabbed a hold of the vine and soon was climbing over the wall.

Cole joined her, and then they both stood quietly for a moment behind a giant bird-of-paradise, its colorful flowers on stalks taller than Shaeleen herself.

Shaeleen surveyed the area. Lighted torches lined the winding walkways of the gardens surrounding the castle. Multiple fountains and statues dotted this landscape between them and the castle. And Shaeleen could see a few guards in front of the castle's large stone entranceway.

Walking carefully through the more dense parts of the garden, they made their way around to the back of the castle, where a smaller building stood, up against the hill. She and Cole stood in the shadows and watched the building for a few moments. The night air was still warm, and the sounds of frogs, crickets, and other night insects were the only sounds that filled the air. It was the darkest part of night and still hours before dawn.

Nothing stirred around them. Shaeleen took a deep breath—she wasn't used to sneaking around in the dark.

"The servants' quarters?" Cole asked Shaeleen, pointing at the building.

Shaeleen nodded. That was her thought also. She crooked her finger at her brother, and they began moving forward silently. The windows were dark, and it would be at least another hour before the first servants woke up to start cooking and to ready the castle for the day's activities.

Walking up onto a short stone porch, Shaeleen put her hand on its smooth wooden railing and moved toward the only door they could see for the building. Placing her hand on the knob, she turned and pushed the door at the same time.

A short creek ensued, and she and Cole froze.

After not hearing any other sounds from within the building, Cole nodded his head for Shaeleen to move inside, where they found themselves standing in a very small foyer. Doors lined a hallway, leading—Shaeleen supposed—into bedrooms. At the end of the hallway, Shaeleen saw a rather large recess in the wall. There, hanging on bars, looked to be a variety of servants' clothes.

Careful to make no sounds, Shaeleen pointed forward, and Cole nodded his agreement. They took careful steps to reach the clothes. Shaeleen was not really familiar with what all the different clothes meant, especially in this foreign kingdom. They each searched until they had found uniforms which appeared able to fit them.

Then they found a small sitting room, where they changed into the servants' clothes and wrapped their older belongings up, putting them into a small bag Cole had found in the foyer.

As Cole joined Shaeleen in the hallway once again, she had to stifle a laugh behind her hand. He glared at her and tried to adjust the clothes around his shoulders. Shaeleen thought, Cole was definitely too broad to fit in the servants' attire he had found. It was stretched tightly across his chest, the top button not even able to reach its buttonhole, and he could hardly move his arms. But he still held his sword in his hand.

"This won't do," Shaeleen whispered with a smile. "Your sword will give you away."

"My sword?" Cole pointed a hand to his chest and whispered, "What about these clothes? I look ridiculous. I'm changing back."

Shaeleen nodded and waited for her brother. She would have to find something else for him. For herself, she had found something which fit quite well, though it did drag on the floor a bit. She looked down at the black, sleeveless tunic over a white dress and adjusted the black bonnet to cover her hair and ears.

Soon she and Cole left the building and moved back to their hiding spot. Shaeleen took a few minutes to figure out what they should do now that Cole didn't have any disguise. She turned to Cole. "You will have to wait outside for me," she said.

"No, Shaeleen." Cole's light blue eyes flashed at her. "I won't leave you again."

Shaeleen admired her brother's loyalty; she had missed him earlier at the compound and on her trek through the jungles of Eyvindr, but all she had to do was slip in and talk to the empress and find out where the tunnels were. She could do it. "It just isn't practical, Cole."

Before she could say more, she heard footsteps and soft voices coming their way. Shrinking farther back under the trees and bushes, she crouched down by Cole and watched. Three men walked by them. Two men began to veer off around the back of the castle, while the third man, the youngest, took a step toward the servants' building.

"Be careful, Fen," said one of the other two men to the youngest one. "If the steward finds out about your late-night visits, you'll be serving down at the docks instead of at the castle."

Fen smiled, his white teeth shining in the torchlight. "You're just jealous, Kaeden."

The other two laughed and turned away. Cole put his finger to his lips to keep Shaeleen from talking. Then, before Fen could get to the servants' building, Cole was at his back. Reaching around him, Cole clasped the palm of his hand over Fen's mouth and then slowly dragged Fen back behind the servants' building.

To Shaeleen, it had sounded like only a slight rustling. She turned and watched the other two men. But they continued to walk away without noticing. In a few moments, Cole came striding out from behind the servants' building, dressed in the guard's uniform. It was still tight at the shoulders, but not enough to draw unwanted attention. Dark blue leather armor and armbands covered the black shirt and pants. Cole's own sword stuck out of a black scabbard that was a little too small for it, but it was ready to use nonetheless.

Shaeleen gave a silent clap and smiled as her brother approached. He appeared quite menacing.

"Stay here," she said to Cole. He needed a cloak to cover up the sword, and his hair was too short. Cole gave her a quizzical look, but she put up her hand and ran back to the small servants' building. Sneaking back inside, and grabbing a hooded, black cloak from the servants' attire, she brought it back out for her brother.

She tied the cloak around his shoulders and pulled the hood up over his head.

"Now, your hair won't give you away."

Cole put his hand up and touched the hood. "Good thinking."

"Now, we wait until dawn," Shaeleen said. "It will be easier to move around the castle undetected when there are more servants up and getting to their duties."

As they both sat back down and leaned against a towering palm tree, Shaeleen glanced up and, in the moonlight, noticed coconuts growing above her. As she drifted off to sleep, the last thing she remembered thinking was *I hope they won't fall on me.*

CHAPTER TWENTY-FIVE

"Shae!"

She felt Cole nudging her awake.

"It's time," Cole said.

Sitting up straighter, she rubbed her eyes and glanced around. She couldn't believe she had actually fallen asleep for so long. A faint light filled the eastern sky behind Mount Eyvindr, and only a few faint stars remained to the west. She could see that a light was on in the servants' building and could hear soft sounds of early morning around the castle complex.

They waited until the servants began walking from their quarters to a back door in the castle. Nodding to Cole, Shaeleen approached the back door with him, not knowing really what to expect.

"Here goes." Shaeleen smiled.

Cole lifted his brows but said nothing. He opened the door for her, and she entered a small mudroom. Sounds of servants and other early risers floated down the hallway located just on the other side of the mudroom.

Although Verlynians spoke the same language as people from Wayland, Shaeleen was worried about not knowing any specifically local words if she spoke to anyone.

Walking out of the room, she found herself facing a tall, stern man. A female servant was just leaving him.

"Yes, Steward," the woman said, bowed slightly, then was on her way.

As the steward turned to Cole, Shaeleen frowned. But, speaking to Shaeleen first, the steward said, "I don't remember any children being part of my staff."

Shaeleen didn't know what to say to that and stammered for a brief moment.

"A favor for Prince Brevin, sir," Cole said, coming to her rescue. Then Cole gave a short bow to the steward.

At the mention of the prince's name, the steward's face turned white, and he looked nervously to the right and to the left. His nervous glances helped Shaeleen hide the pain from Cole's lies.

"Of course, of course," the steward said as he stumbled on his words, turning back to Cole. "Anything for the prince. And, who might you be, sir? Your speech is not from around here."

Shaeleen braced herself for another lie from Cole. *This is going to be a difficult day.*

But Cole smiled widely and put his hand forward to shake the steward's hand. "My name is Cole. I have been living in Galena for some time and have recently returned." He glanced around and then leaned in to whisper to the steward. "You know with all the trouble in Wayland, I thought it better to be here for now." He smiled in a conspiratory way at the steward.

Shaeleen swallowed hard to keep herself from laughing. *My brother really is quite brilliant.* Nothing he'd said had been untrue at all.

The steward nodded knowingly and seemed to relax. He reached out his own hand to shake Cole's. As they did so, Cole seemed to squeeze hard and let out a small spark that Shaeleen saw was traveling up the steward's arm. Then the steward fell limply into Cole's arms.

"Cole," Shaeleen whispered, "that's twice you've used your powers while on the castle grounds. You must be more careful."

Cole shook his head. "I don't think I have to worry as much as you, Shae. I don't hold any stones of power."

Shaeleen thought about that for a brief moment and wondered if it was true. Then she stopped and smiled. *It must be true!* she thought because she hadn't felt any pain.

Another servant came walking by and then stopped abruptly upon seeing the steward lying in Cole's arms. But Cole called the woman over to them.

"The steward has fallen ill," Cole said. "I am new here. Can you tell me where his quarters are?"

The woman nodded her head and motioned with her hand for them to follow her. "He's on the third floor," the woman said, "directly under the empress's rooms."

Shaeleen smiled at their luck. As she followed Cole and the servant up the stairs, others asked to help. It seemed the steward was a man known by all, and, from the attitude of these servants, he was probably a fair and well-liked man.

I hope Cole hasn't hurt him too badly.

As they came to the steward's room, Cole stopped momentarily, as if to catch his breath. The servant leading them opened the door, and Cole carried the steward in and laid him on the bed, which sat at the back of the generous chamber.

"Should I fetch the healers, sir?" the servant asked Cole.

Cole shook his head. "I think he just needs some rest." Then Cole turned to Shaeleen. "Miss, would you mind caring for him and watching over him until he awakens?" Cole said, as if he didn't know her.

"Of course, of course," Shaeleen said. Then, turning to the servant, she continued, "I'm sure you can all get along without him for a bit. Seems like a well-run castle."

The praise seemed to work on the woman, and she smiled broadly. "Oh yes, we serve the empress with all our hearts here." Then a small frown ensued.

"What's wrong?" Cole asked.

"Well..." the servant said and leaned in closer, as if preparing to share a secret. "If you must know, the empress has been quite sick lately. Her grandson is said to be taking care of her, but..." The woman stopped speaking, as if realizing she had gossiped too much already.

"We have helped the steward, miss," Cole continued, his smile warm and inviting. "Please, if something is going on, we need to know. We have just returned here from Wayland and find that things have changed recently.

The servant turned around, glancing at the door and then back at the steward. "He is a good man—the steward—and has served the empress here for forty years faithfully—but he told us to be careful of Prince Brevin." She put her hand to her mouth in apparent fear. "Please forgive me for speaking disrespectfully about the prince, but..."

Shaeleen put her hand on the woman's arm and just let a trickle of her power seep into her arm. "Tell us about Brevin, please."

The woman stiffened slightly. Then she nodded her head. "We are all afraid of Prince Brevin. Every time he visits the empress, she seems to get worse. There is a darkness in her room that wasn't there before."

"Thank you for all your help," Shaeleen said with a sweet voice. "I'll watch over the steward for now."

The woman nodded her head, not even knowing what Shaeleen had done to her, and left the room. Shaeleen jumped up to close the door behind her.

Cole began to look through the steward's room, searching for records or clues that might help them. As he did so, Shaeleen kept an eye on the steward and sat in one of the chairs by a small table in front of the room's window, thinking about what should happen next.

The window faced north, and the morning sun sent a faint stream of golden sunlight from her right hand side into the steward's room and upon the side of Shaeleen's face.

She stood up, faced the window, and stared northwest. She could see the outlines of tall ships in the harbor of Sylvermoor and in the crystal blue waters beyond. But farther out, the strait grew foggy and misty, befitting its name. She closed her eyes and let the morning sun warm her entire face.

Feeling the light creep into her, she drew upon her TruthStone's power and entered the light itself—now much more easily than the first time she'd done so. Her view instantly changed, and she looked down upon herself in the steward's room. Then she took off and flew on the morning rays of the bright summer sun.

Suddenly, Shaeleen found herself outside of the castle, looking down at it from high in the air. She could see the entire city, and she frowned as her view settled on its shadowed quarter to the north. Waves of darkness seemed to be rising from the stone building there, and Shaeleen knew she'd need to hurry.

She flew back down to the castle and went to the window of the room just above the steward's room. Following the rays of light into there, she now stood just inside the room's window. Two servants moved around in the room. One was tidying things up, and the other, an aged woman, stood by the decorative bed. Thin and colorful silk hung down around it from above. The aged servant was talking softly to a woman on the bed. *Empress Veronia!*

Shaeleen took a few steps farther into the room, but the light wasn't as bright there, so she had to step back.

"Empress, how do you feel this morning?" the aged servant asked.

"Help me sit up, Cecilia," Empress Veronia said. "I feel the light strongly today."

Cecilia enlisted the help of the other servant, and together they sat up the empress, pushing plush pillows behind her head. The empress's face was gaunt and pale, but her eyes—a light blue—still held strength. Beautiful, silky, white hair flowed down over her shoulders. The empress looked over at the window where Shaeleen was standing, and she smiled. Then the empress lifted up one bony hand and pointed in Shaeleen's direction.

"You see, Cecilia, the angels are coming to visit me." The empress smiled again.

Shaeleen took a step back and watched the servants carefully. *Could they see her too?* They seemed to ignore the empress's statement and continued their daily routine.

"Can you see me?" Shaeleen whispered softly to Veronia

The empress smiled and nodded. "I've never seen an angel of light before."

Shaeleen would have laughed if the empress didn't seem so serious. *I definitely am no angel.*

Shaeleen felt power radiate from the empress and fill the entire room. Then Shaeleen glanced outside and saw the shadow, off in the distance. *It seems to be moving toward me.*

"Please leave me," the empress said to her servants.

They each looked surprised. And Cecilia opened her mouth as if to respond.

But the empress waved Cecilia away.

As the two servants left the room, Shaeleen waited to see what the empress would do.

"Are you an angel, my child?" Empress Veronia finally said. "I can see you there, in the window's light you know."

Shaeleen shook her head. "I am no angel, Veronia. But you are in danger. There are shadow keepers in Verlyn."

The empress sat still as if thinking about something. "Young Feyn warned us of that last year at the gathering. I have wondered what happened to the boy, but no one seems to know."

Shaeleen didn't know what the old empress was rambling on about. "Veronia, I need to use the tunnels under your castle to get into your grandson's old dwelling place."

"My son?" The empress's eyes seemed to glaze over momentarily.

"No, not your son," Shaeleen rolled her eyes at the old woman. *I don't have time for this right now!* "He's gone, but your grandson Brevin lived in it and uses it now. I'm afraid that he has a ShadowStone."

The empress shook her head back and forth. "No, no. That can't be. Brevin visits me each day. He is a sweet boy."

Shaeleen knew she had to hurry, for the empress was losing her mental clarity. "He's not a sweet boy anymore Your Highness. You must be careful. I am the prophesied one!" Shaeleen said, trying to shock the old woman back to her senses. "I am here to fight the shadow and restore the power of the stones. I need your help."

The empress's eyes seemed to clear, and she opened them wide. "You are so young."

Shaeleen laughed and said, "Don't I know it." She paused before pushing on. "You are in trouble. Brevin and the shadow keepers are taking over Sylvermoor and Verlyn. You must fight them. You must hold on."

"Brevin?" The empress's eyes grew stern. "Yes, he has grown darker, but I have grown weaker. I don't know if I can hold on much longer. My ancestors are calling to me."

As if calling Prince Brevin's name had called the shadow closer, a dark thickness began to gather outside the castle, and the light in the empress's room dimmed slightly.

"The tunnels, Veronia," Shaeleen asked again, her voice growing more urgent. "Where are the tunnels?"

The empress pushed herself up straighter in bed, and her eyes cleared momentarily. "In the far corner of the lowest levels, past the dungeon. There lies a door there. It is disguised in the wall, but there is a small lever that—"

Just then, darkness flowed into the empress's room and a man burst in through the door.

"Brevin!" the empress exclaimed, sinking down once again into the bed.

"Empress, are you all right?" As Prince Brevin gazed intently around the room, Shaeleen saw that shadows crept from his fingers and his eyes were dark. He was dressed all in dark gray, and his slender build looked ready to pounce at any moment.

"It's too light in here, Mother," he said as he closed the shades on one window and then moved toward the window behind where Shaeleen stood.

As he began to close its shades as well, Shaeleen began to dissipate in the growing darkness. Then Prince Brevin paused and cocked his head to one side as he stared at Shaeleen's location.

"An angel of light visited me, Brevin," the empress said. "She was so beautiful."

"Empress, beware of the shadow!" Shaeleen yelled out before she flew back out the window on the final rays of light that remained.

Quickly, she returned to her body and then slumped to the ground. Cole jumped up from a nearby chair and came to her side.

"Shaeleen, what's wrong? You've just been staring out the window for a few minutes. I was getting worried."

"He's here," Shaeleen said as she allowed Cole to lift her up from the ground.

"Who?"

"Prince Brevin," Shaeleen said. "And he holds a ShadowStone."

CHAPTER TWENTY-SIX

Shaeleen and Cole left the steward lying on his bed and raced out of his room. Instantly, Cole ran into a servant carrying a tray of food. As the tray hit the wall, bowls of food splattered the hallway. Then Cole leaned down, as if to help the woman up.

"Cole, we don't have time for that!" Shaeleen yelled at him, glancing back as she headed for the stairs.

Cole glared at Shaeleen and lifted the woman back to her feet. Shaeleen could hear him muttering his apologies and then heard him following her down the third floor flights of stairs.

The castle was more alive now than when they had first entered it. Servants and other early risers walked through the halls, appearing to be hurrying to perform their duties or to get a bite to eat.

Then she heard a loud roaring voice above them. Shaeleen spared a glance upward and saw Prince Bevin hanging over the railing, his arms waving in the air.

"Guards!" he called out. "Catch those two."

Shaeleen stumbled on the stairs, but Cole caught her arm and steadied her. The amount of time she had spent within the light, communicating with the empress, had weakened Shaeleen.

As two guards showed up at the bottom of the stairs, Shaeleen and Cole reached the landing on the second floor above them. Suddenly, Shaeleen felt Cole take her hand and pull her back toward him. Then he got a firm grip around Shaeleen as he grabbed the banister with his other hand, carrying both of them over the edge of the second floor railing.

"Cole!" Shaeleen yelled out. He'd acted before she could even think to do anything else. As she was in midair, falling down to the bottom floor, Shaeleen noticed that their cloaks had floated up around them as they were falling past onlookers on the last set of stairs. Then she saw Cole pointing his hand down and felt a gush of air come up at them from the floor, slowing their descent.

She landed in a crouch next to Cole. Instantly, Cole's sword was in his hands, and Shaeleen heard servants scream as they backed away. Then cries of alarm filled the castle.

Shaeleen turned to a nearby servant. "Where are the stairs to the dungeons?"

"Down there," the woman said with fear in her voice, and she pointed to the other end of a wide hallway before running off in the other direction.

Shaeleen motioned Cole forward.

From side hallways, a dozen men approached them from different directions: tall, lithe, and skilled Verlynian guards. Cole swiped at a few of them, and fire sizzled from his sword. Then Shaeleen called upon the StrengthStone and punched a guard that was about to get to her brother. The guard went flying into a stone wall.

I don't really want to hurt these people, Shaeleen thought. *Unless they follow the shadow, then it is their own faults if they get in my way.*

From behind her somewhere, Shaeleen heard a hiss. Then something hit her from behind, knocking her forward onto the ground. She twisted around on the ground and saw Prince Brevin, his eyes ablaze with anger, coming down the last flight of stairs, black fire erupting from his fingertips.

Shaeleen jumped up and continued to run down the hall as she gathered her own powers. Then she formed a lightning spell and threw it at the prince's feet, causing him to stumble for a moment on the stairs. As Shaeleen neared the end of the hall, she and Cole began to search for the door to the dungeons.

"There!" Cole yelled to her. But two guards stood in front of the thick, oaken door.

Shaeleen nodded and said, "Go!" And Cole moved around her to deal with the guards.

Hopefully these are normal guards and not holders of magic.

Shaeleen drew upon the TruthStone and brought up a thick blanket of green fog behind them, blocking their actions from the advancing prince and his guards. Cole finished knocking out the two guards, grabbed a set of their keys, then unlocked and opened the door.

"Shaeleen, let's go!" Cole yelled.

She turned away from her spell of fog and followed Cole through the doorway. A few candles, in spaced-out sconces on the walls, dimly lit the set of stone stairs that descended below the main floor of the castle.

"You know where you're going?" Cole asked.

"Yes, the empress told me," Shaeleen said, breathing hard as she ran ahead of Cole down the stairs, trying not to trip.

Cole let out a puff of air. "What about the SpeedStone?" he asked. "The prince and his men are not far behind us."

Shaeleen thought about it but said, "I need to conserve my strength for later."

Then the door above them crashed open, and the sounds of guards following them echoed down the stairwell. When Shaeleen had gone down two flights of stairs, she met another pair of guards. But Cole threw out a ball of fire from his hand, knocking the two guards unconscious.

Beyond where the guards had been was a room. Cells lined the dimly lit room on either of its sides, some filled with men and women. Suddenly, Shaeleen recognized Lorelei inside one of the cells. She skidded to a stop in front of the cells.

"Lorelei!" she yelled out.

The master keeper was sitting at the back of the cell on the floor with her arms wrapped around her knees.

"Shaeleen, we have to go!" Cole yelled. "Where is the entrance?"

Men poured into the cell area, and Shaeleen felt the air grow cold and dark.

The ShadowStone!

Cole jumped forward and began fighting the guards, but two other men, one dressed in a hooded black cloak, stepped around him and headed toward Shaeleen. She grabbed hold of one of the bars, to call for Lorelei again, but pain erupted throughout her body, and she fell to the floor.

"They are spelled to block our powers," Lorelei said as she ran to the bars and reached through to Shaeleen. "It's a ShadowSpell."

A sizzling of power leapt from the fingertips of one of the men and flew toward Cole.

"Watch out, Cole!" Shaeleen yelled. "Shadow keepers."

One of the two shadow keepers headed toward Cole, to join the fighting guards. The other shadow keeper turned, his hood covering his head, and scowled down at Shaeleen. Then he took two long strides and knelt down next to her.

Shaeleen shook her head to clear it and then began to gather her powers back to her. She'd reached forward, intending to touch the man with a TruthSpell, when he removed his hood.

"Taegen," Shaeleen uttered, barely getting the word out. She couldn't believe he was here. "What are you doing?"

"I tried to help him," Lorelei said from behind Shaeleen. "But I was caught and put in these cells with the rest of the keepers. The bars block our powers."

"These are all keepers of the stones?" Shaeleen looked around at the other men and women behind the bars. "Yes," Lorelei said. "Many that were on their way to the gathering."

Shaeleen quickly looked around. "Melindra," Shaeleen gasped, and the elder keeper walked forward from another cell and smiled at Shaeleen.

"Solanna turned us in," Melindra said. "I don't know if she fully realizes yet what she has done."

Shaeleen grunted in exasperation, but she was not surprised. The woman was weak—and Prince Brevin obviously had manipulated her.

"Be careful who you trust," Melindra said in reference to Taegen who knelt over her still.

Turning to Taegen, Shaeleen pushed him over and then stood up over him.

How dare he do this to me after I have tried to help him! Her anger fueled her power, and she brought it to bear, preparing to strike Taegen. But he looked up at her, his light eyes burning into hers, and her heartbeats quickened. Even in this light he was beautiful.

I don't need this distraction right now.

"Shaeleen, please," Taegen pleaded. "It's not what you think."

"What's not what I think?" Shaeleen stepped on his arm, keeping Taegen on the ground. Her strength held him tightly there. "Do you still hold a ShadowStone?"

Tears filled Taegen's eyes, and his head dropped down, guilt written all over his face.

"Then you are my enemy," Shaeleen said in a soft whisper as she had to look away.

"Let me up, and I'll help you escape," Taegen said, drawing Shaeleen's eyes back to his. "I didn't know it was you we were chasing, I swear."

"Enough of this," came the loud, booming voice of Prince Brevin just up the stairwell from them. "Do I have to make up for all of your incompetence?" he said to the guards.

"Brevin," Shaeleen whispered. *The man gives me the creeps.* She wasn't sure if Prince Brevin was more powerful than herself or not, but she didn't want to find out right now. So Shaeleen looked down at Taegen once again and then took her foot off his arm. She didn't know if it was the right thing to do, but she needed all the help she could get at the moment.

"If you betray me," she warned Taegen, "I will kill you next time."

Taegen had the sense to only nod and didn't say another word. Standing up, he brought his hands in front of him and pointed them toward Shaeleen.

She felt shocked. *Did he really trick me?*

"Move," Taegen said.

As soon as Shaeleen had obeyed, taking a step to the side, Taegen blasted his dark shadow powers into the cell bars, creating an opening. Then he turned and did the same thing to the bars of the cells on the other side. A dozen keepers of the stones pushed forward and joined them in the fight against the castle guards.

"Go!" Taegen told Shaeleen, placing his hand on her arm.

Then Cole roared toward them, coming at Taegen and yelling, "Get your hands off of her!" Cole brought his sword up to strike Taegen down.

But Shaeleen pushed Taegen out of the way.

"No, Cole!" Shaeleen yelled and then grabbed Cole's other hand. "He's helping us." She glanced sideways to give a look to Taegen that said, *You better not cross me.*

Just then, Prince Brevin entered the chaos. Shaeleen could see him over the crowd, for he was taller than the rest of them.

Cole turned to fight, but Shaeleen pulled Cole farther down the hall, past the fighting guards and keepers.

"The tunnels are here." Shaeleen motioned Cole forward. Leaving the sounds of fighting behind them, they moved into a smaller hallway once again. But she turned her head one last time and caught Taegen looking her way. His eyes seemed to be pleading with her to believe in him. Then he turned and joined the fray.

The hall opened up into what looked like a small storage area. Shaeleen brought up a ball of light in front of her and began searching for the lever the empress had mentioned. In the passage, old wooden crates were stacked here waist high. She began to knock them down, and Cole joined her.

"What are we looking for?" he asked.

"A lever that—" But Shaeleen stopped, feeling the presence of darkness before she could see it.

"Stop right there!" Prince Brevin said.

He was behind them, swirls of darkness flowing around him like a cloak on a windy day.

We have to get away from him. Shaeleen had faced Georrod, Hutchin, and Dunstun before, but she wasn't prepared yet to face their leader.

"Found it, Shae," Cole whispered behind her.

She heard a loud grating sound and saw the stone wall opening slowly. But Prince Brevin brought his hands up in front of him, gathering black fire in his hands. Then he threw it toward Shaeleen and Cole.

But Shaeleen was quicker. She'd pulled upon the power of the small orange Garnet SpeedStone that she held in her pouch and had grabbed Cole's hand, jumping through the doorway, entering the dark narrow tunnel.

She and Cole sped through the darkness, scraping against walls and corners in the tunnels, until they were far enough away to safely stop.

"I need light, Cole," Shaeleen said, bumping into a wall as she slowed down.

As Cole brought forth a ball of light in front of him, Shaeleen could see that, in the tunnel in front of them, other tunnels branched off.

"How will we know where to go?" Cole asked.

Shaeleen thought for a moment. She didn't know for sure how far they were from Brevin or how much further they had to go. The Prince would know the tunnels much better than she or Cole would. Suddenly a thought came to her and she stifled a nervous laugh. "I can follow the shadow. If Diamonique really is in Brevin's old home, there will be shadow keepers there."

"Won't they feel you also?" Cole looked back behind them. "And the prince won't be far behind us."

"At this point, I think they probably already feel me," Shaeleen said. "Our best chance is to get there as quickly as we can using the SpeedStone. But it may tire me out."

Cole nodded and bit his bottom lip. "We must find the princess. We promised to do so. Our own safety is second to that."

Shaeleen rolled her eyes at her brother's chivalry. She herself would put her own well-being before that of Princess Diamonique—a woman she had never even met. But, either way, Cole was right. They had to find the princess and get her safely away.

Grabbing her brother's hand, Shaeleen closed her eyes and drew power from all the stones she had—TruthStone, StrengthStone, IntelligenceStone, and SpeedStone. Off ahead of them the evil coldness of a ShadowStone pushed against the power of her TruthStone. And, as she had touched it with her power, she knew it had recognized her stone too.

"Here we go." Shaeleen breathed out. And, in a flash, they sped through the royal tunnels under the city of Sylvermoor.

CHAPTER TWENTY-SEVEN

Shaeleen felt disoriented from using the power of the SpeedStone in the winding, dark tunnels. The light Cole held in his hand had barely stayed with them as they sped through the underground of Sylvermoor.

Shaeleen tried to stay focused on where they were going, but it was getting harder and harder the closer they came. Whether this was because her own strength was failing or because of the proximity of the ShadowStone, she didn't know.

Soon they came out of the speed, and both she and Cole stumbled forward a few feet before being able to stop themselves.

"I can't do any more," Shaeleen said, breathing hard. "I think the power of the ShadowStone interferes more with my powers the closer I get. But we should be close now—just up ahead and to the right."

As they moved on, Shaeleen noticed that thick moss and trickles of water covered the walls around them. The floor was slick here, and she had to step forward carefully.

"We should have gotten here quickly enough to still surprise them," Cole said. He now kept his sword in his hand, and Shaeleen saw his eyes flicker around, looking for signs of trouble.

"We'll see," Shaeleen said.

"Who was that man back there?" Cole asked. "The one you said had helped us?"

Shaeleen felt her face grow warm, but she hoped Cole couldn't tell in the dark.

"A friend," she finally said.

"Last I heard friends weren't people shooting waves of dark magic at you."

Shaeleen sighed. "It's kind of complicated. He's a shadow keeper who wants to do what is right."

Cole grunted. "Dangerous friend."

Shaeleen wondered, *Is Taegen any more dangerous than I am?* Either way, she hoped he'd made it through the skirmish below the castle without getting hurt. But she didn't know yet if she could really trust Taegen fully.

Shaeleen let out a deep sigh and said, "Why do things have to be so complicated?"

"Focus, Shae," Cole said to her.

Shaeleen realized she had just turned them down a dead end. So she turned back around. But then Shaeleen stopped and turned back again toward the dead end. It made sense that if the other end of this tunnel, in the castle, started as a blank wall, then this end of the tunnel, below Prince Brevin's home, might also.

"Look for a lever, Cole."

She and Cole both felt along the walls for a moment, but they found nothing. Then, as Shaeleen stepped to the side in one corner, the stone below her foot rocked a bit. She knelt down to examine it. Then Cole leaned down and helped her to lift up the broken stone. Underneath it was a small lever.

"I'll pull it. You stand at the wall, and be prepared for whatever happens," Shaeleen ordered her brother.

Cole gave her a stern look.

"Please," Shaeleen added.

"Let's do it," Cole said. He held his sword out in front of him in one hand and a ball of light in the other hand.

As Shaeleen pulled the lever, the stone door grated against the wall, filling the silent tunnel with echoes. Shaeleen heard a shuffle of steps on the other side, but then it stopped. She gave Cole a questioning glance, but he just shook his head.

After the door had opened enough to let them inside, Shaeleen joined Cole at the new doorway. It was dim inside, with only a small candle set in a sconce on the far wall. As they walked forward, Cole's light gave them a better view of what seemed to be a small bedroom. A bed sat in one corner, with a bureau and washbasin off to one side.

As Shaeleen moved forward, to look to her left, someone jumped on her from behind, taking her by surprise. Cole moved quickly and swung his sword wide, but the figure slid under the arc of Cole's sword and swept his legs, taking Cole down and making his light go out.

In the dim candlelight, Shaeleen could see that the figure had shoulder-length hair as it flew at her on the ground. Shaeleen scrambled away, feeling weak from using the SpeedStone to get them there.

Cole also had stood up once again and was moving to grab their attacker.

As the figure yelled out, Shaeleen realized that it was a woman and saw her muscles bulge around her as the woman snaked a hand out and grabbed Cole's sword arm.

"Cole, use your magic," Shaeleen yelled as she moved toward the woman.

"She's a woman," Cole said in surprise.

"A woman that's trying to kill us!" Shaeleen yelled. "Now is not the time for chivalry."

Cole brought his other hand up, and lightning sizzled from his fingers. As he moved to strike the woman down, she pulled his sword arm down, and the blade of his own sword caught his lightning and reflected it over toward Shaeleen, singeing Shaeleen's cloak.

"That's it!" Shaeleen drew upon her last ounce of the SpeedStone's power and moved instantly to the woman's side. Then, drawing upon the StrengthStone, Shaeleen grabbed the woman by the arms and turned her around, causing the woman's back to face Shaeleen.

Holding the woman's hands in her own, Shaeleen felt the woman's muscles bulge. But, pulling upon the power of the TruthStone, Shaeleen held on—if only barely.

Then Cole moved up in front of the woman and put his sword's point at the hollow of her throat.

"Who are you?" Cole said.

The woman gritted her teeth but then seemed to realize something. "You're not one of them," she said. Her voice had a hoarseness to it—yet held a strength that showed Shaeleen that this woman was used to being obeyed.

Cole moved closer and brought up a small flame of light to see her better. Then he gasped and lowered his sword arm. "Shae, this isn't a shadow keeper or a guard."

"Well, she attacked us, so who is it?" Shaeleen asked, still holding the woman from behind.

Cole's eyes were locked on the woman in front of him, and a thin smile formed on his lips. Then he knelt down on one knee and bowed his head to the woman.

"Cole, are you crazy?!" Shaeleen demanded, not knowing what to make of her brother's actions.

"Forgive me, Your Highness," Cole said slowly to the woman with his head still bowed, and then he glanced back up. "Princess Diamonique, we are here to rescue you."

What?! Shaeleen screamed in her mind. Then the woman's arm muscles constricted and grew limp, so Shaeleen let go of her hands and then walked out in front of the woman, standing next to Cole.

Shaeleen studied the woman in front of her carefully. She had dusty brown skin, brown eyes, and shoulder-length, dark hair. Freckles covered her upturned nose, and her lips curled into a smile of wonder. *It is Diamonique, princess of Gabor!*

With her eyes on Cole, the princess put out her hand to him and said, "You may rise, sir."

Cole rose without taking his eyes off of the princess. And Shaeleen noticed that the princess also couldn't seem to take her own eyes off of Cole, looking him over from head to toe and then looking back to his eyes once again.

"And, does my rescuer have a name?" the princess asked.

Cole tried to speak, but then he cleared his throat. "My name is Cole, my lady. My sister, Shaeleen, and I have been sent here to find you and bring you back to Galena."

At least my brother has finally found his senses.

Shaeleen noted that the two still didn't take their eyes off of one another. So Shaeleen cleared her throat.

Princess Diamonique turned to Shaeleen for a moment before returning her gaze back to Cole. "And, who sent you here to find me?" the princess asked Cole.

"Basil," Shaeleen said.

"Prince Calix," Cole said next.

"And your mother, Victoria," Shaeleen added.

"*Queen* Victoria," emphasized Princess Diamonique.

Shaeleen waved her hand in the air. She didn't need another Cole around, reminding her how to say things.

"Look, Diamonique—" Shaeleen began to say.

"*Princess Diamonique,*" both Cole and the princess said at the same time. Then they caught each other's eyes and actually snickered.

Shaeleen couldn't believe this was happening here in a basement in Verlyn. They didn't even know each other. *Just like Basil and me.* The thought jolted her—at least she had talked to Basil more than a few seconds. She pushed thoughts of the handsome prince out of her mind.

"Wake up, you two," Shaeleen said as she slapped both of them on their arms. Before she knew what was happening, Princess Diamonique had grabbed her arm and had twisted her around.

"Ouch, let go of me," Shaeleen said.

"Not until I understand what you're doing here," Princess Diamonique said.

"You're stronger than Dunstun let on," Shaeleen mumbled and wrenched her arm away from the princess.

Cole put a softer hand on Princess Diamonique's arm and called her attention back to him. "Please forgive the rudeness of my sister. She is not one for protocol, as we are."

"As we are?" Shaeleen said in disbelief and stepped away from the princess. "Do you actually hear what you're saying? Get your eyes off each other, and let's concentrate on getting out of here."

Cole blushed, and Princess Diamonique turned away without saying another word.

"This building houses many shadow guards and shadow keepers, with possibly more coming behind us," Shaeleen said.

"Which direction did you come from?" Princess Diamonique asked, finally getting down to business.

"We sped here from the castle," Cole explained. "But Prince Brevin is following us."

Princess Diamonique visibly shivered, and Cole took a step toward her. But Shaeleen flashed her eyes at him, and he stopped.

"Both of you fought me with powers of the stones, and you have used speeding." Princess Diamonique backed up a step. "Who are you really?"

Shaeleen sighed. This woman was barely older than her, and Shaeleen didn't have time for protocol. "We really don't have time for this Monique—can I call you Monique?"

"No," Princess Diamonique said.

"No," Cole agreed. "She is a princess soon to be engaged to a king."

"Very well." Shaeleen was getting tired of all this politeness. They needed to get out of here and back to the docks to get a ship to Galena. "Princess, we can't explain right now. All you need to know is that we have powers of multiple stones between us, but my powers are dimmed by being around the shadow keepers. There must be a ShadowStone nearby."

"Well, *I* can still fight," the princess said.

Shaeleen nodded her head. "Yes, I see you have inherited quite a bit of the StrengthStone. But I don't think we can fight our way out of here—against the shadow keepers in their own lair. That fight has to wait for another time."

"Then what's your plan, Shae?" Cole asked. "They must know we are here."

As if his words had called them, voices sounded outside of Princess Diamonique's room. Shaeleen could feel the cold presence of the shadow, and she swayed to one side. But Cole hopped next to her side and held her up.

"The tunnels!" Shaeleen said and then motioned. "They must eventually lead to the docks."

Just then, the doorknob to the cell began to turn.

"Go," Cole told Shaeleen and Princess Diamonique. "I'll hold them off."

Shaeleen started to protest, but then the door began to open.

"I am your guardian, Shae—don't forget that," Cole said as he pushed her toward Princess Diamonique. "Get the princess to safety. Remember the mission."

Shaeleen knew her brother was right. So she grabbed onto Princess Diamonique and dragged her into the tunnel as the princess tried to pull away.

"Cole," Princess Diamonique said.

Cole turned and smiled at the princess. Then he turned back to the doorway to meet the onslaught of shadow guards. As she left, Shaeleen saw that only one shadow guard at a time could get through the door. And so, for a few moments, Cole should be able to hold them off.

Shaeleen's legs could barely hold her up, but she pulled on the StrengthStone, along with the power of the SpeedStone. Before the second guard had come into the room, Shaeleen and the princess had sped back into the tunnels and had turned the opposite direction than she and Cole had previously come from.

At one point as she ran, Shaeleen heard a loud boom, and it shook her out of the speed. She and the princess stumbled and fell to the ground.

"Cole?" Princess Diamonique said as she looked back down the tunnels in the direction they'd just come from.

"We need to keep going." Shaeleen tried to stand, but she felt so weak.

Then Princess Diamonique swept down with her arms, seeming to pull upon her own powers of the StrengthStone, and picked Shaeleen up.

"I can walk." Shaeleen tried to squirm out of the princess's arms.

"Don't be stupid," Princess Diamonique said. "You can barely stand."

Shaeleen felt embarrassed but said nothing more as Princess Diamonique ran through the tunnels with her in her arms, letting Shaeleen direct her at each turn. And, somehow, the TruthStone helped Shaeleen know what direction to go each time. *I'll never live down the embarrassment of this!*

After half an hour had passed, Princess Diamonique's strength seemed to ebb, and she put Shaeleen down. Now that Shaeleen was farther away from the shadow guards and the ShadowStone, Shaeleen was beginning to recover her powers more quickly.

Shaeleen came up to a door. After carefully pushing it open, they found themselves in some kind of cellar. Shaeleen could see barrels of ale, sacks of potatoes, and crates of other foodstuffs lining the space around them. On the other side of the room she saw another door. She pushed it open, and they climbed a short set of stairs, emerging into a kitchen.

Their sudden appearance brought gasps from the lips of the cook and her helpers, for Shaeleen had the eyes of a Verlynian but was way too short, and Princess Diamonique, who was only a few years older than Shaeleen, was obviously not from their island.

"Hey, where did you come from?" shouted the cook, a tall, elderly woman, who held a spatula in her hands. "Guards," she yelled to men out front. "We have intruders from Wayland in here."

Shaeleen let out a deep breath and said, "Great, here we go again. I can see we're not wanted here, Monique." The princess gave her a dirty look, but Shaeleen pushed her toward the back door and whispered, "You don't want them to know your real name, do you?"

Princess Diamonique let out an exasperated sigh and rushed to open the door in front of them. But Shaeleen stopped and turned around, smelling something sweet, and her eyes glanced in quick darts around the room.

"Shaeleen!" Princess Diamonique called out.

Finally, Shaeleen spied what she was searching for. So she took a few steps back toward a counter and grabbed two pieces of cake and then turned and followed Princess Diamonique out the door.

CHAPTER TWENTY-EIGHT

Hiding in the shade of a group of gigantic palm trees at the edge of the Eyvindr jungle, Shaeleen and Princess Diamonique sat down to scan the docks below them. By now, it was later in the afternoon, and the sun was reflecting off the deep blue of Sylvermoor Bay. Shaeleen knew that they needed to find a ship to sail back to Galena on as soon as possible. But Shaeleen handed the princess a piece of cake and took a bite of her own piece.

Rolling her eyes with delight, Shaeleen took a moment to rest and savor the sweetness of the Verlynian cake. It had a different kind of appeal and was so moist it seemed to melt in her mouth.

Princess Diamonique kept glancing back toward the city. And Shaeleen had noticed that, although her hands sat in her lap, the princess was wringing them tightly; the piece of cake sitting by her side uneaten.

"He'll be all right," Shaeleen said. "He'll find us."

Princess Diamonique nodded her head but still looked away for a moment. Turning back to Shaeleen, the princess seemed to grow serious. "What did you and your brother mean about both Prince Basil and Prince Calix sending you to bring me to Galena?"

Shaeleen groaned inside. This was a line of thought she had purposefully tried not to think about. She licked her fingers after finishing her last bite of cake. But her silence seemed to prompt Princess Diamonique to ask her another question.

"Are you hiding things, Shaeleen? If you won't answer my previous question, then who are you?"

This time Shaeleen groaned out loud. "It's not very easy to talk about—either answer. But I have announced myself to your mother, and, as heir to Gabor, you deserve to know also."

Princess Diamonique's eyes went wide. "Go on." She waved her hand at Shaeleen, with a look that suggested her expectation of full answers.

"Your mother is not doing well," Shaeleen began. "Commander Kerr is trying to take over. All of the kingdoms are being disrupted. In the kingdom of Shema, I hear, they have closed up Lightfort with all the rulers inside the city. In Mistport, two of the heirs have been killed and the third is missing. Also, a group there is trying to outlaw magic."

"Outlaw magic?" Princess Diamonique's eyes grew stern. "They can't do that."

Shaeleen laughed. "Likely not. But the influence of the ShadowStone has grown stronger as the stones of power in the kingdoms of Wayland have grown weaker."

"What about in Galena? You did not mention them," Princess Diamonique prodded.

"No, I did not," Shaeleen said.

"You said I deserve to know. And, if I am going to marry Prince Basil…"

Shaeleen bent over in pain and almost threw up. Her heartbeats sped up, and her head throbbed behind her eyes.

"Shaeleen, what's wrong?" Princess Diamonique asked as she moved closer to Shaeleen.

"Stupid stone," Shaeleen said, tears filling her eyes.

Can't I ever escape the lies that have been told?

"Stone?" Princess Diamonique looked genuinely worried.

"TruthStone," Shaeleen said. "I hold a TruthStone."

"You're a TruthSeer? One of the five?"

Shaeleen shook her head. "No, not one of the five. I have a special task." Shaeleen wouldn't elaborate any further at the moment.

"And, about Galena?" Princess Diamonique asked again.

"You're quite determined, aren't you?"

"I have been raised my entire life to rule. I guess it comes with that. Why were you and your brother sent to find me and not someone more experienced?" Princess Diamonique turned and looked for Cole once again.

"You care for my brother, don't you?" Shaeleen asked with a sigh.

Princess Diamonique blushed. "Is it that obvious?"

"Yes. But you are going to marry the next king of Galena, Diamonique," Shaeleen said firmly. "You must forget about my brother, Cole. He is a good man—and I can see you share his propensity for decorum and etiquette—but it can never be."

Princess Diamonique's eyes grew hard, and she fixed them on Shaeleen. "Don't preach to me. I know my role in life and will do what is expected of me. Don't doubt that."

"Even if it means you will marry Calix instead of Basil?" Shaeleen blurted out. She hadn't meant to tell this secret in such a way, but Princess Diamonique's haughtiness seemed to have brought it on.

The princess's face turned pale for a moment, and then her mouth grew thin. "If that is what it takes to keep peace in Wayland, I will do what is needed."

Shaeleen's eyes grew moist. Could she ever give so much of herself for others as Princess Diamonique was prepared to do? "You are a unique woman, Princess Diamonique," Shaeleen whispered.

The princess smiled in obvious appreciation of Shaeleen's use of her full title and name. "I think you must be quite a unique person also, Shaeleen, for Prince Basil to send you here with your brother. Whatever you are, I am sure you will do what is needed also."

Shaeleen grunted. What exactly was it she was supposed to do? Would she be able to tell Basil when the time came? Could she find all the stones and destroy the shadow keepers? The questions kept piling up on her. "We'll see about that. You see, Calix is actually the oldest brother of the twin princes of Galena. He is the lawful heir to the throne, but I haven't been able to make myself tell Basil yet."

Princess Diamonique's eyes opened wider, but she didn't say anything.

"Basil is kind, considerate, and charming. He loves his people and would be a wonderful king," Shaeleen said. She looked off into the bay for a minute. She brought Prince Basil up in her mind but found an image that mixed him and Taegen together—both men vying for the attention of her mind. Taegen was a shadow keeper and Basil a prince! *Silly girl!* Neither would be hers. She shook her head to clear her thoughts

"Someone thinks quite highly of Prince Basil," Princess Diamonique teased.

Shaeleen felt herself blush. "No, no. It's nothing like that." Shaeleen immediately felt a pounding begin in her head, and then she gasped at the implications. "No!" She tried to push the thoughts away by saying, "We will find a way for you to marry Basil. We will find a way for him to rule Galena."

A quake of pain surged through her, and Shaeleen knew for sure now that none of her hopes and wishes for Galena would come to be.

Princess Diamonique put her hand on Shaeleen's shoulder. "We all carry burdens, Shaeleen, but if those burdens save our people, they are not actually burdens at all."

Shaeleen shook her head. "How can you think like that? How can you give so much of yourself that you would actually marry Calix—a self-absorbed, power-hungry, thoughtless fool?"

Princess Diamonique laughed out loud. "That great, huh? You are talking about my future husband."

"Sorry," Shaeleen said. Then she spotted the familiar flag of Abby's father, flying on a ship at the docks. She stood up in surprise. *He must have found a new ship!*

"What is it?" Princess Diamonique asked and stood up with her.

"I think I know how we are getting back to Wayland. Come with me."

"What about your brother?"

Shaeleen closed her eyes for a moment and searched for his presence. *Cole, hurry!* she called out to him, and she felt him pick up his pace. She smiled. "He'll find me."

Shaeleen and the princess ran toward the docks. With all the ships Shaeleen had seen from Wayland in the harbor, she decided that their nationalities wouldn't stand out as much down there. After they'd gained themselves too many looks, Shaeleen had stopped running.

Walking down the docks, Shaeleen called out, "Abby!"

Princess Diamonique gave her a strange look. "Who are you calling for?"

"A friend of mine."

"Here, at the docks?" Princess Diamonique questioned. "How will she hear you over all this noise?"

"Oh, she will."

Shaeleen stood up on tiptoe and tried to see over the crowd. But Princess Diamonique was taller and began to look around also.

"Who are we looking for?" the princess asked.

"A girl about ten or eleven with short, dark hair who walks like a sailor."

"Abby! It's Shaeleen," Shaeleen shouted, once in each direction down the docks. A few dozen ships were anchored there, with sailors loading and unloading their goods and business owners loading up and emptying carts between or driving them from the docks to the city.

Then Princess Diamonique pointed and said, "Look."

Shaeleen stood as tall as she could, but she still couldn't see anything.

Then, through the crowd of sailors, a girl burst out from behind them.

Abby!

Abby ran right up to Shaeleen and gave her a big hug.

"Shae! Where did you go?" Abby said.

Shaeleen laughed. "I'll tell you about it later. Is your father ready to sail?"

Abby smiled. "Last time we sailed with you, our ship was destroyed. Maybe a little less adventure this time? It's taken him a lot of talking today to find a new boat to captain. Luckily, he is well known here, and his credit is good."

Princess Diamonique raised her eyebrows.

"It wasn't my fault," Shaeleen said to both of them. And that was the truth—no pain there.

Abby grabbed Shaeleen's hand and pulled her down the docks toward a medium-sized cargo ship.

Walking up the gangplank of the ship, Shaeleen saw the captain barking orders to his crew, many of whom she recognized. When the captain turned and saw her, his face grew grim. She wondered if he would be mad at her for leaving them without saying anything. Hopefully he didn't really blame the destruction of his ship in the storm on her. *That wouldn't be fair.*

"Hello, Captain," Shaeleen said once she was on the deck.

"Hmmm." The captain folded his arms in front of himself. "Where did you run off to? You know, that boy's uncle wasn't so happy when you two left. When the uncle returned, he didn't look too good."

"Sorry if I caused you any problems, Captain," Shaeleen said. She didn't want to get into the actual events with him at the moment.

Distracted, she turned around and looked back at the city. From this standpoint, she could see the castle on the hill and the shadow, now hanging over a larger portion of the city.

"Does that fog seem to be traveling toward us?" she asked.

The captain shaded his eyes and seemed to take in the city with a quick glance. "What trouble do you bring to us this time, Miss Shaeleen?" Then he smiled, as if to show her he didn't hold a grudge.

Shaeleen waved her hand toward Princess Diamonique and said, "Captain, please meet Diamonique, princess of Gabor and the soon-to-be betrothed of the next king of Galena." Shaeleen wiped her own forehead. The heat of the day and the thoughts of Princess Diamonique marrying Prince Calix had brought sweat to her forehead—but no sickness. That in itself almost made her nauseated for real.

The captain seemed to not quite know what to do or say. Then he bowed stiffly.

"My lady, nice to meet you."

"I request the services of your ship, Captain," Princess Diamonique said. "You will be well compensated, I assure you." Princess Diamonique held her head high, and Shaeleen decided that the princess played her part well.

I could never be a leader like that. It was hard enough for Shaeleen to just tell the truth now. *So formal and polite—yuck!*

Speaking of politeness, she thought as she sensed her brother arriving at the docks.

Moving to the railing of the ship, she looked out at the throngs of people. Her attention was taken away, however, by a company of guards—shadow guards, if she had to guess. They were just entering the docks. Above them, the thick gray fog was rolling even closer to the sea.

"Captain, we need to leave *now!*" Shaeleen turned back around.

"B-but we are not done loading our goods," he stammered.

"You are done now, for your current cargo is more precious than all you could hold in this ship."

The captain stood there for a moment, as if deciding what to do.

Shaeleen could see that the guards were now pushing people out of their way down the docks. Then Cole ran out in front of them, and three of the guards pulled out their bows and shot arrows at him.

There was no time to wait for the sailors to finish loading the cargo. Shaeleen called upon her powers. She drew upon the small IntelligenceStone Prince Basil had given her and ran through all the possibilities in her mind at once. She immediately knew what to do.

Using the SpeedStone, she jumped off the side of the ship and raced to Cole's side, pulling him gently to the ground, the arrows narrowly missing him. She drew Cole back up and sped them both back to the ship.

She drew upon the StrengthStone, kicking the gangplank off the ship. Then she sped around the deck and, with her bare hands, ripped the thick ropes free from the dock. The ship began to float away—forcing a few of the crew to jump from the docks to the ship at the last minute.

Soon Cole stood by her side and, with his sword spewing lightning, repelled each arrow from the shadow guards as they tried to stop the ship.

Shaeleen drew upon the TruthStone, raising her hands up in the air, and called forth the last rays of light from the sun before they succumbed to the shadow. With their burst of strength, she pushed the shadow from the bay and back over to the city, leaving her and the others on the ship standing in sunlight once again.

Cries from all the shadow keepers echoed through Sylvermoor. Their powers began to push against hers. Standing in sunlight now, Shaeleen sent her soul soaring into the sunlight. She sailed over the city. Each shadow she met she pushed back with the power of the light.

Soon she came over the castle. Running out of the castle was Lorelei, Melindra, and the rest of the other keepers.

"Stay true to the stones!" Melindra yelled out to her fellow keepers. Then Melindra and Lorelei looked up and seemed to behold Shaeleen's light in the sky. They smiled.

Shadow keepers were also leaving the castle. Then she saw him. Separate from both the shadow keepers and the keepers of the stones, at the back of the group, lagged Taegen. His face looked drawn.

At the moment, no one seemed to be paying Taegen any attention. So Shaeleen directed the light down toward him. He jerked in his stride and almost tripped. As a reaction to the light, Taegen sent dark curls of shadow to push back against the light. Taegen groaned and then gazed up.

Shaeleen sent the light to warm his face, and he smiled with what seemed like a knowing look. Did he know she was there?

With an extra boost of power, Shaeleen shoved the light into Taegen's body and tried to rid him of the shadow. But, would this time be just like it had been with Orin? Did she have enough power yet?

Taegen fell to the ground, his body convulsing, his mouth held open in what seemed to be a silent howl of pain. Shaeleen knew that, with enough time and power, she might be able to get the shadow out of Taegen. So she pushed the light further, but it didn't seem to be enough. He still held the ShadowStone and it pushed back against her own powers.

Taegen faced the sky and bellowed, "You're killing me."

Shaeleen pulled the light back, feeling tears drip down her face back at the ship. Then a shadow passed over her, and she turned and looked back out over the city.

On a hill above the docks stood Prince Brevin. Five shadow keepers—Georrod, Dunstun, Hutchin, and two others—stood at his sides. Prince Brevin pulled a stone from his pocket, and the others followed suit. As they thrust their stones high in the air, a gust of wind shot forth from each ShadowStone, sending black tendrils of power roaring forth and racing toward the light where Shaeleen now watched from.

Shaeleen glanced down at Taegen. He was now standing, and a look of relief had filled his face. But then, as the power of the shadow keepers flew over Taegen, his face darkened. As if without thinking, he too pulled a small stone from his pocket and held it up in the air. Shadow poured forth from Taegen's fingers and joined with the rest of the shadow keepers' black tendrils of power.

Shaeleen screamed down, "No! Fight it, Taegen!" Then she threw one last flicker of light his way.

Taegen glanced up, and his shadow tendrils faltered momentarily. But, before Shaeleen could do anything more, the sky all around Sylvermoor filled with streaks of shadow from all the shadow keepers. The sky had darkened too much for her to stay there any longer.

"Fight it, Taegen!" she said again. Then, flying on the remaining light with the power of the SpeedStone, Shaeleen raced back to the safety of her body on the ship. With her soul crashing back into her body, Shaeleen felt Cole and Princess Diamonique grab her arms to keep her from falling down.

"TruthSeer!" Brevin yelled, his deep and hollow voice filling the air around them. "We will come for you after the gathering!"

CHAPTER TWENTY-NINE

"Incredible," Princess Diamonique said under her breath as Shaeleen felt herself being lowered by the princess and Cole onto a bench.

Shaeleen let her shoulders sag, with her energy all expended. Her heart ached for Taegen, and she hoped he would be strong enough to break free. She knew Taegen had sensed her power of light and truth there. *But will it be enough?*

Twisting around on the bench, Shaeleen glanced back at the island of Verlyn. They were now moving rapidly away from the coast.

I have done what I can for the moment.

She hoped that seeing the clashes of light and shadow over the sky of Sylvermoor and the freed keepers of the stones would awaken the people of Verlyn to what was happening in their kingdom. She also felt the truth in Prince Brevin's threat. There still would be a final confrontation between shadow and light before this was all over. But for now, Shaeleen and Cole had rescued Princess Diamonique and had saved her from any further harm.

Abby gave Shaeleen a drink of water in a small tin cup. Shaeleen gulped it down greedily.

"Where to?" the captain asked as he stood over Shaeleen, clearly still annoyed about having to surrender his newly commissioned ship to her and about having to leave much of his cargo behind.

Shaeleen stood up and stared northwest. She really wanted to go back to Mistport and check on Orin. She still felt guilty about what she had done to him. But then she shifted her body farther north and pointed there instead.

"Home," she said. "Take us home, to Stronghaven."

The captain nodded, barked the orders, and moved up to take the helm from a crew member. Shaeleen knew that they would soon encounter the infamous mists that always seemed to cling to the waters between Verlyn and Wayland. But Shaeleen hoped they wouldn't encounter any problems this time.

Cole came up next to Shaeleen as she looked toward the bow of the ship, where Princess Diamonique stood alone, her shoulder-length, dark hair fluttering around her head in the ocean breeze.

"I told her, Cole," Shaeleen said without turning. "She knows about Calix."

Cole let out a long sigh. "And what will she do?"

Shaeleen gave Cole a melancholy smile. "She will do her duty, Cole. You would have been proud of her words."

Cole smiled. Then, as he turned and looked back at Princess Diamonique, Shaeleen continued standing in silence next to him for a few moments. Shaeleen could see the longing in his eyes.

"Sometimes life is not fair," Shaeleen finally whispered.

Cole only nodded his head, his lips held tight. She could hear him breathe in deeply and then let out a long breath.

"And will you tell Prince Basil, Shae?" He turned and looked down at her, fire in his eyes. "Will you finally do *your duty?*"

Shaeleen took a step back. Cole's eyes crackled with power, and their color was almost opaque. She noticed that his fists were clenched at his sides and his firm jaw was set hard. His shaggy hair blew around his face in the wind, almost obscuring it from her. She wanted to distract Cole, to tell him to just go cut his hair or something, but she knew now wasn't the time for deflection. So she glared back at him, her own powers rising up to meet his if need be.

She felt the ship rock to the side, and both she and Cole grabbed for the railing. A mist of water sprayed over their heads as the fog began to gather thickly around them. Shaeleen put her other hand on her stomach. The lies she carried around with her in regards to Basil and Calix caused her continual pain—pain she was getting used to living with. But she knew she could reduce the frequency of that pain with a few words to Prince Basil: the kind, compassionate, would-be king of Galena.

"Shae?" Cole asked again, this time with more pleading than anger in his voice.

Tears filled her eyes, and she gave a short nod of her head. It would kill her to tell Prince Basil he would never be king. She didn't want to see the look in Basil's eyes. It would crush her.

"I will do my duty, Wizard Guardian."

Shaeleen turned and walked away from Cole. She knew he was right to make her say the words out loud. But she didn't like Cole very much for it at the moment. She moved over to the other side of the ship and watched the mists cover her view of Sylvermoor. Only the snowy peak of Mount Eyvindr, still poking up over the low-hanging mist, was still visible.

After a few moments of wallowing in self-pity, she pushed those feelings aside and turned to go find a place to lie down. Her own pains and problems were nothing compared to what was happening in the kingdoms of Wayland. She stood taller and drew on the familiar power of the stones. She would need to be stronger in the coming days. As she did so, she saw two silhouettes at the bow of the ship, standing together in the thickening mists. *Cole and Princess Diamonique.* They stood so close together that the backs of their hands brushed each other. But duty and decorum had stopped them from doing anything more than stand there.

As Shaeleen watched these two that could never be, a surge of the TruthStone's power brought Shaeleen a flicker of a thought: *Or could they?* She almost jumped with the revelation.

Is this how true TruthSeers live their lives? Seeing possibility after possibility—the truth of the future changing with every decision and action of the present?

Shaeleen realized that there were many futures ahead of them. Which one will they live in? She allowed herself a brief smile as she turned away from the two and headed to a bunk downstairs. She was exhausted and needed to renew her resources—both physical and magical.

There was still a significant confrontation for her to deal with in Stronghaven.

Only a few more days, she reminded herself, *until the seventeenth birthday of Calix and Basil."*

* * *

Two and a half days later, the captain began moving the ship into the docks of Stronghaven, which were as busy as usual on an early summer morning.

Shaeleen stood near the bow of the ship next to Cole, Princess Diamonique, and Abby. She felt a homesickness she hadn't realized before. She missed her parents and her younger sister, Alva, terribly and wished all this mess of gathering the stones would be over so that she could return to her simple life as the daughter of a carpenter.

"Our lives will never be the same again," Cole said, as if he were having the same thoughts.

Shaeleen took a deep breath of the salty morning air. She had rested well on the ship, and so now, as she pushed away these melancholy thoughts, the powers of truth, intelligence, strength, and speed filled her mind and body. A soft glow of green began to build up around her, and she felt peace at who she was becoming. The stones lifted her spirits, and she drew more of their power into her.

"Shae!" Cole said and warned her with a look, and Princess Diamonique stepped back from her.

Shaeleen twirled, her dark cloak billowing around her, and said, "Cole, I'm not hiding anymore." Then she proceeded to climb up onto the railing. Balancing her feet carefully, she put her hands up in the air.

"Is she always this crazy?" Princess Diamonique asked Cole.

"Yes, but I think the power has gone to her head now." Cole shook his head, but they both laughed.

"Wayland!" Shaeleen yelled out at the approaching docks—only a few hundred feet away—as the ship moved very slowly toward one of the empty slips. "Your TruthSeer has arrived!" Clapping her hands together, she sent a blast of green, blue, red, and orange light flashing up high into the sky—a column of light announcing to all that she was there.

Shaeleen was enjoying the power coursing through her veins, but then she looked up at the castle, and her delight began to be dampened. Duty loomed large in front of her now.

Still standing on the railing, she noticed Princess Diamonique looking in the same direction, Cole standing protectively by the princess's side. A tear rolled down the princess's flawless face, and Shaeleen took a moment to share in the grief the princess must be feeling.

Then she saw Cole put his hand softly on Princess Diamonique's arm and lean in.

"I will always be here to protect you," Cole said.

As he glanced at Shaeleen out of the corner of his eye, she gave him a sharp look. He was *her own* protector and guardian.

He nodded his understanding, but his face revealed conflicting emotions.

"I hear ships coming," Abby said to Shaeleen as Abby pointed northward. "Large ones."

At first, Shaeleen didn't understand, but then she remembered—Abby had the powers of the HearingStone. Shaeleen jumped down from the railing and ran up the stairs to the ship's bridge. The captain stood there, still overlooking the docking of the ship. But she asked him for a spyglass and then put it to her eye.

"He's coming!" Shaeleen yelled out.

Cole turned toward her. "Who's coming?"

"Calix! And he brings Kerr and their armies," Shaeleen yelled as she pointed northward. "Only an hour away at most!"

Shaeleen saw Cole's face twist in what Shaeleen knew must be from his conflicting duties to Prince Calix and to Prince Basil. So Shaeleen ran back down to Cole.

"We go to Prince Basil first," Cole said. "He has a right to know the truth."

Shaeleen only nodded her head, knowing how her brother's loyalty and sense of honor were being stretched.

Shaeleen waited impatiently for the ship to fully dock. Soon Prince Calix's ships were visible without the spyglass. Shaeleen could count at least six ships, which she was sure would be full of soldiers—from both Gabor and northern Galena.

"Commander Kerr will hang for his treachery," Princess Diamonique said, her lips tight as she spoke. "There is no excuse for this."

As if in answer to her threat, a loud boom sounded, and then a cannonball hit the end of the dock. Splinters of wood flew into the air amid the yells of dockworkers and sailors.

Shaeleen turned to Abby and the captain. "Thank you for your help, but you should get off the ship. I will make sure payment for our passage gets to you."

"And a new ship?" the captain said, looking at her sternly, clearly afraid his new ship was going to be destroyed soon.

Shaeleen offered him a grim smile and nodded. "And a new ship."

Abby leaned over and gave Shaeleen a quick hug.

"Let's go!" Cole yelled, and Shaeleen followed him and Princess Diamonique off the ship, jumping the last few feet—from the port side of the ship onto the docks—before the ramp was set up. The people on the docks were in chaos, and it was difficult for Shaeleen's group to get through the throng. Cole pushed through in front of Shaeleen and the princess. Then he stopped abruptly. Princess Diamonique and Shaeleen ran into his back.

"Cole!" Shaeleen yelled. "Get moving!"

Then she moved out around him and saw why he'd stopped. Standing in front of them was Orin, with an older gentleman at his side. Orin glared at Cole, but Cole held his ground.

"Orin!" Shaeleen said. And, without thinking, she ran forward and grabbed Orin into her arms, the top of his head reaching Shaeleen's nose. But she felt his body stiffen, so she let go.

"Orin, I'm so sorry."

Shaeleen then looked up at the man next to Orin. He wasn't as tall as Cole but was taller than Shaeleen. His hair was the color of Orin's, but his eyes were lighter. He stood in a dangerous pose, his hand on the hilt of his sword.

"Marcus, I presume," Shaeleen said.

Prince Marcus nodded his head. "Orin has told me about you, TruthSeer."

Shaeleen groaned, and she frowned. Rather than responding to this accusation, she changed subjects. "Calix is attacking Stronghaven.

Princess Diamonique stepped forward and gave a short bow. "I am Princess Diamonique of Gabor. You are the heir of Antioch, Prince Marcus?"

"It appears that way." Prince Marcus didn't smile as he turned his attention back to Shaeleen. "Our ship is too big to get out of the docks without being attacked."

Another boom sounded, and a ship at the end of the dock blew up—wooden planks and people flying into the air.

"Shae, we need to go now." Cole grabbed her arm. Then he turned to Prince Marcus and Orin and said, "We can take you to Prince Basil. He can protect you."

"Can he?" Prince Marcus asked.

"Orin, you know you can trust Basil," Shaeleen said as she turned to Orin, who still stood with a grim look. "He's a good man."

"And, will you hurt him too?" Orin jabbed at her.

Her heart fell, and tears came to Shaeleen's eyes as she realized what Orin meant. "That's not fair, Orin, and you know it. I didn't ask for any of this."

Orin's eyes softened somewhat, and then he stared down at his feet. When he looked up again, he nodded his head, apparently feeling ashamed for what he had said. But he didn't offer any other words.

Just then, two huge ships crashed into the docks.

"Shae!" Cole yelled out.

As chaos rained down around them, Shaeleen saw that three more ships were coming quickly behind the first two. So she put her hands out in front of her and said, "Everyone, grab on."

"Shae, you can't take that many people," Orin said in disbelief.

"I have no choice," she said. "Now, grab on."

Cole, Princess Diamonique, Prince Marcus, and Orin in turn grabbed onto one of her hands.

With the stones already at the surface of her thoughts, it didn't take much for Shaeleen to pull upon her full powers. A flash of light, followed by a loud boom, exploded from her hands, sending colors flying around them. And then she pulled all the power of the SpeedStone she held in her possession—lending it the strength, intelligence, and truth of the other stones.

Then she felt a surge to her powers and realized Prince Marcus also had powers of the SpeedStone in his blood, though not as much power as his son used to have.

Shaeleen grimaced at that thought. The overseer had stolen Orin's powers. Shaeleen had vowed to do all she could to make the overseer pay for hurting her friend.

All five of them sped off the docks and then up the numerous streets and a small hill toward the castle. Orin roared but still held on, and Shaeleen felt his pain, for the shadow still had a hold on him, and it fought against Shaeleen's power. Then Shaeleen saw the gates of the castle loom up in front of them.

"Cole!" she yelled.

He understood and immediately brought forth his own power, blasting the gates open without Shaeleen stopping. They sped through the courtyard and up to the steps of the castle, only stopping right at the front doors. Shaeleen fell over Cole as she tried to stand up and get reoriented after using the SpeedStone.

Orin rolled on the ground in pain, and his father leaned over to help him up—sparing a brief moment to glare up at Shaeleen.

Shaeleen groaned inside but, at the moment, could do nothing more.

Then, in front of them, came a group of guards, with swords pulled out in front of them and grim looks on their faces.

Shaeleen pushed her way forward. "We need to see Basil now."

A guard's sword swiftly moved to block her way. "And, who are you?" the guard asked.

"I am a TruthSeer." Using her powers, Shaeleen pushed her hand forward, and the sword flew out of the guard's hand.

"And I am Princess Diamonique," the princess said, pushing forward herself more courteously than Shaeleen had, somehow still looking all put together. Then Princess Diamonique smiled warmly and said, "Prince Basil is expecting me."

CHAPTER THIRTY

A steward motioned Shaeleen's group forward, toward a sitting room, and said, "I will get the prince for you."

But Shaeleen shook her head. "No need," she said. "There is not enough time." The others in her group looked at her quizzically.

She closed her eyes and immediately used the TruthStone to jump into the light from the windows in the room. Calling upon the SpeedStone, she immediately located Prince Basil, for he was in his study with the regent and Lord Gregory, the prince's military general.

"Basil, come downstairs now!" Shaeleen ordered him.

The prince stiffened and glanced around curiously.

"Now!" Shaeleen repeated, and both the sitting room, where her body was, and the prince's study shook with power.

Rushing back, she opened her eyes—it having only been the space of a few blinks.

"He's coming," Shaeleen said.

The steward gasped. But within moments, they all heard a commotion on the stairs.

"Shaeleen!" The prince's voice filled the castle as he ran toward them. "How did you—"

Sliding into the sitting room, Prince Basil stopped and then looked around. He nodded at Shaeleen, Cole, and Orin. Then his eyes moved to Prince Marcus.

"Prince Basil, I am Marcus, heir to Antioch—my son is Orin."

Prince Basil lifted his eyebrows in surprise. Then he turned and saw the last person in Shaeleen's group. His eyes widened, and his face became flushed.

Shaeleen noticed that, even after a three-day journey on a ship, Princess Diamonique looked regal.

Princess Diamonique smiled and bowed low as she said, "Prince Basil."

"Princess Diamonique?" Prince Basil said, his voice catching in his throat.

Shaeleen felt a thread of unexpected jealousy at the way the prince had looked at the princess.

Probably without even realizing it, Cole had moved closer to the princess's side.

The steward left, and the door closed behind him.

Then Shaeleen cleared her throat. "Basil, we have some things to discuss."

Both Princess Diamonique and Cole gasped at Shaeleen's impudence, and even Prince Marcus seemed to have stiffened somewhat, though Shaeleen did notice that Orin's lips had cracked a small smile.

"Yes, yes," Prince Basil said. "My brother is attacking and trying to take the throne for himself. Our birthday is two days away, so I must hold out until then."

As everyone in the room looked at Shaeleen in silence, the prince noticed their grim looks and turned to her as well. His beautiful, dark blue eyes searched hers, and she turned away, thinking, *I can't do it! I can't destroy such a good man!*

"Shae," Cole whispered with compassion. "The truth is your duty."

Shaeleen stomped one foot. "Curse the truth and the TruthStone! All it has brought me is pain."

Off in the distance, at the docks, another boom sounded, signaling to Shaeleen the continued attack on the city. Prince Basil looked in that direction then back at Shaeleen.

"He will not take the throne," Prince Basil said.

Shaeleen fell to the floor, racked with pain. Her entire body shook, and a burning heat from the TruthStone seared into her side. It seemed that the stronger she felt the powers of the TruthStone, the harder the lies were to bear.

Cole was the first she saw reach down to her. But Prince Basil followed suit. Shaeleen closed her eyes and tried to regain control. Finally, she opened them again, and Prince Basil held her eyes in his.

She couldn't turn away this time. Her heart beat faster, and tears filled her eyes.

"Shaeleen, I can't bear to see you in so much pain." Prince Basil grabbed her hands in his. Then he said softly, barely above a whisper, "Please tell me what is causing this. I can handle the truth."

Could he? Shaeleen thought. *Maybe he could—he was strong. But can I handle it?*

"Remember when you sent us to North Bay to find out the truth about your brother?" Shaeleen said as she let Cole and Prince Basil help her sit up on the floor. "Well, I didn't tell you everything yet."

Shaeleen glanced at Cole, and he nodded. Then Shaeleen noticed Cole was holding onto Princess Diamonique's hand for comfort. Shaeleen closed her eyes again, trying to regain her composure.

As she looked at Prince Basil again and made sure she had his attention, she felt herself being swallowed up in his deep eyes and in what she saw there—compassion, caring, love for others, good-heartedness—and then she took a deep breath. She was going to shatter it all.

"Calix—" Shaeleen paused to gather her emotions. "Calix is the firstborn, Basil. By law, he is the heir to the throne…" She broke eye contact with him and looked at Princess Diamonique before finishing by saying, "And he will be king and marry Diamonique."

For the space of a heartbeat, the entire world seemed to stop.

Then Prince Basil fell back off his knees, Shaeleen's hand sliding out of his. He sat down on the floor, staring off into empty space.

Eventually, he turned his head back toward her, and she had to look away. There was too much pain in his eyes.

"Are you sure?" he whispered quietly.

"I spoke to your mother," Shaeleen said back. "She and your father had originally lied to protect Calix, the heir. But, as you both grew and as Calix's personality became apparent, your mother continued the lie because she thought you would be a better king, that maybe something would change to allow it. But eventually she had to tell Calix. I suppose it might be hard for her to see you, but she does love you very much."

Prince Basil nodded and then stood up. He looked from one person in the room to the next. Then he settled his eyes on Princess Diamonique. Tears glistened in her eyes.

"And, my lady," Prince Basil said, "do you understand what this means?"

Princess Diamonique turned and looked at Cole, but Cole couldn't meet her eyes. Then she turned back to Prince Basil and stood up straight. "I do, Prince Basil. I have been raised to become the betrothed of the heir of Galena."

Shaeleen watched as Princess Diamonique stopped for a moment and swallowed hard. The princess held herself together with such poise that Shaeleen suddenly felt ashamed to be in her presence. Shaeleen could see now why Cole liked Princess Diamonique.

"I am prepared to fulfill my duty," Princess Diamonique said to Prince Basil.

"As am I." Prince Basil looked each person in the eye, settling finally on Shaeleen. "My brother, Calix, is the oldest and, by law, the true heir. But I give no promise of my generals or my people." His eyes grew hard. "My brother is a cruel man, and this kingdom doesn't deserve him. But I will obey the law and step down and allow him his right."

He turned back to Princess Diamonique with a grim smile and said, "But, I surmise, my people will fight this. Are you prepared for that?"

"I will do what I can to lessen the impact on the people, Prince Basil. I am the heir to Gabor and will order Commander Kerr home, to be put on trial for his traitorous deeds." Princess Diamonique stood straight and tall. "Over time, I hope your people will come to accept me."

"You are a remarkable woman," Prince Basil said, and Shaeleen felt another bout of jealousy at the prince's attention on Diamonique. She barely heard him continue. "The people will learn to love you, if not my brother. Maybe you can help him be a good ruler."

Princess Diamonique nodded in silence.

Then Prince Basil turned to Cole. "And, Cole, did you know about this as well?"

Cole flinched but nodded his head. "Your brother told me that he was the oldest and then asked me to bring Princess Diamonique to him. As a prince of the kingdom—and now, as heir—he ordered me to tell no one else."

Shaeleen had thought Prince Basil would be angry with her brother for his deception, but the prince smiled at Cole instead.

"You are the most honorable man I have met, Sir Cole," Prince Basil said. "If you would kindly escort Princess Diamonique to my brother, maybe we can lessen the amount of harm to our city."

Cole nodded.

"Then I would ask you to return to me," Prince Basil said.

Cole raised his eyebrows in surprise. "And where will you go, my prince?"

"I am still a prince of Galena," he said. "There is much good I can do. But, I'm afraid I will have to leave Stronghaven for a time, until things settle down." He then turned to Shaeleen. "Where to, TruthSeer?"

This question surprised her and completely caught her off guard. *Prince Basil still trusts me after all I have done?* She couldn't believe it. *How can someone be that good of a person?*

She paused for a moment, bringing up the powers of the IntelligenceStone, and thought about the war with the shadow, still looming ahead of her.

"The kingdom of Shema. We go to Lightfort in Shema," she said with certainty. "I have two more stones to gather before we face our real enemy."

Prince Basil gave her a quizzical look but only nodded. "To Lightfort, then." He turned to Prince Marcus and Orin, who had remained quiet during the conversation. "And, will you accompany us also, Prince Marcus and Orin?"

Prince Marcus thought a moment. "I'm afraid that using the port in Stronghaven will be difficult for now—especially for me. We will accompany you west, to the Myr River, and then take it south, to Mistport. I need to return to my father and help Antioch."

"Orin?" Prince Basil asked.

Orin looked from his father to Prince Basil and then to Shaeleen—his gaze holding a mixture of pain and hope. "I don't know," Orin finally said. "Let's see what happens."

Orin stood on his own now, and Shaeleen thought she saw a small tendril of shadow float off behind his head. But no one else had seemed to notice it.

She vowed again to herself that she would help Orin. Then Shaeleen smiled at him, and he smiled back to her, warming her heart.

Prince Basil called upon a company of guards, instructing them to escort Cole and the princess in a carriage down to the port after allowing them to clean themselves up somewhat first. Then Prince Basil went to gather some belongings and prepare to leave.

Shaeleen found herself alone in the sitting room, and she sat down on a chair. She closed her eyes for a moment, but she opened them again as she heard footsteps in the room. It was Orin.

Seeing that he held out something in front of him, she broke into a laugh. "Oh, Orin," Shaeleen cried as she reached out and took a tasty looking sweet cake off of the plate. Then she took a bite. As chocolate frosting met her lips, she groaned in delight.

"I want to be friends again, Shaeleen," Orin said with a grim smile. "But it's not going to be easy for us."

Shaeleen wiped away a tear and offered Orin a bite of cake. "None of this is easy, Orin, and things are going to get a lot more difficult before all this is over. But I do feel better with you around."

Orin took a bite and then nodded to her. A small smile crept over his lips.

* * *

Two days later, Shaeleen, Cole, Prince Basil, Prince Marcus, and Orin stood on the rooftop of a nondescript building near the castle before the ceremony. Below them, gathered around the castle gardens, were throngs of people trying to see the ceremony also. Raised platforms held dignitaries from towns all over Galena, as well as a few from the neighboring kingdoms.

Shaeleen saw Commander Kerr and TruthSeer Apprentice Erwin, from Gabor, standing in the background. Council members sat to the side of the dignitaries, dressed in all their finery. But Shaeleen noticed a few were missing, for some had already voiced their opposition to what was happening. Guards filled the perimeter and tried to keep the masses under control.

Then the doors to the castle opened, and Regent Warin, the princes' uncle, strode out front. He raised his hands for the people to quiet down.

"Welcome, citizens of Galena," he said, his voice tight and his mouth grim. "According to the laws of Galena and Wayland, as set forth by King Wayland at the founding of this great land, I announce to you the next king of Galena." The regent paused and looked around.

Then the door to the castle opened again, and Prince Calix emerged. His hair looked newly cut, and he was dressed in black military garb from head to foot. He strode out and stood next to the regent.

"Prince Calix has reached his seventeenth birthday and, as the oldest child, is now named King Calix of Galena." The regent brought forth a silver crown and laid it on the new king's head. "Hail the king," the regent said, though his voice held little enthusiasm.

"Hail the king!" cried some. But many others looked on in apparent confusion. They had expected Prince Basil as their next ruler. And most of the citizens did not seem to understand the reason for bringing his warships or for the destruction at the docks.

Chaos broke out, and the guards had to step in to regain control—if only barely. Shaeleen glanced up at Prince Basil, who stood next to her. His face was hard to read.

Prince Calix raised his hands for silence and then said his first words as king. "As is our custom, as your new king, I also announce my betrothal to Princess Diamonique of Gabor."

The princess came out of the castle door, her dark brown, wavy hair cascading in curls to her shoulders, her dusty brown skin glowing in the sunlight. She wore a beautiful gown of red—the color of Gabor's StrengthStone—and she looked every bit a queen. Her presence seemed to calm down the crowd for a moment.

Then behind Diamonique Shaeleen saw Lady Judith and frowned and then mumbled, "Why that dirty…"

But Cole turned to her, as if questioning her words.

Shaeleen pointed back toward Princess Diamonique. Standing directly behind her was Lady Judith, one of Prince Basil's most outspoken opponents. Shaeleen couldn't seem to get completely away from that horrible woman. How had she weaseled herself into the new king's household so quickly?

Cole grimaced also, but Shaeleen noticed he soon had eyes only on the princess herself, a princess that would soon be wed to the new king of Gabor.

"Where is Prince Basil?" a lonely voice said, and its sound rang out in the crowd. "He is our king."

Pandemonium broke out again, and the people surged forward. A line of guards formed between Prince Calix and the people. Then a man threw something at Prince Calix, and a guard stepped in and manhandled him, taking the man down.

As chaos ensued, men began fighting, women were trampled, and the cries of children filled the morning air.

Shaeleen glanced at Prince Basil through the corner of her eyes. His expression still seemed stoic, but tears streamed unabashedly down his face. As Shaeleen watched, his lips parted slightly.

"My people," he whispered. "My people."

Shaeleen broke, feeling angry. *What have I done?* To spare herself the pain of lies and to succumb to the honor of her brother, she had told the truth to Prince Basil, a truth that now caused her—and him—more pain than the lies ever could have. The lies had caused physical pain, but the truth caused a pain in her heart that wouldn't stop. She should have had Calix killed weeks ago. *Better late than never!*

Then power filled her soul. She pulled it all in to help dull the anger—truth, strength, intelligence, speed—and then she let it fill her to the brim. She looked down at Prince Calix, his face smug, and she thought about what she could do right then to end it all. As Shaeleen watched TruthSeer Apprentice Erwin step up behind King Calix and put a hand on the newly crowned king's shoulder, a black shadow caressed King Calix's neck.

A ShadowStone!

Anger filled Shaeleen's heart, and the power raged for a release inside her. Raising her left hand in the air, she prepared a TruthSpell that would destroy the new king, Commander Kerr, Erwin, Judith, and everyone else that got in Shaeleen's way.

A breath away from releasing this spell, Shaeleen felt soft fingers grasp her right hand tenderly. Prince Basil's grip felt warm and strong and made her head swim with emotions.

Then Prince Basil leaned in closer to her and said in soft, barely audible tones, "Not now, Shaeleen. Now is not the time." He paused a moment and then added, "Let your anger go. They are still my people."

Then she felt Cole put his arm around her, and Prince Marcus and Orin stepped closer to the prince. Shaeleen's soul fought between love and anger. She tried to regain control of herself, but it was difficult.

Being a TruthSeer is difficult.

"TruthSeer, take us away from here," Prince Basil said to Shaeleen with sudden fierceness. "It's time for us to go."

Shaeleen glanced over at Orin for a moment. Each time she had used her powers on him, he had felt pain from the shadow. He gave her a sour look but nodded his head to her, signaling his willingness for her to do what was needed.

Shaeleen was glad to do something with her power. As she pulled on the power of the SpeedStone, they all grabbed hands. In the blink of an eye, she had whisked them away from the crowds and screams of the city of Stronghaven, a city that would have to remain strong to survive what the future now held for it.

* * *

This is the end of ***TruthSpell,*** Book 2 in The TruthSeer Archives.

To continue the adventures of Shaeleen, Cole, Orin, and Basil, read **TruthSeer**, Book 3 in the TruthSeer Archives.

Having magical abilities is exciting…

…and dangerous.

How much power can one person hold and still stay in control?

The TruthStone has been a heavy weight for Shaeleen to bear, but she must continue to gather all the stones of power and restore them to their original glory – how, she is still not quite sure.

Evil Shadow Keepers are creating chaos at every turn. But there are many that do not even believe in their existence.

The weight of her mission begins to take its toll and she begins to question what is right and wrong.

At the moment of decision will she find it easier to succumb to the seductive lure of the shadow and become all powerful or will she discover a way to save all she loves?

Read this stunning and decisive conclusion to The TruthSeer Archives and find out what truths survive in the end of this magical journey.

Other Series By Mike Shelton
The Alaris Chronicles

For 100 years it protected them…

…and now the magical barrier is about to fail.

What waits on the other side?

Bakari is nerdy and awkward. At 15, he's lived at the Wizard Citadel for most of his life. Everything seems to be working out like he'd hoped. He just got promoted to Level 1 and despite being painfully shy, he has a friend.

Kharlia knows medicine. And he really likes her.

When Bakari finds an ancient map that marks a source of power, he must check it out. With Kharlia by his side, they wander through the Kingdom toward the spot on the map. The trip isn't what they expect.

Magical creatures have made it through the barrier. Should they fight or flee?

Bakari knows they are in trouble. He isn't a battle wizard. As they struggle against the beasts, the worst thing Bakari can imagine happens.

Will they survive?

You'll love this first book in *The Alaris Chronicles,* because of the beautifully woven story with diverse characters, great adventure, and political intrigue.

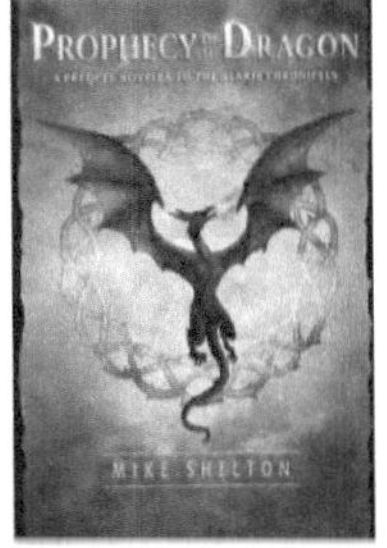

Sign up on Mike's website at www.MichaelSheltonBooks.com and get a copy of the prequel novella e-book to The Alaris Chronicles, Prophecy of the Dragon.

Protect the youngest heir of the Dragon King. That is the mission given to Imari in this prequel novella to The Alaris Chronicles.

The Wizard Academies

He lost his family...

...He's got voices in his head.

And he's more powerful than they ever imagined.

Fifteen-year-old apprentice Kyril is sick of being bullied. And after a tragic fire leaves him orphaned with out-of-control thoughts and powers, he can't wait to escape constant taunting at the wizard academy. So when a dicey faction entices him with companionship, he ignores the grim warning signs.

Even as Kyril's power grows within the group, he's left out of the crew's dangerous plans to derail the authorities. And when being accepted comes at the expense of making questionable choices, he fears his newfound friendships aren't worth the deadly price.

Can Kyril master his new magic before his shady companions send him to his doom?

Mark of the Medallion is the spellbinding first novel in The Wizard Academies YA fantasy series. If you like sword and sorcery, enchanted adventures, and suspenseful coming-of-age stories, then you'll love Mike Shelton's action-packed tale.

About the Author

Mike was born in California and has lived in multiple states from the west coast to the east coast. He cannot remember a time when he wasn't reading a book. At school, home, on vacation, at work at lunch time, and yes even a few pages in the car (at times when he just couldn't put that great book down). Though he has read all sorts of genres he has always been drawn to fantasy. It is his way of escaping to a simpler time filled with magic, wonders and heroics of young men and women.

Other than reading, Mike has always enjoyed the outdoors. From the beaches in Southern California to the warm waters of North Carolina. From the waterfalls in the Northwest to the Rocky Mountains in Utah. Mike has appreciated the beauty that God provides for us. He also enjoys hiking, discovering nature, playing a little basketball or volleyball, and most recently disc golf. He has a lovely wife who has always supported him, and three beautiful children who have been the center of his life.

Mike began writing stories in elementary school and moved on to larger novels in his early adult years. He has worked in corporate finance for most of his career. That, along with spending time with his wonderful family and obligations at church has made it difficult to find the time to truly dedicate to writing. In the last few years as his children have become older he has returned to doing what he truly enjoys – writing!

mikesheltonbooks@gmail.com
www.MichaelSheltonBooks.com
https://www.facebook.com/groups/MikeSheltonAuthor/
https://www.facebook.com/mikesheltonbooks/
http://www.Twitter.com/msheltonbooks
http://www.Instagram.com/mikesheltonbooks
https://www.pinterest.com/mikesheltonbooks/